THE
COMPANION
Lloyd A. Meeker

Published by
DREAMSPINNER PRESS

5032 Capital Circle SW, Suite 2, PMB# 279, Tallahassee, FL 32305-7886 USA
http://www.dreamspinnerpress.com/

This is a work of fiction. Names, characters, places, and incidents either are the product of author imagination or are used fictitiously, and any resemblance to actual persons, living or dead, business establishments, events, or locales is entirely coincidental.

The Companion
© 2014 Lloyd A. Meeker.

Cover Photo
© 2014 DWS Photography.
cerberuspic@gmail.com
Cover design
© 2014 Paul Richmond.
Cover content is for illustrative purposes only and any person depicted on the cover is a model.

All rights reserved. This book is licensed to the original purchaser only. Duplication or distribution via any means is illegal and a violation of international copyright law, subject to criminal prosecution and upon conviction, fines, and/or imprisonment. Any eBook format cannot be legally loaned or given to others. No part of this book may be reproduced or transmitted in any form or by any means, electronic or mechanical, including photocopying, recording, or by any information storage and retrieval system, without the written permission of the Publisher, except where permitted by law. To request permission and all other inquiries, contact Dreamspinner Press, 5032 Capital Circle SW, Suite 2, PMB# 279, Tallahassee, FL 32305-7886, USA, or http://www.dreamspinnerpress.com/.

ISBN: 978-1-62798-849-0
Digital ISBN: 978-1-62798-850-6
Library of Congress Control Number: 2014940017
First Edition July 2014

Printed in the United States of America

This paper meets the requirements of
ANSI/NISO Z39.48-1992 (Permanence of Paper).

To Victor J. Banis,
front-line pioneer of gay fiction and a master storyteller,
whose scope of work—with its emotional depth,
imagination, and quality—
is likely to remain unsurpassed for a very, very long time.
Thank you for being such a generous mentor.

Acknowledgments

To the countless storytellers who've shown us
how the inner journey gives meaning to the outer;
to Dr. Grant Johnson for sharing his
expertise in Ericksonian hypnotherapy;
to my writing buddies whose insights made
this story so much better, especially
Martha Ragland and the rest of
my wonderful "Oregonian" critique circle;
and to my husband Bob, for his loving patience—
heartfelt thanks.

Chapter One

"I can't wait," Bill Smith wailed, his head thrashing from side to side on the bed. "I'm going to explode! I'll die—I can't!"

I wasn't worried about the noise. I'd had my studio soundproofed as soon as I bought it. Bill could have screamed, and nobody would have heard much at all. The thick fragrance of our sweat, our breath, and the sage we'd burned at the beginning bore us up, up, into prayer.

He brought his hand to his penis to stroke it, but I pushed it away. "No. Don't make it happen. You don't have to. Just let it happen. Keep your eyes open. Listen to me. Let your body break all the way open, it's good." After weeks of practice, he was ready, so ready.

"See yourself opening to the sun, like a lotus," I coaxed, undulating inside him. "Not to me, or me inside you, but to the whole universe. Give yourself to sun-fire, petal by petal. Keep your eyes open, breathe from your belly, let the mystery take you."

He bucked, his eyes wide and fierce. He clamped his legs around my waist and dug his fingers into the sheets. He stopped breathing.

"Breathe out, now, all the way. Give all your beauty away. Now!" I pushed in all the way, and his breath burst out of him in a ragged prayer to "Oh, God!" as he came. His body arched and shuddered, beautiful and holy in release. Magnificent. I loved this work.

For a while, neither of us moved, just sweating, still joined. The only sound was our breathing as it slowed. After a few minutes, I leaned forward to kiss his throat softly as I reached for a small alabaster jar beside the bed.

"Thank you," he said shakily, as I wiped him clean and slowly anointed his heart and belly chakras with sandalwood oil from the jar. "Fifty-some years since puberty, and I've never come without someone or something touching my dick before."

"And?" I asked with a smile. I knew the answer already.

His belly convulsed as I slid out. "Amazing."

BILL'S WEATHERED face still glowed as he tucked in his shirt, smoothed down the fabric. His hand stopped just below his solar plexus. "I can still feel that," he said, his voice soft with wonder. "My breathing goes all the way down, wide open. Powerful."

"Isn't it wonderful?" I said, toweling my hair dry. "Breathing," I repeated from our very first session, "is our first and most primal sex—welcome in, as deep as we can; pour out, twice as long as in. Twice as much time giving as taking. Without breath, we have nothing, are nothing."

I came up behind my client to give him an affectionate peck below his ear. I rubbed my clean-shaven cheek along his neck, wondering how long he'd stay this pliant, this gentle. "You did great today, Bill."

I knew what Bill Smith's real name was. I took on clients only by referral and then only after a thorough background check, but I honored professional convention. He was a relatively new client and, so far, preferred the pretense of anonymity. If that made him feel safer with me early on, no problem—his comfort made it easier to do the work. We could go deeper into the mystery.

He caught my eye in the mirror and held it, as only a tough, silver-haired airline executive could. Very used to being in charge. "You didn't answer the question I asked in the shower," he said. "But I'd like an answer. Do you ever regret being so beautiful?"

"Not that I'm aware of." I hesitated, cautious about where this might lead. "Why?"

He shrugged, his smile disappointed. "I would have preferred you to say yes. It's selfish of me, but the world would seem a little more just if once in a while you felt there was a downside to your looks. Even here in Los Angeles, your physical perfection is… unnerving. When we're together, I'd rather not be the only one in the room who felt a little awkward about that, at least once in a while."

Involuntarily, my hand rose to cover the three blood-red spots of the birthmark that lay along my neck. "I'm not perfect."

His laugh carried a hard edge. "You," he said with quiet accusation, "are more physically perfect than any human being has a right to be." His gaze flicked to where my fingers lay. "And those things serve only as punctuation, like an eighteenth century beauty mark."

I laughed too, just to deflect him. "Okay, then. But that's not really what my coaching is about. Would you be less interested in working with me if I were less attractive physically?"

He pulled the knot of his tie into place, looking thoughtful. "It might have mattered to begin with. Not now, certainly."

"That's because you're beginning to experience your own beauty, inside." I waggled a finger at Mr. Smith's reflection. "But I'm hearing comparison and competition creeping back into your language already, and you're not even out the door."

"Competition makes the world go around," he said, showing teeth.

"Not with me, not here in my space." I hugged his trim, mature body from behind, catching a rich whiff of sandalwood, and whispered into his ear, "You are unique. That's what makes you a pleasure to be with, for whoever you're with."

"Huh. I'll bet you say that to all your customers."

"Clients," I corrected. It was almost the same thing, but not quite. Certainly not to me. I gave him another smooch on his neck, on comfortable territory again. "Of course I do. Because it's true. My work is to help a man discover how true that actually is."

"By having the most spectacular sex imaginable."

"Exactly!" I squeezed and pulled away. "Can you think of a better way to discover your sacred inner beauty?"

Bill shook his head, finally surrendering a real smile. "Trust me, I'm not looking for a better way."

I winked into the mirror at him. "Me neither."

After he left, I massaged my chakras using lavender oil as I always did to separate from a client. I did some stretching, showered again, and dressed slowly.

His question about beauty had touched a nerve. From childhood, I'd been keenly aware that people thought me beautiful. I was. It had been one of Mother's favorite topics of conversation with her martini friends. But in spite of Bill's curt dismissal, I was also marked by ugliness.

I stared into the mirror at the rough red spots that lay on my neck like blood spatter. As they had since puberty, when I'd first started having the nightmares, they whispered to me of grisly, violent death. Mine.

Any number of times I'd decided to have them removed, but I'd never been able to go through with it. Always—once as late as actually settling onto the table with the plastic surgeon standing next to me—I decided it would be wrong to cut them out. They were a true part of me, somehow, even though I hated that they were. I didn't want to be beaten to death like the nightmare promised.

My throat tightened and began to ache. I'd looked at them too long. Sweat beaded on my forehead. I shut my eyes and breathed into the rising swell of nausea. *I'm safe right now*. I began a silent affirmation. *This is my studio. I choose my clients. I'm safe here.*

I wouldn't let that prophecy of violence and death become reality, even though it had marked me from birth. I had the resources to make sure it didn't. I took all the precautions.

I wiped my face with the damp towel and shrugged into a fresh shirt. I needed to schedule another appointment with Reggie, my therapist, to work on that again. But right then, I was due for lunch with Stef at Chez Henri. My reservation was for two o'clock, and they wouldn't hold a table even for a regular like me.

Chapter TWO

I LEFT the keys in the Maserati for the parking valet and stepped into the elegant, restrained clamor of Chez Henri. Stef stood waiting for me in the vestibule, looking a little nervous. His face lit up when he saw me, and I'm sure mine did the same. We hugged. He was such a great kid.

"They kept looking at me like I'd snuck in through the kitchen," Stef said with his brightest aw-shucks grin. "Guess they don't want an Oklahoma farm boy here unless he's trussed up on a platter with an apple in his mouth. They should've asked—I'd'a said sure, for the right price!"

He glanced around the room. "Could be fun, with some of these guys."

Stef was naïve, way too open for his own good, but I wasn't sure how to teach him more caution without damping the irrepressible spirit that made him so special. I'd lecture him about it over lunch. Again.

"The Scottish wild salmon is particularly fine today, Mr. Bucknam," the *maître d'* murmured as he seated us at a window table.

"Thank you, William. Your 'particularly fine' must translate to 'heavenly' for the rest of us."

One corner of William's urbane lip curled heavenward at the compliment, maybe as much as a millimeter, as he withdrew into the flow of his domain.

I watched Stef tuck into his steak the way he did just about everything—with unabashed enthusiasm. I could list plenty of reasons why I felt so protective of him, why I enjoyed being with him so much, wanted to teach him how to flourish, succeed. I wanted him to be happy.

He was a good kid, smart and dangerously generous of heart. His love of adventure electrified everything he did. He made me laugh, more than I had in a long time. I also considered him my protégé, which was something new for me. I found my proprietary attitude surprisingly satisfying. He loved our work and would become superb at it.

Six months ago, Stef had tried to pick me up at a party as he worked the room—so new to LA he was still wearing cowboy boots and a belt with a giant silver and brass buckle, his straw-blond thatch headed in half a dozen directions without any help from hair product. I'd been mildly offended at first, but then as we talked, I became intrigued—and ultimately charmed.

For his part, Stef had been miffed when he discovered that he wasn't going to make any money off this particular trick, but by then, he was too interested to say no. We had a truly wonderful time.

He was special. From that first night, he'd been eager to learn how to grow beyond just hustling. He was imaginative, playful, and talented too. He possessed the intuitive empathy that enabled him to listen to another man's body. He was an excellent listener.

I took a bite of salmon. It really was heavenly. I lost myself in the melting texture and flavors for a moment. Beautifully delicate, with just the right whisper of tarragon in the butter.

"Wherever you went, I could tell you had a good time," Stef said with a leer. "I swear, sometimes food is just as good as sex." He waved his fork at me and winked. "Except sex with you, which is better'n food any day. I think I need another lesson soon."

"Have you been doing your meditation and breath work?"

"Every day." Stef dropped his eyes. "Well, nearly every day. I like it. Makes me feel good." He looked up, his eyes soft and thoughtful. "It really does. I feel like I glow afterward."

He cut off another bite and stuffed it in his mouth. "Mercy, that is fine," he mumbled around it. "And speaking of sex, is it okay if I use the studio later this afternoon? I've got a high roller."

"Sure. I was there just now, but I didn't clean up. Camilla won't be in until tomorrow morning, so you'll have to tidy up before your appointment." I paused, weighing whether I should ask. Stef got skittish if he felt I was crowding him. "Anyone I know?"

"Nah, it's not even someone I'm supposed to know, but I do. This is our second time. First was at a hotel a couple days ago. But I saw him on the news yesterday going on about some big project. Political guy. Wild man in the sack, though. Big dick, knows how to use it."

Stef impaled a spear of asparagus. "Isn't it kinda stupid to stack these up in a tepee like they do? I mean, it's the first thing I pushed over getting to the—"

"For god's sake, don't let on you know who he is." I grabbed Stef's fork hand so hard the asparagus jarred free and fell back onto his plate. "If he doesn't want you to know who he is, then trust me, you don't want to know either. You've got to play by the rules. You could get into serious trouble if you don't."

I let go of Stef's hand with a squeeze, a little embarrassed at feeling—and sounding—like an overprotective parent. "I care a lot about you," I said, trying to explain myself. "I should start screening all your clients."

Stef shook his head firmly and picked up the dislodged asparagus. "I know you mean well, Shepherd, that's a sure thing." He popped it in his mouth and chewed. When he looked up, his eyes told me he'd dug in and wouldn't budge.

"I know you got the finest corral I can imagine all ready for me, but I still can't abide fences. Even yours." He looked sad. "I get spooked every time I see a fence. I just ain't ready to give up the right to pick my own guys."

"I understand that." I smiled and held up my hands, backing off. "It was wrong of me to put it that way. It's just that I get scared for you sometimes, Stef. Los Angeles is a very different place from Oklahoma City. Bad things happen to men like us every day here. There's good reason behind my paranoia."

"Geez, you're really serious about this, aren't you?" Stef grinned at me as if reassuring a baby brother afraid to get up on the big scary tractor. "Don't worry, dude. His secret is safe with me. I've got nobody but you to tell."

OUTSIDE THE restaurant, Stef seemed to hang back when the valet brought my car up, its engine rumbling, impatient for the street.

"Where's yours?" I asked Stef. I tipped the valet but closed the car door to stop the warning bell from dinging.

Stef blushed. "I'm already parked at the studio. I figured you'd say yes."

"Not a problem. That's why I gave you your own set of keys. How did you get here, then?"

"Walked. It's only a mile or so."

"Nobody walks in Los Angeles," I laughed. "Jump in—I'll give you a lift."

Stef laughed and climbed in. "How can I say no?" The doors clunked shut, and we buckled up.

"Sweet." He ran a reverent hand over the burl paneling. "Dude, you have no idea how much I love riding in this thing," Stef sighed. "A bad-ass Maserati. I'd send my folks a big ol' photo of me in it just to annoy them, but my dad wouldn't even open the damn envelope."

We pulled into traffic and turned up a back street toward Westwood. After a few blocks, we were stopped by a patrolman waving his arms. Lights from two police cars flashed. Another cop was stringing up yellow tape.

An ambulance siren got louder behind us, coming up fast. Something bad had happened; I could feel it. My stomach knotted. "Oh, damn," I whispered to no one, bracing against the first wave of dread and nausea.

"It's okay, he's saying just go around," said Stef. We crept forward. I kept my eyes focused on the street. Maybe I could get through this without a disaster.

"Look—just follow his… holy crap, check it out!" Stef crowed, pressing his face against the window. "The guy on the ground, he's in cuffs. Look at all the blood! Cripes, how can he still be alive? He must have tried to… shit—there's another guy, no cuffs, nothing. Not moving at all. Man, he's gotta be dead already, lying twisted up like that. What a mess!"

I sped up, tried to escape it, tried not to look—but I did. One glance was all it took. I tasted thick salt, leaned forward, and lost my wild Scottish salmon through the steering wheel, onto the floor between my knees.

"Jesus, dude!" Stef shouted, laughing nervously, putting down the window. "What the fuck was that?"

I wiped my mouth with the back of one hand, steering the car past the crime scene with the other. "Sorry." I smiled tight-lipped, afraid I might hurl again. "Violence. Makes me sick."

"No kidding!" he coughed, his face screwed up in disgust. "You gotta get that taken care of."

"Trust me, I've tried. Still can't crack it. At least not yet."

"Throwing up in a car like this, though. Jeez, that's gotta be a federal crime all on its own."

I shook my head. "The dealership can take care of it. It's happened before. They'll make it like new."

We drove to the studio in silence through the hot Los Angeles afternoon. Even with the fan on high and windows down, the car still stank. I pulled into the garage and stopped at the elevator.

Stef leaned back in through the open window, looking worried. "You gonna be okay? Really?"

"Yeah, I'll be fine." I gave him a feeble thumbs-up. "You be careful, okay?"

"Sure thing, boss. I'll call you later tonight."

"No, call me tomorrow. I've got a club dinner and concert tonight. I probably won't get home until after midnight."

Stef nodded, returned the thumbs-up, and headed for the elevator, whistling.

Stinking and clammy, I headed home, calling on the hands-free to get the car scheduled for cleanup.

Chapter Three

I FIDGETED with my gym bag in front of the wall of glass in my condo's living room, ignoring the fifteenth story view across Wilshire to the UCLA campus. I itched to get going, but Camilla hadn't shown up yet, and I wanted to ask her about increasing her schedule to three times a week as well as give her a check. It had a bonus in it.

Being late was completely unlike her. She was scheduled to clean the studio and come here to do my apartment afterward. Usually, she'd have arrived an hour ago, and I'd be at the gym, well into my workout by now.

I called her again—no answer. She always answered. Always.

Maybe it was traffic. But if it was only traffic, then she would have called. She would have called if she was sick, too, but she'd never done that. Never had to. No, something was wrong, and it was making me edgy. I hated feeling like I was full of static electricity frantic for a ground.

I checked my phone again in case I hadn't heard a message arrive—nope. I gave up pacing and parked in a chair again, leaning back and closing my eyes, wishing I could see Reggie today instead of tomorrow. Right now, actually. When I was anxious and off-center like this, our sessions helped a lot. He was intuitive, humorous, inquisitive, and gentle—more effective than most of the therapists I'd worked with.

Even so, I'd always felt secure talking with a therapist. Even with the first one, after I came back from school in Switzerland. That was when Mother, in her perpetual alcoholic fog, had decided I was emotionally adrift, never stumbling over the brutal irony of her martini-fueled wisdom.

She'd been afraid I was fooling around with drugs, she said, or that I lacked career goals. But I wasn't adrift at all.

More importantly, I'd already found my true calling. I'd been practicing for years on classmates, teachers, fathers of classmates, my skiing coach, a couple of priests, strangers on trains or at cafes—any man at all who fired my interest.

I'd become an explorer, mapping the erotic rivers and jungles of men, and an acolyte, celebrating the divine power men's bodies contained. As for drugs, my calling was the only high I needed. But I'd been naïve back then, indiscriminate and undisciplined. A dilettante in my art—so much to learn.

That first therapist Mother hired had introduced me to tantra, though, and to Body Erotic. That marked the beginning of an eclectic procession of practices and teachers I encountered, once I'd begun my journey toward becoming a Daka. Unconscious as it was, that start was one of Mother's few gifts that had meaning to me.

Sharp raps on the door startled me back into the present. That couldn't be Camilla; she had a key... I got up and looked through the fish eye. It was a stranger—jacket and tie. This couldn't be good.

"Yes?" I called through the door.

The man held up a shiny badge. "Detective Marco Fidanza, LAPD. Please open the door, sir."

Gripped by new dread, I did as I was told.

Detective Fidanza strode in, moving like a panther on the hunt. He was overwhelming, took over the room. His dark eyes sparked vitality and intelligence. "Are you Shepherd Bucknam?"

"Yes." I struggled against his seductive power and grace, his thick black hair, and classic cheekbones. Or his great jaw. "What's the matter?"

"Do you own the property at 10574 Ashton Avenue—unit 407?"

"It's my studio. What's this about?"

"Uh-huh. Studio. Is that what you call it?" His voice was cold, even scornful. "I've just come from there. I know what it is, Mr. Bucknam. It's remarkably well-appointed, for a hustler's playpen."

I refused to go on the defensive. "Call it what you like, Detective. Camilla Perez, my cleaning lady, was there this morning. Are you the reason she hasn't called? Are you holding her? She's fully documented, so I hope, for your sake, you're not violating her rights."

Fidanza gave me a mirthless smile. "I know exactly who was in your little hideaway this morning."

"So why were you there? Why are you here? You need to tell me what's going on."

"No, I don't."

I felt a power dance begin, and my adrenaline jumped. Power play between men was so sexy. I softened my voice to a dangerous murmur. "Do I need to call my lawyer, Detective? He's very good, and not at all afraid to take on bullies. He'll represent Camilla, if need be."

He must have heard the promise of battle, because he looked up from his notebook. His nose had been broken, and a scar cut a pale ditch through his left eyebrow. It was damn sexy. If he wasn't going to answer my questions, I'd start a different conversation with him. His mouth opened, but I cut him off.

"Do you enjoy sex, Detective?"

He snorted. "Not with prostitutes."

I ignored the deliberate insult. "You'd be amazed at how many men don't enjoy sex, don't know how. Mostly, men love orgasm, and it doesn't matter much what they do to get one."

"Is that so?" Fidanza looked amused.

I got the uneasy feeling he might be playing me, but I pushed on. "In my experience, yes. Real sex is a mystical journey that few men explore, let alone become skilled at—probably because they never learned what sex is, never had anyone actually lead them into the real wonder. That's what I do. I'm a Daka. I coach men in sexual ecstasy."

Fidanza smiled, a thin, cynical curl. "And I'm sure you're paid very well too." He tilted his head at the stainless steel kitchen. "This place isn't exactly a slum. And DMV shows you have three cars: a Prius, a Mercedes sedan, and a Maserati. Nice."

I was winning round one. I knew this dance perfectly. "I do get paid well. But I don't do it for the money."

"Bullshit. The cars aren't financed. There's no mortgage on this place or your so-called studio. I had them checked. The Maserati alone must've cost over two hundred fifty grand. To say nothing of maintenance."

"It probably doesn't fit your prejudice, Detective, but I'm not a Daka for the money. I inherited more money than I'll ever spend, even with this very expensive apartment and a Maserati. In fact, I donate the cash equivalent of one of those cars to charity every year. I do my erotic coaching because it's a sacred art, and I'm good at it. I've practiced, experimented. Trained. Studied with tantric masters for years. I still do."

His eyebrows lifted. I watched him take time to let that sink in. "You're shitting me."

"Detective, you're far too attractive to bullshit."

The man's face slammed shut like a cold steel door. "Don't try flattery on me, Bucknam. Or worse, seduction. You're assuming I'm attracted. That could be a mighty dangerous mistake."

"Not an assumption." I shook my head. I had him. "You're too angry with me to be straight. I've learned to read men's bodies. A straight cop would just smile and treat me like any other nonperson he had to deal with. He'd risk nothing, being here. You're too tense—your breathing is a little fast and shallow, and your grip on the pen is too tight. I'm guessing it's because you're more personally affected than a straight cop would be."

Fidanza barked out a curt laugh. "Well, good for you, Sherlock." He glared at me, and I felt the energetic wallop. We were attracted to each other. A lot.

"So what?" he snapped. "Yes, you look nice. Feel better now? Is that what you wanted me to say?" His lips curled into a delicious, hard-jawed sneer. I wanted to lick the corner of it slowly, softly until the lips parted—just a little.

"But I'm not interested in taking that mystical journey with you," he said. "Thanks just the same."

He was lying.

"So now," he said, returning to his notebook, "playtime's over. Where were you last night?"

A chill crawled across my shoulders. "You still haven't told me what this is about."

Fidanza grinned. He was winning now, didn't even look up. "And I don't have to. Not yet, anyway." His voice hardened. "Where were you last night, and who were you with, Mr. Bucknam?"

"I was with my concert club." My face warmed. It sounded too effete, when said aloud in front of him. I tried to fix it. "It's not really a club, we just call it that. Four or five of us get together for dinner and a concert every now and then."

"When was that? And where?"

"The concert was at Disney Hall. We met there for drinks and appetizers around six thirty. After the concert, we had dinner. I got home a little after midnight."

"What was the concert?"

I looked around. "I think I have the program somewhere." This was bizarre. "It was a performance by the Los Angeles Master Chorale. They did a contemporary piece called *The World in Flower*. It was lovely. I forget who it was by. Second half was the Brahms' Requiem. Why are you asking me this?"

"Did you stay to the end?"

"Of course. Nobody walks out on Brahms' Requiem."

"Not if they love music," he agreed, not looking up, which took me completely by surprise. He made a note. "I'll need names and phone numbers."

"Sure. But why were you at my studio, and why are you grilling me like a criminal?"

"All in good time, Mr. Bucknam."

"Right now is a good time. You'd better tell me what this is about now, Detective, or I'm calling my attorney."

Fidanza looked at me like I'd just spat in his food. "About six o'clock this morning, we got a call from your cleaning lady, who'd discovered the body of a young man there. He'd been shot twice. What can you tell me about him?"

The world crumbled away beneath me, and I fell into the nothing it left behind. "Stef? No!" It wasn't true. But I knew better. "No! Oh, my god, Stef...."

"She found him naked, duct-taped to a chair," Fidanza growled, pushing into my space so close I could smell the coffee on his breath. "He'd been tied up quite a while, long enough to make him piss on the carpet. He cried a lot before he was killed—had salt streaks all over his cheeks. What can you tell me about that, Mr. Bucknam?"

"Don't!" I staggered backward as if he'd hit me. "Stef was my friend. Oh, damn. I'm going to be sick...." I raced to the bathroom. I made it just in time.

Fidanza stood in the doorway watching me heave, calm, as if this happened to him every day. Maybe it did.

"Who was Steven Lewis to you, Bucknam?" The detective's voice cut through my retching, hard and cynical.

"I told you, he was my friend. Like a younger brother," I panted, flushing the toilet. I blew my nose, wincing at the burn. "I let him use the studio... I was teaching him to...." I imagined him bound to a chair, helpless, crying. I felt his despair. I watched ugly dark bullet holes appear in that lithe, lovely body. I gagged and heaved again.

"Maybe you were his pimp. You were farming him out. Maybe he was freelancing on you so you shot him."

I hacked out a wet cough and looked up at Fidanza's silhouette in the doorway. I wanted to laugh at the notion, but couldn't. The pain in my chest wouldn't let me. "Even if I were desperate for money," I croaked, "you have no idea how impossible that is."

I retched again, but I was already empty. I'd seen Stef for the last time. I wasn't prepared. It wasn't fair. My throat burned.

I'd said good-bye to Stef yesterday, and I'd had puke all over me then too. I pulled off a bunch of toilet paper to wipe my mouth and began to cry—naked, lost, groaning sobs. All I could do was sag against the bathroom wall and cry.

He must have stood in the doorway quite a while longer, though I had no idea how long. When he spoke, his voice was still hard, but kinder. "Get me the contact info for your concert buddies, and I'll leave you alone. For now."

Still dripping tears, I flushed the toilet again, splashed water on my face, and stumbled to the kitchen where I'd left my phone.

I gave him the names and numbers he wanted, and he handed me his card on his way out. My chest ached—as if my heart had been torn open and Stef ripped out, leaving a gaping pit. I had no idea losing him would hurt like this. I had no idea I'd lose him at all.

Chapter Four

The next morning, I headed to my therapist's office far too early. After a night of staring at the bedroom ceiling, I felt better doing something else, even if it was sitting in my car waiting for the clock to say 10:00. Then I poured out my pain to Reggie while he sat perched on the tan sofa, legs folded under him Buddha-style, a thin, mocha-skinned cross between Puck and Yoda.

"You've got a lot going on right now," he said softly when I fell silent. That was Reggie-speak for "I can see you're up to your ass in alligators, old son," and I was grateful for the acknowledgment. I was cried out for the moment, but still hurt more than I had in years.

I'd grieved when Mother died, I really had. She was my mother, after all. But there'd been no shock in her passing. She drank herself to death, and it was a long, ugly descent, taking far too long, longer than any of us wanted, including her. She'd wanted to die. It was a relief when she did.

Stef hadn't wanted to die. His murder had sunk me into can't-focus-can't-eat pain I hadn't experienced since Danny, and that had been, what, eighteen years ago? Yes. We'd both been seventeen when he jumped from the school bell tower.

Sweet Danny. Although I knew why he'd jumped, his parents wouldn't listen. Instead, they raged at me, accusing me of lying, slandering him. They couldn't bear to hear that their son had been in love with Rory Neville, captain of the rowing team, who had seduced him, used him for weeks, and then outed him for a laugh. Danny showed me how love can tear away all pride, all hope, and then kill you. Just like that.

"Yes, I do," I said, pulling myself back to Reggie's office but shivering at the memory.

"You went somewhere else just then. What was that about?"

"Danny. This is stirring up some old stuff."

"Mm-hmm. How is Stef's death like his for you?"

I had to sit with the question a while, until I understood. "They're not, really. It's mostly the loss. Someone else I loved. Taken away, through no fault of theirs. Or mine."

"So you loved Stef."

I had. I needed another tissue. I'd loved him. That wasn't really a surprise—more like an unexpected confirmation. "I never said so out loud, but I must have. But not like a lover. More… gods, I was going to say like an uncle. That would be wrong, for sure."

"Mmmm." Reggie made his little noise of empathy, making a note. "Not like Uncle George."

"Not in any way like Uncle George." The comparison was hideous.

"But not like a lover," he prompted.

"No. More like a kid brother. I thought of him as my protégé. I was proud of him. He felt like a natural part of me. We had sex, of course, but I was coaching him. He was a natural and learned almost effortlessly. He was special. Uninhibited, happy, generous—and wild, in some very healthy, basic way I didn't really understand. I loved that part of him, but I don't know how he kept it. Some of his stories about his childhood were horrible."

Something else pushed from deep inside my ache, insisting on being said. "I felt… parental." That sounded odd, but it was true. "I wanted him to be happy and successful. He deserved to be happy and successful."

"So that's all about Stef," Reggie said gently. "What about Shepherd? How are you going to take care of him?"

I shrugged. "I can handle the police investigation. I called my attorney yesterday right after the police left, and he's poised if needed."

"That's good, but that's not really what I meant. What are you going to do to take care of yourself? What do *you* need?"

What did I need? I didn't know. Sometimes it's hard to tell when you look inside and see only the empty space caused by death. "I need a different studio. I can't go back to the one where…." I couldn't bring myself to say, *where Stef wept, duct-taped to a chair for so long that he peed on the carpet before he was shot, where his good-hearted blood splattered everywhere.* "… where he died. I'll call my real estate agent this afternoon."

"That's a good idea. What else? What do you deserve?"

"I deserve to be normal." The words were out of my mouth before I could choose them. "Or at least as normal as possible. I've got to get past this insane reaction to physical violence, but I've run out of memories for us to explore." I looked up, feeling lost. "What *am* I going to do next, Reggie?"

He sat quietly for a little while, and then said, "I'm not sure. It may be that the key experience is blocked. I have a colleague, a friend who's had good results with hypnotherapy techniques. I'd like your permission to discuss whether that might be a good modality for you."

"Sure. I'm willing to try just about anything."

Reggie got up and studied his desk calendar. "What do you think about getting together again next week? That'll give me time to talk to my colleague."

"Perfect. That will give me time to take care of Stef's funeral. I've got Juergen Hostler, the PI who does my client screening, looking for his family to get their permission." I'd never arranged a memorial service. Mother had organized every last detail of her own with the funeral director who'd taken care of Dad's. I'd use someone else for Stef.

"I'm sure the memorial will bring up issues too, but I've got to do it. I owe Stef proper closure. I owe it to me too. That's something else I need. Closure. We both deserve that."

Chapter Five

THE NEXT day on my way home from the gym, I called Camilla to let her know I'd take care of any legal expenses she might incur during the investigation. I also wanted her to call me if she felt the police were threatening her or even just pushing too hard. She'd been held by the police much longer than it would have taken her to clean both apartments, and she deserved to be paid for the time she was prevented from being at other jobs. I insisted she send me an invoice.

As I walked into my apartment, my phone rang—it was Juergen. His voice was always the same: calm, unhurried, solid. I found it very reassuring, especially right then.

"I've talked to Steven Lewis's family," he reported.

"That was fast, even for you."

"You gave me his social, a phone number, and a bank account. Fish in a barrel."

"Even so." I looked at my watch. "Where are you now?" I got a call-waiting signal and ignored it.

"At the office."

"Have you had lunch?" I asked.

"Not yet. You want to meet at the diner? I'll be there in half an hour. I'd just as soon deliver my report in person."

"I'm eager to hear what his folks had to say, but I'd prefer that too. See you there." I drank a glass of water and checked voice mail. It was Detective Fidanza. Call, he said, and gave his number. He sounded irritated.

I hit the return call button, and he answered before the second ring. "Fidanza."

"Shepherd Bucknam returning your call, Detective."

He didn't waste any time on social niceties. "You didn't tell me you had a key to Lewis's apartment, or that you cosigned his lease."

It was an accusation, and I resented it. "I had my head in the toilet most of the time you were asking me questions, but I answered each one. I don't recall you asking me about the lease on his apartment. Did you?"

He ignored me. "This makes you tighter with Lewis than I thought. I want you to come to the station. I've got more questions. I figure it'll take you less than half an hour to get here."

"I'm sorry, but I'm on my way to get something to eat. What about tomorrow morning?"

"You're going to eat all afternoon?"

Pushy. I wasn't in the mood to be pushed. "I'd prefer to come down in the morning."

"And I'd prefer you to come down this afternoon," he said, his voice a sarcastic slap through the phone. "Strongly prefer."

It wasn't worth fighting about. "All right. I'll be there around three."

He grunted acknowledgment and hung up.

I headed for my car.

To say Juergen's favorite diner was a noir Hollywood PI's cliché wouldn't be entirely fair. The line cook wasn't dressed in a greasy white T-shirt and didn't have a cigarette dangling from his mouth. Although the waitress who took our order had to be in her fifties, she didn't have big red hair. She wasn't even chewing gum. Still, an argument could be made. The air was thick with smells declaring that deep frying was a specialty of the house, and had been for decades.

The decor had none of the chrome and turquoise Formica that had sprouted up in nostalgic retro chains a decade ago. This was just plain ugly—dull, worn, without a trace of imagination. There were no weight-watching or heart-healthy graphics on the menu, which hadn't changed in the years Juergen had done background checks and other research for me—and probably in all the years before that when he'd been a cop. The most outstanding feature of Sandy's Kitchen was that it was completely unremarkable, but it was Juergen's favorite place to eat.

"I have a theory about why these places appeal to you guys," I said.

"Yeah?" Juergen even sounded like an ex-cop turned PI—unhurried, wry. His ice-blue eyes always seemed a little dangerous. Ready to smile, ready for trouble. "What's that?"

"Some men crave variety and excitement in a restaurant, maybe because their lives are too full of routine. But for men whose lives are already unpredictable and full of other people's dramas, the last thing they're looking for is more variety and excitement. What they want is something that doesn't change, no matter what. Something familiar that doesn't demand anything from you. Like this place."

"Huh." He poured a packet of sugar into his coffee as a faint smile tugged at his heavily lined face. "Thank you, Dr. Freud. I feel much better now."

"I'll send you an invoice this afternoon."

"Don't." He made another tiny smile. His eyes smiled too. "My wife would never understand if I started paying you money." He put on his reading glasses and thumbed through the notebook next to his plate.

"Steven Harold Lewis. Born 1990 in Crescent, Oklahoma. Father Harold, mother Deborah. His parents still live on what's left of their farm. Property records show sale of most of the land parcel in 2007. Only sibling is sister Laurie, four years older. She's a hairdresser in Oklahoma City. She says Lewis left home at 16, the year before the parents sold most of the land. I suspect that's part of the story."

He handed me a blue folder, the kind he always used to deliver his reports. "All the data's in there. No point in contacting the parents again that I can see. The father's response to the news was"—Juergen looked down to check his notebook—"'He's been dead to us for a long time. The devil took that boy early and never let go. We've already done our grieving.'"

"Stef—Steven often made comments that he and his parents fought," I said. There were so many ways parents could shove their children away. At least mine hadn't driven me away in disapproval—just shipped me off to boarding school in Switzerland. By the time I came back to stay, Dad was dead and Mother had weighed anchor on her tanker of martinis, never to set foot on dry land again.

I put the folder beside me. "I'll call Laurie about funeral arrangements. Any other relatives or close friends there?"

Juergen shook his head. He folded his reading glasses and set them beside his notebook, aligning them precisely with its top edge. He was done with his report. "No other relatives that the sister mentioned. Looks like Lewis cut all ties except Laurie when he came to LA." He closed his notebook. "I take it you've met the investigating officer on the case."

"Detective Marco Fidanza. He wants me to come down to the Butler Avenue station this afternoon. He has more questions."

"Uh-huh." Juergen looked at me carefully. "I know him. Know of him, actually. Tough, honest cop. But stay alert around him."

"What do you mean?"

"He comes from a big police family. Very into the tradition 'to serve and protect.' Maybe that's the only reason he stuck it out when he was getting serious shit about being gay. He had a rough time of it, there's no doubt." Juergen took a sip of his coffee. "You said it yourself. Most cops don't like different."

"That's not much reason to be cautious around him."

Juergen shrugged. "Maybe there isn't any. On his first case as detective, he offered to date a gay suspect as a form of surveillance. He palled around with the guy for a month before he got what he was looking for, then they busted him. I think that's why he's accepted by his brethren now." He smiled. "That and a couple of serious fights." He scratched the back of his twice-as-much-salt-as-pepper brush cut. "Policemen prefer simple solutions to their problems."

A chill dribbled down my spine. "Is that even legal? The dating thing?"

"Completely at the discretion of the investigating officers. His partner would have to agree, and it's entered in the case notes. Thorough ass-covering ensues. Probably discussed at the homicide table with his lieutenant. Doesn't happen often, but it can." Juergen sat back in the booth, looking concerned. "I've still got good sources over there. So far, you're the only lead they've got."

"But I didn't kill Stef! I… I couldn't."

"And you've got a solid alibi. Doesn't matter. Fidanza doesn't have anyone else to pay attention to at the moment, so be careful." He picked up the check. "He's attractive, so I'm told."

"More than attractive. He's scorching. Industrial strength mojo."

"He's smart too. Very. Don't underestimate him."

"Thanks, I appreciate it. And for lunch too."

He nodded, tucking his glasses into his shirt pocket, his smile wry. "No problem. All covered by your retainer. Good luck with Fidanza."

Chapter Six

I climbed into the car and headed to the police station where the scorching and dangerous Detective Fidanza apparently plotted to incriminate me. I appreciated Juergen's warning. I wouldn't let Fidanza get too close.

Juergen had also given me the number for Stef's sister, Laurie, in Oklahoma City. It took a few rings for her to answer.

"Hello?" She sounded fragile. I could understand that.

"Laurie, my name is Shepherd Bucknam. I'm a friend of Stef's. Steven's. You talked to my investigator Juergen Hostler recently."

"Stevie told me about you." Silence. Cautious. I could understand that too.

"I'd like your permission to take care of his funeral, and fly you out here to attend, if you'd like that."

She was quiet for a while. "Sure. I guess I'm it, aren't I? My folks don't want nothing to do with him, that's a sure thing."

"I gathered that."

She was silent for a moment. "I'd like to come, but I can't afford it."

"I'll take care of your ticket. Glad to. You can stay at my apartment if you like, or if you'd rather, I'll put you up in a hotel."

"You're gay, right?"

"Yes," I chuckled. She was smart to ask. "You're safe with me. I'd be honored if you'd stay at my place."

"Thanks. That's nice of you."

"Stef—Steven—was very important to me. I want to see this done right."

"Okay. But don't you bury him, you hear?" Her voice rose, hurting and certain. "Cremate him and spread his ashes somewhere wild. No hole-in-the-ground grave for my Stevie. He'd hate that." She began to sob quietly. Right then, it wouldn't have taken much to make me start, either. No corrals for Stef, and no coffin, either. Free-spirited Stef.

"Thank you for letting me do this." I had to clear my throat as I turned off Santa Monica onto Butler. "I'll call you again with dates, and arrange a ticket."

She snuffled. "Okay." Then her voice shifted. "Look, my next appointment just came in. I've got to go."

"No problem. I'll call you later. Or you can call me anytime you feel like it. Really. Anytime at all."

I DIDN'T see any visitor parking at the police station, so I took a meter on the street and reported to the desk. Five minutes later, Fidanza appeared and steered me to what could only be an interrogation room. Two chairs and a metal table with a welded bracket in the middle—for restraints, I guessed. Not even a wastebasket. That was it. The air smelled of pine disinfectant, but I didn't want to think of why the place might have needed disinfecting.

He pointed to a chair. "Have a seat." He put a recorder on the table and sat across from me. He spoke in a brusque monotone into the recorder: date, time, people present, case number, murder of Steven Lewis.

Using the same voice, he read me my rights and asked if I understood them. I said yes, and my attorney was waiting for my call if needed.

He studied the open file in front of him as if he hadn't heard what I'd said or its warning. But then I'd threatened to call my lawyer yesterday. He probably heard that all the time.

"You say you were a friend of the deceased." He sounded nonchalant, even bored. Even without Juergen's warning, he didn't fool me for a second.

"Yes, I was."

"How close a friend?"

"I was his mentor. We were intimate friends."

"Physically intimate?"

"Certainly. Once a month, sometimes more often. For his lesson."

Fidanza looked up, and his lip curled. "A lesson in sex."

I shook my head. "A lesson in sexual intimacy."

"Come on, Bucknam. You're saying he didn't know how to do it?"

"Can you sing Happy Birthday, Detective?" I smiled. "I'll bet you can."

He scowled. "On the right occasion. What's that got to do with this?"

"Dmitri Hvorostovsky can sing happy birthday too. Even though he sings the same notes you do, I think you'd agree it's a very different song when he sings it."

I leaned forward on the table and stared into Marco Fidanza's glare. "Most men know the melody of sex and can stumble through it, pretty much in tune. I teach them how to sing their sexual intimacy like Hvorostovsky sings opera. At least as far as they can go, and as far as I can take them."

The air crackled between us. I could tell I'd gotten to him, and it was clear he didn't like being bested on his own turf. A small ragged vein on his temple pulsed, and his lips pressed to a thin line. I sat back in my chair.

"Very clever," he grumbled. "So you were teaching Lewis to sing sexual opera."

I nodded. "He was incredibly gifted—a natural—but still dangerously naïve." I fought a lump in my throat. "We were working on that too."

"Yes, I'm sure you're not naïve in the least, Mr. Bucknam."

He was good. I folded my arms and replied with silence.

"Did you introduce him to customers?"

"Yes, a few. He had no trouble finding his own, though."

He drew some rectangles in a corner of his notepad. "Did you get a cut of that action?"

"No. He offered, I refused."

"His car had no loan. Was that your doing?"

"Everyone in LA needs a reliable car, Detective. We agreed it would be a loan."

"What about him using your, ah, studio?"

"What about it?"

"Did he pay you for its use?"

"Detective, you seem fixated on money issues. That may make sense in other investigations, but it doesn't in this one. We didn't have any money issues. I would have covered all his costs without a thought, if he'd let me."

He looked up, searching my face for something. "But he didn't."

"He was a free spirit. He didn't like being fenced in."

Fidanza nodded. "Were you trying to fence him in?"

"Not deliberately. And he had no trouble telling me when he felt like I was."

He went back to his doodling. "How did you stay in touch?"

"Phone mostly. Sometimes a text."

"What did you do together besides your, um, opera lessons?"

I couldn't help but laugh. "Not very much." Then I wanted to cry. The truth was that we hadn't done anywhere near enough together. We could have done so much more.

"He loved his independence, as I said. We'd eat together once a week, maybe twice. Occasionally, we'd attend a wine tasting or some other event. One weekend, we went to a gay rodeo in Palm Springs. He loved that."

He glanced at the papers in front of him. "So part of your, ah, mentorship included cosigning his lease and holding a key to his apartment."

"Yes. He'd arrived in LA with nothing. No credit, almost no cash reserves. Sometimes, he was sleeping in dangerous places. He needed a place of his own. I wanted him to stay safe."

"Right," he said, his voice cold and dry. "That worked out well for him, didn't it?"

"How—" I gasped, blindsided by the deliberate cruelty. "I suppose you say that to the children of every officer killed in the line of duty. You must be a real hit at police funerals."

"I thought that might get a reaction from you." He looked up, smug. "I was right."

"Brilliant. You get a reaction by hitting someone with a sledgehammer. Such sophistication. Such finesse."

My heart hammered against my ribs as I leaned forward, hating that he'd found where I hurt most. "Maybe I could have done more to protect him. I wish I had. But if you think I didn't want the best for Stef, you are *wrong,* Detective. Very, very wrong."

He shrugged, unrepentant. The door opened and a heavy-set Hispanic man, probably early fifties, with a tired, fleshy face and a soft middle came in, half dragging a chair. He parked it facing the table, sat, and sighed as if his feet had hurt all day and he'd just discovered the solution.

Fidanza cocked his head at him. "This is my partner, Detective Tomás Alvarez. He's here to make me behave." He picked up the recorder and turned it off before stuffing it in his pocket.

I smiled tightly at Alvarez, still stinging. "You've arrived too late for that, I'm afraid."

He lifted his shoulders an inch, clearly used to the failure. "I do what I can." He looked at his partner. "Malena called. Nicki's over, and the little one is sick. If I want to eat, I've got to buy stuff at the store on the way home. I want to eat."

"You go ahead. Mr. Bucknam and I have one more task," Fidanza said as he closed the file and stood. He stared down at me, and I could tell he was watching for something. "I need you to identify the body, down at the Coroner's Office. You can ride with me, if you like."

Sweat pricked along my neck. I didn't want to see Stef's body. Then I surprised myself. Yes, actually I did. I wanted to say good-bye. We both deserved that. What if I got sick again? Then I got sick, it didn't matter. I wasn't going to try to get out of it. That's probably what Fidanza was hoping for.

There was no way I was going to ride in his car, though. He would just try to nail me again to see how I squirmed. I shook my head. "Give me the address. I'll meet you there."

FIFTY-FIVE MINUTES later, I pulled into the visitor parking lot of the Coroner's Office on Mission Road. Fidanza was waiting for me. He'd rolled up his sleeves, exposing his forearms. Even through the dark hair, I could see how they cabled and bunched when his hands moved. His open collar and loosened tie made it evident there was more of that dark hair underneath the white T-shirt. Yes, industrial strength mojo.

Even so, I'd spent the drive preparing myself to see Stef's body. Now was not the time to be admiring Detective Fidanza's forearms and speculating about the beckoning mystery of his dark forest. I refused to be distracted, but I had to admit he looked hot.

"This won't take long," he promised, all business. I wondered how many times he'd brought someone here to identify a corpse. He'd lost count long ago, no doubt.

We checked in and followed a serious gray-haired man in a lab coat into a cavernous, incredibly slow elevator and down to a room lined with the refrigerated lockers like I'd seen in all kinds of crime shows. It was eerie, being here in real life. Except for the rushing sound of ventilation and our softly echoing steps, the place was silent.

The place smelled like... nothing. Formaldehyde. Chemically preserved nothing. Maybe death had no smell of its own. Decay would be another matter, but that was more life at work, not death. Here, all that was held at bay, at least for a while. Our escort pointed to the wall on our right, and we let him lead.

I worked to keep my breathing even and deep, pushing the tension out of my solar plexus. It didn't help much. The man pulled out a drawer and stepped away. Fidanza strode up to it and crooked a finger at me. I made myself step forward slowly until I was standing opposite him, the rolling slab between us. He pulled back the cover, and there was Stef.

His face had a soft blue cast to it, serene as young Arjuna in a Hindu painting. I touched his cold, stubbled cheek, missing him like hell, wanting him to wake up and laugh, to make one of his corny jokes. And then I noticed that I felt fine, which was a complete surprise. Not even a twist of sick nerves.

I lifted the cover until I could see the gunshot wounds in his chest, even the long, ugly autopsy incisions. That made me queasy, but it wasn't at all the same as my panic nausea. I didn't understand. I let the cloth sag back and smoothed it out tenderly.

"Stef," I whispered to his empty body, "I'll do everything I can to see this resolved. Doesn't matter how long it takes. That's a promise."

With a start, I remembered I wasn't alone. I looked up, feeling embarrassed. Fidanza was staring at me with disturbing intensity. "I'm sorry, I forgot...."

"Never mind." He waved me off. "That's Steven Lewis?"

"It's his body," I corrected. Seeing his corpse made it clear that who Stef really was had left town two days ago.

"As you say." He signaled to the attendant who stepped forward, closed the drawer, got a signature from Fidanza, and escorted us back to the elevator.

On the slow ride up, I said, "You know, Stef mentioned something else to me about the client he expected the night he died. A politician. That night wasn't his first appointment with him. Stef happened to see him on the news and recognized him. He never did say who it was."

"We know who it was. Lewis's phone was taken from the scene, but we have his phone records."

"Who was it?"

Fidanza stared at me for a second before shaking his head. "Don't get involved, Bucknam. Leave this to the professionals."

"And simply knowing who his client was would be getting involved?"

He nodded. "With you, I have a feeling it would." His face hardened. "You do not want to start meddling in this investigation," he growled. "Take my word on that."

I recognized a real threat when I heard one. It fired nerves all the way down my spine. I nodded.

Once outside, we stood in the parking lot for a moment, not moving. It felt to me like Fidanza wanted to say something, and I was in no hurry to face the long drive home.

"Are you finished at the studio?" I asked. "I want to sell it."

"Yeah, we're done there. Go ahead." His voice was warmer, even kind. Maybe.

"I talked to Laurie, Stef's—Steve's—sister in Oklahoma City. She's given me permission to arrange cremation and a memorial service. I've posted on his Facebook page that he's dead and to contact me for details about the memorial if anyone's interested."

"No reason to delay." He turned to face me. "Look, do you want to get a coffee somewhere?"

I could feel myself do a double take, incredulous. "Really? A little earlier this afternoon you were abusing me and enjoying the hell out of it."

"Hey," he said. It was the first time I'd seen his smile. It was a killer. "I was hard on you. I had to be, it's my job. But after watching you downstairs, I'm willing to start looking elsewhere for the murderer."

"Not to mention I have an alibi."

"There is that," he said with a soft chuckle. "So are you up for that coffee?"

"To tell you the truth, no. It's been a harrowing day for me, and I'm exhausted. I don't think I'd be very good company." I smiled back to let him know it wasn't a full refusal. "Rain check, though?"

"Sure." He pulled off his tie. More of the crisp black hair at the base of his throat called out for friendly attention. He stuffed the tie in his jacket pocket and grinned. "Punching out, off duty. I'll call you soon," he said and walked away.

I sat in my car for a minute, eyes closed and head back, missing Stef and unnerved by Fidanza's invitation.

It sounded like the police were making progress. Still, I owed Stef... something. Action of some kind. I sighed and turned the key, and the Maserati came to life with its throaty rumble. It was such a great sound.

There was no point getting onto the 10 at this time of day. I decided to go through downtown and make my way to Wilshire instead. I pulled out of the parking lot and headed toward fifteen miles of stoplights.

Once on Wilshire, I dialed Maddie, the virtual assistant I used for research and odd admin jobs.

"Make It So Services," she answered on the first ring. "Good afternoon, Mr. Bucknam. How can I help you today?" Her cheerful efficiency was always a lift, and her performance was every bit as good as she sounded. She got things done.

"Hi, Maddie. I need you to research some local service charities for me. The focus should be on helping gay teenagers at risk. Abuse or rejection at home or school, bullying, trouble with the law, whatever. Preferably not a primary focus on drugs. If they have strong fresh start programs that would be a plus. Maybe find three with solid reputations and e-mail me a two-page summary on each, including contact information."

"Certainly, Mr. Bucknam." I could feel her typing in the assignment. "Anything else?"

"Don't think so. But do check news archives for stories about each of them. Good or bad."

"Got it. How soon do you need this?"

"Any time in the next week is fine."

"Terrific. And has any of your contact info changed?"

"Nope. Same old, same old."

She laughed. "I'll get right on it. Would you like a progress report in a couple of days?"

"No, not necessary."

"Okay. Thank you, Mr. Bucknam. You have a great day," she chirped, and hung up.

I needed music that was big and cathartic, so I put on Sibelius's Second Symphony, listened to the whole thing, and then drove in silence another half hour before I got home. I took a shower, did some stretching, and meditated. It felt like the middle of the night. I poured myself a glass of stony, bracing Chablis, ate some fruit, and collapsed into bed at ten.

Stef visited my dreams. He smiled and laughed a lot, joking with me. I didn't really understand anything he said, just that we were happy to be together again. Like a powerful drug, his sunny affection sank me into my first deep rest in two days.

Chapter Seven

There was so much to do in the next few days I didn't really notice that Detective Fidanza hadn't called. In fact, he would have been a distraction—one I didn't need while arranging cremation, memorial space, and flowers; unleashing my real estate agent to get the studio cleaned up and listed, then to look for a new one; suspending client appointments; and picking up Stef's sister, Laurie, at the airport and getting her settled at my place. I was grateful to be so busy.

I recognized Laurie as soon as she walked past security. Her hair was dark, probably dyed, and she was heavier and softer than Stef, but her face and eyes were unmistakable. Stef's sister.

At her request, we drove directly to Stef's tiny West Hollywood apartment and spent a tender afternoon going through his things. She swore and broke down in tears when she saw the battered stuffed horse he kept on his bed. It had been her Christmas gift to him when he was five, she said, and he'd never parted with it. She carried it like a sleeping infant as we went through the apartment.

Although he owned almost nothing, she found things that were important to her—two small framed photos, one of the two of them with their arms around each other, mugging for the camera. She wanted his cowboy belt with its flashy buckle, his music CDs and iPod, some books, and picked out a couple of his western-style shirts.

We set them all aside to take back to my condo for packing up. I told her I'd sell his car and send her the money, and ship his laptop once the police released it.

I asked her if she wanted some of his trendier clothes, items he'd bought since coming to LA, but she said no, she didn't really want to imagine him in those. On impulse, I asked her if I could have his cowboy boots, and she said yes.

Laurie looked exhausted. The next day was the memorial service, and I figured she could use some quiet and rest. I didn't want to rush her, but suggested that when she was ready, we take her things back to the apartment and go out for an early dinner.

She nodded, looking lost, still clutching the stuffed horse she couldn't put in the box yet.

"I hate cooking," she said as if we'd been talking about it for a while. "Stevie liked it, though. He was pretty good, too, although I have no idea where he picked it up." She laughed, wiping tears. "Not from Momma, that's a sure thing. If it can't be fried in smashed cornflakes and Crisco, she don't want no part of it."

"I had no idea he liked to cook." I wished I'd known that. I felt a little cheated that he hadn't told me. An important aspect of his life we'd never shared, one we could have enjoyed together. Stef hadn't kept it a secret, though. He hated secrets. It was my fault for not finding out. "I enjoy cooking, too."

"You guys always seem to," she said with a rueful grin, running her hand across the plastic cutting board beside the stove. "He'd get recipes off the Internet, then try them out on me. Back home I got a whole kitchen full of gadgets I'll never use." She started to cry again, and I put my arm around her shoulders.

"It hurts, doesn't it?" I said softly. "He was an amazing young man, and we're lucky to have known him as well as we did." I wiped my eyes with my free hand, not letting her go.

She looked at me sideways and grinned. "You better save some of that for the memorial tomorrow. I don't want to be the only one cryin'."

I gave her a squeeze. "I can guarantee you won't be. I'll make sure there are plenty of tissues handy."

On the way back to the apartment, Laurie stared out the car window, silent for a long time. "You folks have to drive everywhere, don't you?"

"Pretty much."

"I don't think I could live like this. I need to be able to walk places, I guess."

I grimaced. "Apologies ahead of time, but we'll have to drive to the restaurant tonight too. If you'd rather not go out again, that's fine. We can order in, or I can see what I've got in the fridge."

She patted my right hand, which rested on the gearshift. "No, I was just thinkin' out loud. Shoulda kept my mouth shut, probably."

"Not at all," I said firmly. "I hope you'll think out loud to me anytime."

"Thanks," she said, pulling back her hand with a shy smile. "I 'preciate it."

"YOU COME here a lot?" asked Laurie as she looked around Chez Henri. "That head waiter guy knew your name."

"Yes, fairly often. I like it. The food is very good, and the more trend-worshipping herd usually grazes elsewhere." I decided not to tell her that my last meal with Stef had been here, just two tables from where we sat.

She looked over the menu. "Stevie said you were rich. You'd hafta be, just to eat here."

"I am rich. I was born rich. I was born gay. I have no excuses."

"You don't need to make no excuses to me, that's a sure thing." She looked me in the eye, as an equal. "Stevie said you were good to him, and I'm real grateful for that."

We ordered, the wine steward poured, we talked about Oklahoma City. Laurie liked being a hair stylist. She had regulars who liked her. She didn't have a boyfriend at the moment, but she didn't mind—most of the time they were a nuisance anyway. She wanted to learn Spanish and was thinking of an evening conversation class at the library near her apartment if she could get Wednesday nights off for two months.

When the food came, we ate mostly in relaxed silence, broken by discussion of the food and more talk of her life at home. But halfway through, she put her fork down and waited until I looked directly at her.

"You know what, Stevie admired you, and it wasn't about your money. Well, maybe a little it was, but not mostly. He liked you a lot. I can see why. You're a nice man, Shepherd."

I could feel myself blush into my scalp. I couldn't remember the last time that had happened from a compliment. "Thank you," I said, lifting my wine glass in a salute.

"Like I said before, I want you to take care of Stevie's ashes, spread them somewhere natural. Free."

My neck stiffened. I hadn't expected the responsibility. What if I made the wrong choice? "I have no idea what to do with them."

"Take your time." She smiled, and a flash of Stef's roguish humor sparkled in her eyes. "He's in no hurry, that's a sure thing. Just let me know what you do, so I'll know too."

"I can fly you back out for that, if you want."

She shook her head. "I don't want to come back here again. It's too much—of everything." She pursed her lips. "Besides, Stevie living in the big bad city is not part of my story with him."

"Are you sure you don't want to take the ashes home?"

"Back to Oklahoma?" she snorted, looking horrified. "No way. I promise you, that is the very last place on earth Stevie would want to end up."

She swirled her wine around in the glass, studying its rhythmic golden wave. "No, you pick the right place out here," she said, looking at me over the glass, closing the subject. "That's part of your story with him, I think. I trust you with that."

She gazed at me, and the burden of the task settled in my heart. It was something I could do for Stef. It felt good.

"Only when you figure it out, and the right time comes. Then let me know it's done." She smiled, wistful. "Send me a nice picture of the place."

Chapter Eight

The memorial chapel bounced to one of Stef's CDs. Laurie had picked it out—Edward Sharpe and the Magnetic Zeros. As unusual as it was for a memorial, I had to admit it was perfect. So Stef. Part country, part Zydeco, part rock, with compelling, happy rhythms. It was a terrific beginning.

I'd asked the florist to make the arrangements big, sunny, upbeat, and informal. They even smelled sunny. There were sunflowers, daisies, roses, freesia, gladiolas, snapdragons, even orchids. Every shade of yellow or orange imaginable illuminated the room, offset with a little red and white and lots of green.

A blow-up of my favorite photo of Stef laughing, one I'd taken in front of a roller coaster, sat in front of a scarred wooden lectern. Happily, extravagant sheaves of gladiolas served as camouflage for the lectern itself. Only its long neck microphone and a churchy-looking brass reading light stuck above the blooms.

To my surprise, I'd received six messages in response to my post on Stef's Facebook page. I'd replied to each, giving them the time and location of the service. Four twinkish young men I didn't recognize stood clustered around Laurie, chatting, and I assumed they were here because of that. I don't know how many I expected to show up, but I wanted more than this handful.

Also to my surprise, Detectives Fidanza and Alvarez had walked in twenty minutes before the service was scheduled to start. They sat on opposite sides of the center aisle at the back looking respectful. Alvarez looked respectful and tired. Fidanza looked respectful and dangerous in a classic-cut navy suit, pale blue shirt, and midnight blue tie.

When it was time to begin, I caught Laurie's eye and pointed to my watch. She nodded, and her little group migrated to the chairs.

I signaled for the music to stop and, as it faded, walked to the lectern. Counting me, there were eight people in twenty chairs, in a room that could hold seventy-five. I wanted the place to be packed with mourners. Who here would remember Stef two or three years from now? Probably just Laurie and me. At least the open spaces had been broken up with oversize floral arrangements.

"Good afternoon, and thank you each for coming," I said, already fighting the lump growing in my throat, "to take some time to appreciate Steven Lewis—Stevie to his family—whom some of us knew as Stef."

I cleared my throat. "My name is Shepherd Bucknam, I'm honored to serve as MC today." I tried to smile and felt like I almost succeeded. "Not that there's going to be much ceremony for me to manage. Before we go any further, I'd like to thank Stevie's sister, Laurie, for coming to LA. It's been a pleasure getting to know her a little, even under these painful circumstances."

She gave me a tight smile, dabbed her nose with a handkerchief, and nodded. She was ready. "There'll be time for each of us to say something about Stef—Stevie—if we want," I continued, "but Laurie said she wanted to speak first."

Laurie made her way to the lectern, looking determined. "I figure there are two parts to Stevie's story," she began in a shaky voice. "There's the back home part that I know most about, and then the LA part that you know most about." She blew her nose. "So we can all learn something more about him today."

She pulled out a piece of paper and studied it for a moment before looking up, grinning with the same humor that I'd loved in Stef. "I made notes, but this is all stuff that I sure ain't never gonna forget. Stevie was born in 1990 on our little farm in Crescent. That's north of Oklahoma City. I was four when he arrived, and I loved him from the first minute I saw him. Somehow, I just knew we were supposed to be together.

"As we grew up, we became best friends. Before he was old enough to go to school, I'd get off the bus and he'd be waiting for me, his nose pressed against a window. Not just once or twice. Every day."

She folded the paper and squared her shoulders. "Mostly today I want to talk about how brave Stevie was. He knew he was different way back in grade school. He didn't get picked on much, 'cause he'd fight anybody who looked at him cross-wise, even if he knew he'd lose bad. The bigger kids respected that and let him be. For the most part, anyways.

"It was hard for both us kids at home, but especially for Stevie. I moved down to Oklahoma City when I turned eighteen, waited tables to make ends meet and earn money for school. I'm a hairstylist now. I knew it would be hell for Stevie at home after I left, but I just couldn't stay any longer, even for him.

"Daddy was always way more strict with Stevie than he'd ever been with me. Kept sayin' Stevie had the devil in him. And he kept trying to beat the devil out of him with that big ol' belt of his. Wasn't a week would go by that Stevie didn't have marks on his back. When he was little, he'd sometimes sneak into my bedroom after everyone was in bed and lie on the floor next to me and sob. Wouldn't even climb into my bed. He refused to cry in front of Daddy, but he'd let loose with me. We kept no secrets from each other. Heck, we even talked about the boys we liked.

"Then one day, more'n a year after I'd left, maybe a year and a half, Daddy got set to beat him like regular. But Stevie just yanked that belt out of his hands, rolled it up, and held it for a while, right up in front of his face. Told Daddy never to touch him again or else, then handed his belt right back to him. He was one tough kid. Stevie said Daddy never did hit him again.

"My folks wanted Stevie to take over the farm, but everyone knew that wasn't going to happen, even Daddy. I think that's one of the reasons he was so hard on him. Anyway, a few months after Stevie stopped the whuppings, he came to live with me in the city. I was really glad." She pushed her hair off her cheek and tried to smile. "He never set foot on the farm again, and as far as I know, never spoke to our folks again, neither.

"I kinda stayed in touch with Ma and Daddy for a while, went to dinner or church with them every now and then, but mostly it was too depressing. And Daddy never once asked after Stevie, even though Ma did sometimes, when Daddy wasn't in the room.

"They sold most of the farmland to a neighbor about a year after Stevie left. Daddy couldn't keep it going, and I'm certain he never forgave Stevie for not taking on the farm as much as for standing up to him like he had. After a while, I saw that Ma and Daddy didn't really feel happy with me coming around, neither, and I'm pretty sure that was because of Stevie. So I stopped. It was a relief for me too."

Laurie took a deep breath and looked around, as if daring anyone to pass judgment on her brother. "Stevie was barely sixteen when he came to stay with me. He waited tables to begin with, just like I had. And things got a lot easier with us sharing the apartment and food expenses.

"But soon I could tell he was making more money than he could get from just waiting tables. I asked him if he was selling drugs, and he said not unless I counted his dick as a needle." She laughed through her tears, and I joined her in both. So like Stef.

When the gentle laughter faded, she continued. "He said he'd started meeting men at the restaurant, and word got around in a hurry. Stevie was real generous to me—paid most of my beautician's ticket—and I'll always be grateful to him for the help. I couldn't have done it without him.

"Anyway"—she took another big breath and smiled—"he and I shared a place for four years or so. It was really good. I could tell he was getting restless toward the end of that time, though. He started talking about Los Angeles and West Hollywood, things he'd seen on his computer. First, he got his own place in Oklahoma City, but that wasn't enough to scratch his itch, neither.

"So last year, he packed up and moved." Her voice quavered. "I was afraid for him, 'cause I knew what he was gonna do to get by, but there was nothin' I could say to him that would change his mind. And I knew he was just being Stevie.

"You can imagine my relief when, a few months later, he phoned to tell me about his new friend Shepherd." She looked at me and smiled, blinking away tears. "I'm gonna look like a raccoon in a minute if I'm not careful."

She stared at the lectern for a moment, swallowing until she could talk again. "That was five or six months ago, I think. Every phone call after that, he sounded happier, and more in his groove. He told me about how good Shepherd was to him, what he was teaching him, and it sounded just so natural for Stevie, like he'd been born to that kind of work. He said it was a sacred art, and I could tell he was totally into it.

"So I want to thank Shepherd for making Stevie so happy. Maybe for the first time in his life, happy all the way through."

She looked around at each person in the room, including the detectives. She was delivering a message. "I've asked Shepherd to scatter Stevie's ashes somewhere nice, someplace wild and natural, where he can be part of everything. Free. That's the way he was, deep inside. Wild and free. That's what he would have wanted."

She blew a kiss at me and slowly made her way to her chair. One of the boys put his arm around Laurie, and although she didn't lean into him, I saw her relax. For a long while, nobody moved.

Eventually one of the boys stood and spoke. He'd met Stef just a week off the bus from Oklahoma City, he said. They'd shared an apartment for a while, and Stef was great company. After Stef moved into his own place, they'd stayed in touch by getting takeout and going to clubs every now and then. He wished he'd made more effort to spend time with Stef. He always assumed there'd be plenty of time for that later.

Two of the other young men said essentially the same thing. Stef's adventuresome nature, his generosity, and his good heart were all recurring themes. Everyone nodded in agreement every time those comments came up.

When it was clear that everyone who wanted to speak had had their say, I stood up again and spoke a bit, and in spite of my best efforts to keep the tears down, cried more than Laurie had. I thanked everyone again and signaled to have Stef's music put back on.

Laurie and I stood together near the lectern, my left arm around her shoulders, a reception line of two. Maybe that was presumptuous of me, but I certainly wasn't going to let her stand alone. The boys shook Laurie's hand and mine, then melted away.

Marco Fidanza came up to Laurie to shake her hand while Alvarez hung back. "Thank you, Ms. Lewis, for your touching story. I'm sorry I didn't get to meet your brother. We intend to meet whoever killed him, though."

"Thank you, Detective," she said quietly.

He turned to me. "I'll want whatever contact information you have on the boys."

"Sure. Have you found anything new?" I asked. Fidanza stiffened, and his eyes narrowed. "I meant no criticism," I added hastily. "I'm just asking."

The guarded look didn't go away. In fact, he seemed angry. "Not much. We're doing the best we can."

"I have no doubt. And thank you for that."

"Any information you can provide will help. Like the information on those four guys."

I nodded. "I'll e-mail you right after I take Laurie to the airport."

LAURIE STARED out the car window at the crawling traffic around us. "Detective Fidanza bats for your team, doesn't he?"

I couldn't stop my smile. "Yes."

"You gay guys always get the cream of the crop. Too damn good-lookin' to be straight. So unfair." She turned and grinned at me. "I think he's into you. He kept staring at you when you weren't looking."

I wanted to believe that was the reason but wasn't convinced. "That's probably because he's still wondering if I killed your brother."

Her eyes widened. "He thinks that? He can't! That's just plain stupid."

"Apparently, most murders are committed by people the victim knew. There aren't many here who knew your brother at all besides me."

"Did you do it?"

"No! I swear."

"Good enough for me." She turned back to the window and was silent for a while.

Traffic on the 405 slowed to stop and go. "I will *not* miss this place, Shepherd," she announced. "This is pure torture, but nobody seems the least bit bothered by it."

"There are good things about LA too."

She made a dismissive noise. "Maybe, but give me Oklahoma City any day. At least when I get in my car, I know I'll go faster than I can walk."

I hugged her good-bye at the curb, and felt another pang as she disappeared through the doors, as if I was losing another piece of Stef. I wondered how long it would take for Fidanza to track down the killer. At the moment, all I could do was wait, and trust that he would.

Chapter Nine

As soon as I got home, I sent Fidanza the e-mail addresses of the young men who had responded, identifying the two who had responded but hadn't shown, and the one who'd come but hadn't spoken. While I was doing that, Maddie's research on charities working with at-risk teens popped up in my inbox.

I read through them. She'd been thorough, as always. I liked the feel of Off the Street best, and settled on them for my donation in Stef's memory. I'd make sure his name wouldn't vanish, at least as long as I was alive. I called the director to set up a lunch.

I set the amphora-style urn holding Stef's ashes on my coffee table. What was I going to do with it? I had no idea. I certainly wasn't going to put it in a closet—symbolically unacceptable. No, his ashes would stay in my living room until I could figure out where to spread them.

The urn sat like a person in the room, asking me what I was going to do to find out who had done this to Stef. I needed to help the police if I could.

I called Fidanza. "I was thinking," I began, "that if I went through Stef's phone with you, I could give some background on the people whose numbers I recognized."

"The phone was taken the night Lewis was shot. I told you that the other day."

"But you also told me you had the records."

"Please don't tell me how to do my job, Bucknam," he said, sounding tired and frustrated. "We do have the records. We're working on it."

"But I'm sure I could help. Time is slipping away. Isn't it true that most solved murders are solved in the first forty-eight hours? It's already been a week."

There was a silence on the phone. Then Fidanza said, "Look, I know you mean well. But leave the legwork to us professionals. If something comes up in the phone records that we'd like your input on, believe me, you'll get a call."

Leave this to the professionals and have a nice day. Okay, I would. "Thanks, Detective. You're right, I should back off. I'm just trying to help solve the murder of my friend."

He ignored my sarcasm. "No, keep your ideas coming. You never know." Then his voice shifted into a sultry promise. "I'm still going to call you for coffee as soon as I can, but I've been tied up, as you might imagine."

I was embarrassed at how quickly I was prepared to forgive him, but I couldn't resist. "I can imagine you tied up, but that doesn't look like coffee to me."

He chuckled. "You wish. Talk to you later."

The image did have its merits. Its merits were giving me a very pleasant stir.

I didn't have to wait for the police to call for my help, though. I had another way of leaving it to the professionals. I called Juergen.

"I was wondering," I said. "Can you get a copy of the texts and phone history from Stef's number?"

He was quiet for a moment, but I could feel him thinking. "Maybe. It's delicate. Dangerous, actually. Could be expensive."

"I don't care about the expense, but I don't want you to do anything that would jeopardize your license."

"Don't worry about that. We're not going there."

"Good."

"I'll see what I can do," he said and hung up.

My phone clinked a text alert. It was from Reggie. *Call me about tomorrow's appt.* So I did.

"About our session tomorrow," he said. "How do you feel about having Alana, my hypnotherapist colleague, join us? You both can get a feel for each other, and you can decide whether to go forward with her."

Somehow, I'd assumed that his colleague would be male. I was a little embarrassed about the assumption. "Sure. That sounds right to me."

"I'll arrange it. See you tomorrow."

Chapter Ten

Dr. Alana Phillips sat in a chair at the opposite end of the couch from Reggie, dressed in a quietly tasteful gray suit. Her blonde hair was gathered loosely at the back of her neck, which accentuated her wide-set green eyes and generous mouth. She radiated calm intelligence as she turned her attention to whoever was speaking, projecting her engaged interest without the slightest ruffle of opinion or concern.

When introductions and small talk were finished, I watched her watching Reggie as he referred to his notes. "Did anything come up for you around the memorial service that might have a bearing on your somatic response to violence?"

"I didn't have an attack, if that's what you mean." I thought back through the events.

"I did have one surprise, though," I said. "Detective Fidanza asked me to identify Stef's body. I think it was some kind of test to see if I was the killer. I was pretty nervous going to the morgue but when I actually saw Stef's corpse, I didn't have the slightest reaction. In fact, I felt incredibly calm. I even lifted the sheet to see the bullet wounds and the autopsy incisions. I did get a little squeamish then, but it didn't feel like it originated from my problem. There was no pain in my throat, for one thing."

"I'd suggest it's a perfectly normal response to feel a little squeamish when viewing a body after an autopsy," Reggie said blandly. "Have you ever looked at a post-autopsy cadaver before?"

"No," I said with a joyless smile. "That was a first."

"Then I think you deserve full marks for being normal." Reggie grinned as he looked up at Alana, who nodded.

"I agree," she said. Her voice and her smile bathed me in warm encouragement and comfort.

"So Shepherd," Reggie said, "I'm wondering if you would describe your recurring dream to Alana."

Suddenly, I was awash in sadness, and it wasn't just the dream. *Here we go again,* I thought. *I've gone over this again and again, and still I can't break free. What if I never will?* The thought was crushing.

"Sure. If you think it will make any difference."

I sat back in the chair and closed my eyes, summoning the memory as I had done a dozen times before in this room, putting it in journal-speak present tense. "I am walking somewhere in a big city. The weather is warm. It feels like spring. It's daytime, and the narrow street is busy. It doesn't feel like Los Angeles, more East Coast. I'm happy and confident. In fact, I'm in love. I'm walking with a bit of a swagger, and I'm full of anticipation.

"Then something happens nearby that I don't see, off to my right, and a shadow falls across the sidewalk in front of me. My happy mood vanishes. I feel confusion, pain, and fear. I lose my balance. The ground crumbles under my feet, and I'm falling into a big hole. I'm angry, like I've been robbed, but I know that's not true. More like something precious has been taken from inside me. It feels like betrayal. By someone I know.

"Then I'm in an alley. Angry, dangerous men about my age start to gather around me and I'm defenseless. I need what I've lost to protect me, but somehow, they've taken it from me. I know they mean to hurt me.

"I can't see clearly, but I know I'm cornered. There are too many of them, and they've cut off any escape. They are laughing, and I'm weak, completely humiliated.

"One of them has a heavy stick. He swings at me, and I put up my arm to protect my head. The blow breaks my arm, between my elbow and wrist. It bends backward at a horrible angle. There's nothing I can do, so I just stand there. Then he hits me here." My hand went, as it always did, to where my left collarbone joined the sternum, right on top of my red birthmarks.

"I feel another bone break, maybe more than one, and the pain is terrible. But I can't cry out, my voice is crushed, and I can't breathe. The circle of men are laughing and joking. They take turns kicking me until I die. Then I wake up. No matter how I try, I can never wake up until I'm dead."

I knew I'd started to cry. I took a moment before opening my eyes, willing my heart to slow down. Then I reached for a tissue and wiped my face and the base of my neck with a shaky hand. The whole collar was damp. In fact, the sides of my shirt were clammy with sweat.

After a while, Dr. Phillips spoke softly. "I can see this dream evokes great sadness or anger in you, maybe both. And you can't remember anything like this happening to you?"

"Not only do I not remember, but my medical records prove I've never even broken a bone. This hasn't happened to me." I made myself voice my real fear. "Yet."

"Just to clarify, you believe that this may happen to you in the future?"

"I'm certain of it. I know the dream belongs to me. It just hasn't happened yet."

"I'd like to help you explore your beliefs around this, Shepherd," she said, smiling gently. "I think hypnosis could be a useful tool for you. I'd like to see if you can reclaim a sense of ownership of your future. As we do that, I can help you develop your inner resources for when you experience these challenging emotions." She smiled at me, and I saw no fake promises there, just care, ready to help. "If you think that might be helpful."

I smiled back at her, feeling a flicker of hope. "I'd like that too. I'd like that more than anything." We made an appointment.

Chapter Eleven

Driving home from Reggie's, I got a call from Fidanza. "I'm wondering if you'd like to get together this afternoon for that coffee you agreed to," he said, his voice warm and playful, "or better yet, maybe a drink."

Again, Juergen's warning came back to me. But I wasn't guilty, and I wanted to see him. If I were looking for a lover, which I wasn't, Marco would be a serious contender. I must have taken too long to respond.

"Well, what do you think?"

"Sorry, I'm driving. Hands-free phone, of course, officer," I added with a short laugh. I did a quick scan of possible choices—something nice but not too fancy. The last thing I wanted was to make our meeting place about money. We agreed on Bar and Kitchen at the O Hotel downtown, at five o'clock. I called ahead to arrange for a table away from the bar.

Getting together might be ill-advised, but I wanted it. I'd get firsthand insight into what made Detective Fidanza tick. He scared me. He also stirred me in ways I hadn't felt for a long time. This would be an adventure.

It was 5:30 when Fidanza arrived, but it didn't look like he'd been late by choice. "You look like you've had a hard day, Detective." I smiled up at him as he sat.

"Yes, I had a hard day. I often do." Our eyes locked, and I felt the wallop again. It lit me up. "Call me Marco. Please."

"Marco. Does that mean I'm scratched off the list of suspects?" I pretended to be playful. "This isn't official?"

He grunted as he scowled at the happy hour menu. "If you confess to killing Lewis, I'd take you in." He looked up and shrugged. "But I don't think you will."

"So this *is* official, since you avoided my question."

He sighed and returned his attention to the menu. "I'm on duty all the time. It's one of the many reasons I'm single."

I waited until he looked at me again. "I didn't do it."

"I believe you." He didn't blink.

I wasn't sure I believed him but decided not to challenge him. "I'm single too."

"I know."

The waiter appeared. I ordered a glass of pinot noir, and he ordered a microbrew IPA.

"The calamari is really good here," I said. "Everything is. Do you want to nibble on something hot?" His head jerked up from the menu, as if I'd baited him with innuendo. Maybe I had. He made it very easy to flirt.

He stared at me, jaw clenched hard. "Calamari sounds good."

As the waiter left, I took a risk. "Are you angry with me?"

He pulled the knot of his tie away from his throat without breaking eye contact. "Shall we jump in the deep end right away and make this a truth-telling happy hour?"

I had no idea what that meant to him, but I grinned, feeling brave. "Let's. Is that like speed dating without a bell?"

"No bell, no games. Fasten your seat belt." He kept staring, and I started to feel less brave. "I am angry, but at myself. I shouldn't want to haul your ass to bed the way I do right now. It's a really bad idea—the last thing I need, personally or career-wise. But I do."

"Truth-telling is good," I said, unable to ignore the warm pleasure spreading through my core. "I'm in the same boat. The last thing I need or want is to be attracted to a man who calls me a prostitute and might still think I'm a killer. But I *am* attracted. He's insanely hot and seems like a smart, decent guy."

I stopped when the waiter brought our drinks, and waited for him to go before continuing. "The difference is that I'm not mad at myself for it. I'm scared. I see nothing but disaster ahead."

We lifted our glasses and, in the same instant, tilted them toward each other, laughing in unspoken mutual salute. "Here's to looming disaster," Marco murmured in a voice that had become rough and bedroom thick.

Why not? Caught up in the swirl of wanting/not wanting and its adrenaline buzz, I clinked his glass. "To looming disaster." I took a reckless gulp.

"While we're immersed in this truth-telling plunge," I continued, "let's take turns asking each other serious questions. No holds barred, okay?" I raised my hand, riding the dangers of the adventure. "I ask first."

"You never let up, do you?" He leaned forward, his lips slightly parted. "I like that."

He sat back in the chair, knees wide apart, hands up. "Ask away."

"What makes you really angry?"

His eyebrows lifted, as if that surprised him. Maybe he was expecting a question about sex. He nodded, and I saw respect in his face.

"I hate cheaters," he said. "Maybe that's why I'm a cop. But it's not just crime. Anyone. For example, I'm thrilled that none of the big dopers, especially Barry Bonds, was elected into the Hall of Fame this year. I hope they never make it. Ever. I cheered when Lance Armstrong was stripped of his titles."

The hardness in his voice scared me. Cheaters unmasked. He'd seen me in a similar light, at least at first. Maybe he still did. "You're sure Bonds was doping?"

Marco's laugh was little more than a sneer. "Everyone knew, even the Giants. That's why when he was rounding the bases after breaking Aaron's record, they shot all those fireworks into the air. 'Put these big asterisks next to every record this man holds!' they shouted from above McCovey Cove."

He took a swig of beer. "I hope to hell they reinstate Aaron's home run record." He leaned forward. "My turn now."

"Your smile is showing too many rows of teeth, officer."

He showed them all. "And I bite."

I grinned and stuck my hands forward, wrists together. "Cuff me, then."

He shook his head, laughing. "Only if you're a really bad boy and earn them." He turned serious. "What kind of long-term relationships have you had, how did they end, and do you want one now?"

"Wow. You get right to it, don't you? And that was three questions."

He didn't say anything. Didn't even smile. He just stared at me, waiting for me to answer.

I took a deep breath. "I had a few affairs when I was a teenager—"

He cut me off. "Adult relationships, I mean."

"Don't tell me how to answer." I bristled. "If you want my truth-telling, you're going to have to let me give you my answer."

"Fair enough." He nodded, more thoughtful. "Go ahead."

"My last teenage affair was with a boy at school. We were lovers for a while. Four months, maybe—a long time for teenagers. We even talked about the future. Then he was seduced by the captain of our rowing team who fucked him raw and slapped him around for a couple of weeks. Finally outed him in the cruelest possible way. Danny jumped from the school's bell tower the night that happened."

I stared into my glass of wine. "He would come back to me after being with Rory, and I'd hold him for a while and help him clean up. He was usually bleeding, but he couldn't stop going back for more."

I fought my way out of the memory, sat up, and met his eyes. "Since then, I've been... cautious. My long-term relationships have been unconventional ones. My longest relationship has been with one of my tantric teachers. Peter. He's in his seventies, and he's a pleasure to be with, in every sense of that word."

Marco's face had hardened into a mask.

"You've met him," I said. "Peter Karspek. He's part of the group I called our concert club. You questioned him about my alibi, I'm sure."

Marco nodded but didn't say anything. The calamari arrived. Under the crisp peppery coating, I could still taste the sea in them. We polished them off in a hurry. "Should we order dinner?" I asked.

"Yeah," he said. "Sounds like this will take a while."

I signaled to the waiter, who fetched menus for us. We ordered right away and picked a bottle of wine, as if neither of us wanted another interruption later.

"So to finish my answer," I began again, "that relationship has lasted almost fifteen years, and it's not over." I waited for a minute until I was ready to answer the last part. "Do I want a traditional long-term relationship now? I don't think so. Maybe. But it's not been a priority for me. Am I ready to pick out china with someone tomorrow?" I shook my head. "No."

Marco nodded and snapped a breadstick, looking angry.

"My turn again," I said. "Same questions for you. Long-term relationships."

Maybe he was reconsidering his interest in me or even preparing to bolt. There was no way he could rationally think I was relationship material. Whatever his reason, he took a while, which was fine with me. I was unnerved, even though this reckless honesty felt right. We weren't kids. We were mature adults, strong enough to talk about our inner landscapes, experienced enough to have earned some scars.

"I've had one," he said, his voice sounding sad and far away. "It lasted five years. We bought the china, the whole nine yards." He cleared his throat and took a drink of water.

"It ended badly three years ago, a year before I made detective. It tore me up." He looked up, unapologetic. "He was too young, and so was I. We grew up in different directions. I've tried a couple of times since, but they didn't pan out. Yes, I want another one. And I'm ready now."

"What are you most afraid of?" he asked. He picked up his wine and smiled as if he'd just asked my opinion of a movie.

That one shook me. My face must've shown it, too, because he nodded. "Take your time," he said. "It's a hard question, I know."

I did take my time, because I didn't really want to answer. If I told him the truth, it would make me more vulnerable, and his intensity already frightened me. But we'd started this, and I couldn't bail now just because he'd picked a tough question.

I looked him straight in the eyes. "I have a recurring nightmare. I'm beaten to death after being betrayed by someone I love." I held his eyes and took a deep breath. "I'm afraid it's prophetic, that it'll happen. Because of that, I'm terrified of physical violence. I panic and throw up when I encounter it."

His eyes never left mine. He didn't even blink, but I could see he was thinking at warp speed.

"Which is why I'm not big on traditional relationships, and also why I couldn't have killed Stef." I slumped back in the chair. "So now you know my Achilles' heel," I said with an apologetic smile. "Not the best emotional foundation for a capital R relationship." I looked away and took a big gulp of my wine. I hadn't felt like damaged goods for a long time.

I felt his fingers on my chin, turning my face back toward his. "Hey," he said. "Every man has fears, and it takes a brave one to say them out loud. You're a brave man, Shepherd Bucknam."

"Just another feature of the looming disaster," I said, trying to make a joke of it. He didn't smile. His eyes scolded me for several heartbeats before his face softened.

He pushed out his tongue between his lips as if he were licking something sweet off the upper one. "You've shown me yours, so now I have to show you mine."

His face hardened. "I have my own set of terrors," he said quietly, not waiting for me to ask. "I'm not afraid of death. I'd be in the wrong profession if I were."

I watched his Adam's apple slide up and fall as he swallowed. "I'm afraid of letting down the people I love," he said softly. "That's with me every day, my constant companion."

I felt the surprise on my face, but I knew he wasn't done so I waited, holding his gaze just as he'd held mine.

"My family has produced a lot of policemen," he said. "A tradition, you could say. All of them honest. All except one—a second cousin who resigned ten years ago, under suspicion of graft." He sipped his wine.

"He wasn't prosecuted because nothing could be proven, but he was guilty as hell. Everyone knew it. He was shunned by the family. Banished. His pictures disappeared from mantelpieces, he was excluded from every event, his name was never mentioned again in my hearing except as an object lesson in shame. It was like he'd never existed. I don't know where he is, or even if he's still alive."

Marco shook his head, a small, tight smile on his lips. "I couldn't survive that kind of exile. I'd end it. My extended family is a part of my body, and I don't just mean biologically. I mean in living terms. I carry them all with me on every shift. They're watching me all the time, on duty and off." He spread his hands open wide. "Marry me, marry my family."

Marry? His family? Is that really where he wanted to go? How did we get there so fast? This definitely qualified as plunging into the deep end—this was barely a first date. I was going to make a joke, but a hard light came up in his eyes, silencing me.

"Be clear that's not why I'm an honest cop, though," he said. "I told you I hate frauds, and I won't be one. But you need to know that I become part of the people I love, and they become part of me. That's not just a nice line from some drug-store greeting card."

That sounded a lot like a warning I didn't want to examine right then. "So your family didn't exile you for being gay."

"My family respects every form of honesty," he said with Delphic ambiguity. He didn't elaborate.

Our food arrived, and we both seemed ready for a change of pace. Maybe we'd both had enough truth-telling for one evening. I certainly felt I had.

The food was good. Not spectacular, but then we weren't there for the food. Through the main course and dessert, we talked about travel, music, sports, and politics. He was a Dodgers fan and followed the Kings. Neither of us were movie buffs or fans of musical theater, and we laughingly agreed our gay cards might be revoked if anyone found out.

Regardless of topic, the attraction simmering between us was inescapable. The first time our fingers touched, I nearly dropped the oil cruet. Every contact triggered an electric shock. I hadn't experienced anything like it for years and avoided asking myself why.

We sat talking long after the check arrived. He reached for it, saying it was his invitation, but I insisted on splitting it. And still we talked after it had been paid and the wine was gone. The waiter gave up refilling our water glasses because they stayed full. It was clear neither of us wanted to stop.

Finally, Marco sighed. "Well, I need to get off this chair and go home." He grinned at me. "We'll save the really tough questions for another time, okay?"

I laughed. "Good plan."

MARCO AND I walked to his car slowly, as if we'd agreed to take as much time as possible to get there. It felt warm and comfortable to be next to him. "This has been a strange and disturbing evening," I said. "Thank you. I've really enjoyed it."

He threw his jacket onto the passenger seat and turned to me with a hungry look. "You are a strange and disturbing man, Shepherd. I'm going to kiss you."

He put his hand on the back of my neck and pulled my face to his. I stepped into him and breathed in. From underneath the recent aromas of wine and dinner rose the rich scent of his body—his sweat and hard work, laced with faint traces of deodorant and cedar, maybe cologne. My hands dropped to his waist, and we connected—arc welded into full contact, actually—our bodies meeting in all the important places.

We kissed longer than we should have in a hotel parking lot, before he finished with a not-so-soft bite, pulling on my lower lip. "Want to come to my place and try out my handcuffs?" he growled, breathing hard.

I wanted to say yes. "I think that would be a really bad idea. I'm already—"

"You're right," he said quickly. "Bad idea. Way too fast." He laughed. "Let's not rush looming disaster."

He rubbed his neck and looked around. "Where's your car?"

"It'll be brought around by the valet."

He stared at me a few seconds. "I won't be just a rich man's diversion, Shepherd. I deserve to be taken seriously."

"Yes, you do. Believe me, I have—from minute one." Taking Marco Fidanza anything but seriously had never occurred to me.

"Please don't make my money an issue," I said, matching his tone. "It's not worth it." I stroked his cheek, and his stubble shot needles of heat into my fingertips. "And I won't be just a police detective's quarry. I deserve to be taken seriously too."

"Right. Point two—don't make my job an issue. That's a deal-breaker for me."

"Duly noted." I didn't think I should say the same thing, although making my job an issue was probably a deal-breaker, too. I wondered briefly what kind of deal that left for us to make.

We kissed again, feasting, and lightning fused our mouths together until he pulled away. "You're scaring me, Shepherd, and I don't scare easy."

I tried to keep my voice light. "Can we be scared together?"

"Why not?" He climbed into his car. "Let's talk soon," he said, closing the door before I had a chance to reply. He backed out and drove away without a wave.

I already felt his absence, and I didn't like that. I didn't like the absence, and I didn't like that it felt so wrong.

Chapter TWELVE

THE NEXT day, it was easy to rationalize that I thought about Marco so much because he was investigating Stef's murder, but I knew better. When I thought of him, it wasn't as a detective, not even a naked one. He was an enormous electrical storm closing in around me, and all I wanted to do was run outside barefoot, wrapped in copper wire.

I needed some time to regain perspective. Yes, he was lightning-bolt powerful and sexy, but our lives were too different to do more than intersect briefly. Looming disaster.

I decided to wait until he called me. That resolve lasted almost forty-eight hours. I knew because I had counted most of them. Then I called Marco.

"Fidanza," he said in his professional tone, but I could tell by his voice that he knew it was me.

"Do you want to play hooky this afternoon?"

"What do you have in mind?" he asked, his voice cautious.

"There's a farmers' market I like on La Cienega on Thursday afternoons. I thought I could meet you there. We could buy some produce, and I could cook you dinner."

Several seconds of silence ensued. "I can get away," he said. "I'm not convinced it's a good idea, but I think I can arrange it."

"Of course, it's not a good idea. It's a looming disaster, remember?" I kept my voice nonchalant. "Glad you can make it. I'll be there by three, so anytime between then and four, we could meet. What would you like to eat?"

Marco snorted. "I'd say you, but that would be a cheesy cliché. Worse yet, it would be true. That would be very embarrassing for me, so I won't say that. Something relatively simple. I'd prefer if it isn't a big production."

"Great. We can decide what we feel like having once we get together." I realized that sounded dangerously like innuendo too. When you find yourself in a hole, stop digging. Unless you actually want a hole, in which case dig harder. "Give me a call when you get to the market. It's at Eighteenth and La Cienega."

I got to the market just before three and scouted around to find produce that looked especially interesting. I loved farmers' markets—wandering around the stalls, reveling in the colorful abundance of fresh food, seeing the variety of what people poured their effort and aspirations into. I'd just sat down with an espresso when my phone rang. It was him.

"Hi," I said. "I'm at Tom's Espresso. Here, I'll turn on my locator." I fiddled with my phone. "Do you want a coffee?"

"Thanks, I've had too much already." In a second, he spoke again. "Okay, I've got you. Be there pronto."

I finished my espresso, threw the paper cup in the trash, and started walking down the lane toward where I figured he'd parked.

"Trying to escape the long arm of the law?" Marco grabbed my upper arm from behind, making me jump. He seemed pleased at my reaction—certainly more pleased than I was.

"I thought I was walking toward you."

He grinned. "I took a short cut. I was in a hurry."

It felt good to be next to each other again. As we strolled around, we picked up fresh chanterelles from Marin County and debated various specialty items. We decided purple beans weren't worth it since they turned green when cooked, and neither of us liked them raw. Besides, the regular green beans we found couldn't have been out of the garden more than a day or two.

"I've got an enormous rib eye steak at home I thought we could split," I said. "Unless you're really hungry, or in case you don't like your steak rare-medium-rare—in which case I can call the butcher for another one and pick it up on the way home."

"I'd love to share," he said, a hungry look making his eyelids heavy. He tilted his head back toward the stalls. "Let's get some salad makings and call it good."

"What about these baby carrots?" I asked, stopping at the next booth we hit.

"Why not?" He grinned. "We'll have a feast."

"Do you like sweet things?" I asked.

He laughed and shook his head. "You're impossible. However I answer that, I'll just get into trouble."

I laughed too. "There's a place down this way that has terrific pastries—even mousse."

The electricity between us, charged with both promise and magnetic inevitability, made me shiver. Cooking dinner together at my place was going to be intense. I didn't want him going back to his place tonight.

As we headed toward the desserts, a hand caught my arm, and I jumped. Again. This time, the hand belonged to an obese white woman in a vast magenta muumuu with a long turquoise scarf wrapped around her head like a turban and flowing down over one shoulder. Her lacquered seed-pod necklace heaved up and down with each breath.

"Excuse me," she said. Her flesh was clammy and chilled mine. "I've been watching you, following you around for the last half hour wondering if I should say anything, but Guidance says go for it, so I'm taking this chance." She drew closer, and her voice took on a confidential urgency. A cloud of patchouli enveloped me. Combined with her body's perspiration, it was not pleasant.

"You have unfinished business from a past life," she said, as she dabbed a white handkerchief against her forehead with her free hand. "It's hobbling you in this one."

At the edge of my vision, I could see Marco rolling his eyes.

She tucked the handkerchief back into some hidden recess of her bosom and began speaking faster. "I know these ideas aren't for everyone, but you are in such pain and Guidance tells me to speak up. There is a terrible shadow of violence following you."

I stopped breathing. I could feel the blood leaving my cheeks. My throat started closing. I knew Marco could see the change in my face because he said, "Ma'am, you're harassing him—please move on."

"I'm sorry, that's not my intention, but I have to speak," she said, shaking her head at Marco so hard the wattles of her throat swung back and forth.

Her chest heaved, as if every breath was a great effort. "I do past life readings. This is my card. I'm told I can help you. Give me a call. Please. Your life will be so much better once you understand." She turned away, her ponderous, thigh-rubbing gait making her sway back and forth as she walked. I watched her until the crowd closed in around her.

In a few seconds, I could breathe again. My hand shook as I put her card in my pocket.

"You don't believe that bullshit, do you?" Marco's voice made it clear there was only one right answer.

"I don't know. Probably not." I didn't know what to believe, but something in what she'd said had rattled me—irrational, perhaps, but undeniable.

Chapter Thirteen

Marco made small noises I took to be disapproval in the lobby of my building, as if its luxury was an offense. Without doubt, the blue marble columns with gold capitals that circled the Venetian glass fountain made an ostentatious statement. I wondered if he disapproved any less now than he had two weeks ago when he'd come to question me the morning after Stef was shot. I unlocked my door and pretended it didn't matter to me.

"Just throw your jacket on the couch," I said, heading for the kitchen. "I'll get the desserts in the fridge before they get any warmer." Marco went wandering, while I puttered around the kitchen getting things organized. It was a little early to take the steak out, but it wouldn't be long.

"Are you hungry?" I called out.

"Always ready to eat." Marco's voice drifted from the living room. "I'm a cop, I have no eating schedule. In a perfect world, I'd eat around six-thirty, but I can eat anytime."

He came back into the kitchen, looking pensive. "I see you still have Lewis's—your friend's—ashes. Thought you'd have taken care of them by now."

I put the carrots down beside the sink, slipping into my ache for Stef. This pain made no sense to me. I'd known him less than a year, but I missed him as if he'd been a brother.

I studied Marco's face, looking for clues, and decided he wasn't being mean—just his very direct self.

"I'm not clear on the right thing to do with them yet," I answered. "I want to take my time, find the right place. I'm not sure I can let them go until you catch his killer."

Marco's face darkened, and he blew out a heavy sigh. "You might have a long wait, then," he replied quietly. "We've run out of steam on the case, and I've got a new assignment."

I froze. "Just like that?" I was incredulous. Deserted while I wasn't looking. "You're closing the book on him?"

Marco shook his head, and I could feel his genuine regret. "The case will never go away. A murder stays open forever. Until we make an arrest."

"But in the meantime?"

"We make a complete record of everything we've done, all the way down to our hunches. Tapes, everything. When new evidence surfaces, we'll be ready to pick up exactly where we left off."

"And of course, he was just a hustler. In the meantime, you have more important deaths to work on." Now I was the one being mean, but I didn't care.

He nodded, measured, controlled. "I'll ignore the social commentary. We do the best we can with what we've got. We've given it our best shot. We'll pick it up again the instant we have something new to go on."

"So you didn't find anything useful concerning his last client."

Marco's eyes flashed in the failing afternoon light—dangerous as a jungle cat hunting. "I know you want this case solved. I do too. But please don't question the quality of my work."

His jaw pushed forward. He was giving me a warning. "You have no idea how hard Alvarez and I have worked on this. We've gathered a lot of information, but at the moment, it goes nowhere."

I relented. "I promise I'm not questioning your dedication, your skill, or your thoroughness. I'm just trying to understand."

"But you don't understand," he said, his voice sharp. "You can't. You're not a cop. You don't know what we found. You probably know nothing about following orders you don't like. You sure as hell don't understand the constraints and protocols of official investigation."

He smiled at me, still dangerous, but wistful beneath the danger. "I can't explain further, and not just because you're involved in the case. Unpleasant as it might be for you, you'll just have to trust me on that."

I nodded but didn't say anything more. He was right—I didn't understand, and I felt no obligation to try. Maybe Juergen would find information that could move the investigation forward. I'd turn whatever we found over to Marco, of course, and he could do the rest.

"So," I said, changing the subject, cocking my head toward the temperature-controlled wine cabinet. "A good steak demands a good Barbaresco, don't you think?"

He agreed with a shrug. "My family is from much farther south, but if you say so."

I wiped my hands and pulled out two bottles of the Gaja 1996. "These have been begging to be drunk, but I haven't had a suitable occasion to open them. Tonight feels like it could be the right time. What do you think?"

"Sounds good to me," he said with a knowing half-smile. "I'll open them and let them breathe." His voice thickened, and he licked his lips. "Give them some time to get ready. Open up some."

He rummaged in drawers until he found the corkscrew, raising it like a trophy.

Without saying anything, we'd agreed what would happen later tonight. I handed him the bottles, and our fingers brushed. We grinned at each other like teenagers sharing a secret. I shivered at that charged certainty between us, magnetizing us, slowly pulling us together like two ships circling into a maelstrom. Looming disaster never felt so good.

I got two glasses and watched him open the wine, his hands moving with strong, smooth precision. Large hands—square, powerful, with long athletic fingers, nails clipped short. Very suckable fingers.

He turned and grinned, knowing, telling me he'd felt me watching. And that he liked it. He drew the glasses from my hand slowly, his eyes never leaving mine. "So maybe before we begin to cook," he said, "you could give me the grand tour."

I was ready to let him take a tour of anything he wanted to see.

WHEN I'D shown Marco around the apartment, I had him rub the steak with some light seasoning while I used a damp paper towel to pat the chanterelles clean.

"You seem pretty comfortable in the kitchen," I said. "Do you like to cook?"

"Show me an Italian man who's uncomfortable in the kitchen," he replied, "and I'll show you an impostor."

He turned, holding the steak in one hand and gesturing with the other. "Most life in an Italian household occurs in the kitchen or in the bedroom." He lifted his eyebrows. "I cook in both."

"Good to know," I said softly, enjoying our heat.

He brushed by me on his way to the sink to wash his hands. I stepped in behind him, close enough to make solid contact where it counted, and whispered into his ear. "So do I." He straightened and pushed back into me for a second before heading over to fire the grill.

I had Marco keep an eye on the steak and the sautéing vegetables while I set the table and poured us each a glass of vino, which I brought back to the kitchen.

"Will you accept wine in lieu of flowers?" I asked, offering him the glass.

"What, like a real date?" We clinked glasses and stuck our noses in the bowls.

"Wow," he said. "I forgive you for choosing a northern wine." We both laughed.

After a moment's quiet appreciation, I murmured, "Yum."

"I want to taste it on you," he said. He put his hand on the back of my neck and drove his tongue into my mouth. Very gently, I closed my teeth on it. When he pulled away, there were dots of moisture above his lip. His breathing had deepened. "Yeah. Yum," he murmured and went back to the steak.

"Food in two minutes," he announced. I pulled out plates and a carving board to divvy up the steak.

We served up the food and sat. Everything was perfect. "*Buon appetito*," I said, shaking out my napkin.

He snorted. "My family just says *Mangiamo*. It's more to the point."

We spoke of family—what it was like to have siblings, what it was like to have none. We talked in safe terms about his work and carefully avoided mine. The food disappeared way too soon—there was so much more to talk about.

"Do you want dessert?" I asked.

"Not yet." He stared at me. Hard. "Later."

"More wine?"

"A little. Not much. It's incredible, though."

I felt some tension mounting in him, but he didn't say anything. He just stared into his wineglass, as if there were a message in it that he needed to read. I cleared our plates and sat back down and waited. I put my hand on his, wanting him.

He looked up at me like a wild animal, fierce and wary. He put his wineglass down. "What does sex mean to you?" he asked quietly.

"I think it's essential to a happy life. I'm a big fan."

He scowled. "Don't be cute. I want the real answer."

I was in his interrogation room again, with the recorder running and the pine disinfectant stinging my nose. I took a sip of wine to banish the smell. "My real answer?"

"That's the only kind. Zero tolerance for frauds, remember?"

I tried to lighten his seriousness. "The real answer is complex. I might ramble."

"You can take your time. I need to know."

I took a deep breath. "Remember… you asked," I said.

"Before anything happens between us," he repeated, as if each word weighed as much as he could lift, "I need to know."

I took a deep breath and let it out. "Okay." To my surprise, the truth bubbled up easily, asking me to tell him things I'd seldom told a therapist, and never a date. The sacred essence of my work.

"My first sexual attraction to a man comes in a feeling that somewhere in his body lies a secret, a story I need to learn. Maybe a story he doesn't even know he's keeping."

I looked out the window onto the lights of Westwood Village and UCLA winking in the purple evening, feeling dangerously exposed. But he'd asked, and I'd promised.

"It sounds arrogant to say it out loud, but sometimes, I feel he's asking me for help—can you take the journey to where I keep my secrets? The ones I can't find unless we share our bodies?

"If a man can tell you a story with words, he's giving you one of his surface ones—his history, his wounds, his hopes. Very few of those stories arouse me.

"Can I get to the deeper ones? That's the challenge. Will he let me into the sweet dark archives of his body? The haunted places in his heart? His sacred stories, the powerful, wordless ones, are there, waiting, stored in his skin, his breath, his seed. Those are the ones I love."

I bit my lip, certain this sounded daft to him. I needed him to understand. What if he didn't? Or wouldn't? I looked into his eyes. They told me nothing. Ruthless poker-player's eyes.

"I may sound crazy, but you wanted the truth." He just stared back, not moving.

Gathering myself, I plunged forward. "Somewhere under his skin, stored in some guarded place like a prisoner, lies that memory, or maybe a dream—a longing I can awaken, excavate with my touch, my body, coaxing out his stories aching to be heard. We become allies, then—brothers in some ancient tribe, preparing for a sacred ceremony of spirit and flesh. A ceremony greater than either of us.

"There are clues how to start. He shows me in the way his hand moves, or the stretch of his throat when he turns his head. The way he holds his mouth when he throws back his head and laughs. The way he speaks of small regrets.

"When the ceremony begins, he unfolds as if he's an entire foreign country, a different culture, a story in a strange language I can understand only when my tongue is on his skin, when his flesh is inside me, when his flesh welcomes mine inside him.

"As we go deeper, his body guides me. When did he get that tattoo? What did it mean to him at the time, and what does it mean to him now? When did his eyes become so deep? When the first lines of age creased his face, did he laugh in his strength, or did it take time for him to wear them with grace? When his heart was first broken, where did he store the pain?"

I pointed to Marco's face. "When he got the scar that cuts through his eyebrow, what was he doing?" His eye twitched, but he said nothing.

"Our union forms a unique Rosetta Stone, making us each understandable to the other so long as we're joined. Then we speak the wordless language that men know only when they are filled, overflowing with pleasure and respect. Everything about him radiates his meaning to me, from the folding of an eyelid to the slow unfurling of foreskin, drawing away to reveal more of his power.

"We fall into beauty together. No matter what he looks like, there isn't a man so open and alive as that—so hungry to welcome the mystery of another, so hot to share himself, to know the secrets he can't find in himself except through the Other, secrets to be poured back into him through the breath and pulse and saliva and seed of another—who isn't beautiful to me."

I leaned forward, buzzing with the pleasure of speaking so openly. "Then afterward—very rarely—when a man is soft and vulnerable, in the moments before his breath returns to normal, before he closes himself again to the outer world, putting his outer body back on like insulating armor, I can touch the one who tells the stories, the one who reaches through them to be known, even if only for a moment. I believe that connection lasts forever, and becomes a new, shared story we each, if we're lucky, can tell others."

I had nothing more to say. The AC whispered down on us, the only sound in the room.

Marco drained his glass, not meeting my eyes. I made to pour him more, but he held up his hand to stop me. He stared at the dregs for an uncomfortably long time. I wanted to defend what I'd said, but I'd already said far more than I should have. I'd been an idiot to give him the truth just because he'd asked for it. When I thought about it now, it must have sounded like pretentious bullshit to him.

"Did that happen between you and Lewis?" His voice had cooled and hardened. "Touching the one who tells the stories?"

With a shock, I realized it had. Often. Effortlessly, no excavation needed, so naturally it hadn't even registered as the rare magic I'd been describing. That had to be the reason Stef meant so much to me.

"Yes." I looked away, missing Stef and unable to look Marco in the eye, afraid I'd see his sneer. Even if it meant a sudden end to the evening, I wouldn't let Marco pass judgment on the beauty Stef and I had shared. That was off-limits.

He pushed his chair back and stood. I looked up but couldn't read his face at all. He gestured with both hands, palms up. I stood.

He hooked his fingers inside my belt and led me into the bedroom.

Chapter Fourteen

He wasn't rough, but he'd taken charge without negotiation. My heart raced, unsure. Was he angry? Scornful? I had no idea. He stopped me at the foot of the bed, putting his hands on my hips. Without once breaking eye contact, he began pulling my shirt out of my jeans.

Soft with compliance, I lifted my arms as he drew the shirt over my head. He tossed it on the floor. In the dim light, his fingers traced my throat, pausing at the three bloody marks at the base of my neck. "There is a God after all," he chuckled. "I was afraid you would be too perfect to be real, but now I see you are not perfect, but beautiful instead." His conqueror's smile was dazzling. "Beautiful is much, much better than perfect."

His eyes were dark lamps burning into mine. He found my belt buckle, and he opened my jeans, softly scraped his nails across my skin just above the waistband of my shorts. "Take those off," he ordered softly. I obeyed.

He pulled his own clothes off in swift efficiency and was waiting for me, naked and erect, by the time I had finished. The black hair I'd glimpsed before covered his muscular chest. It dusted his belly, too, pushing into a heavy trail that plunged to his groin, then spread to forest his thighs. He stood, muscles taut, poised—sinuous, dark, powerful.

He put his hands on my hips again and pulled me into him. He lapped the hollow of my throat with an aggressive tongue, biting softly as he grazed.

"Just so you know up front," he said, "you are not going to be digging for my stories tonight. I'm going to shout them into you until you cover your ears and beg for mercy. You will not escape me until you've heard everything I have to tell you." His eyes blazed. "This could take a long time."

I shivered, anticipating something unknown. How long had it been since I hadn't known what would happen next with a sexual partner? I put my arms over his shoulders and kissed him deeply, opening myself to him, tasting the wine in his saliva, calling to the coiled power sparking from his tongue.

I broke away just enough to look into his eyes. "I'm listening," I whispered.

He pushed me backward onto the bed. "Scoot up," he ordered.

When I had, he crawled up between my knees and lowered himself onto me. My legs wrapped around his waist in welcome. His arms closed around me, crushing his chest into mine.

"This," he growled into my neck, "is story number one."

His body began to rock slowly against me, undulating in a rhythm slow and inevitable as the sea, while his mouth roamed from nipple to armpit to neck to ear to mouth to chin to nipple to throat to chest.

Little noises of pleasure-need escaped me at every lick, kiss, and bite. I raked my hands through his hair, down his neck, and across his broad shoulders, reveling in the startling bunch and release of his muscles as he moved, then farther down his spine, settling into the small of his back, clenching, eager to pull him into me. I stroked down the flexing mounds of his ass, letting my fingers fall into the exquisite secret hollow at the inside top of his thighs.

He pushed away to chew his way down my belly, burying his face between my legs. His tongue began a rough dance around my balls and I cried out, ecstatic, bucking upward, opening myself to him.

His mouth closed over my cock, and lights played across the inside of my eyelids.

"I want a turn," I said, trying to roll on top of him.

He didn't budge, just sat up. "Maybe later. But you'd probably try to take charge." He stared at me, his eyes hot and certain. "And that's not going to happen tonight."

He knelt between my thighs and splayed my legs farther apart. "I want in."

I rolled partway onto my side, reaching toward the bedside table, but I was too far away.

"Stay put," he said, and jumped up. "In the drawer?"

"Yeah. Towels are in the bathroom closet."

He collected the condoms and lube, grabbed a towel, and in a moment was back between my legs, right where he belonged. I'd missed him.

"Roll over."

"I want to see you."

"You will," he growled. "Roll over."

He pushed my arms above my head and lay down on me again, wrapping his arms around my chest, possessing me, grinding his jaw stubble against my neck and shoulder, sliding his cock between my cheeks.

I shifted a little, closed my arms tightly around his, and bucked upward against him, impatient, demanding. He moaned his own need into my ear. The scrape of his chest against my back was heaven.

He unwrapped his arms and pulled away, and the sudden chill where his heat had been was awful. "Turn over now."

I did, and rested my legs outside his thighs as he got the condom on and lubed us up. I stared into his eyes, my mouth slack, unable to tell him how magnificent he was, how badly I wanted him in me, how much I needed the crush of his weight on my body again. And then he slowly pushed in, and all I could do was groan his name.

I wrapped my arms and legs around him, holding him tight against me, meeting his thrusts with my own. He bit my shoulder, hard, and I laughed, ecstatic, as we spun into a delirium of lips and sweat, eyes and tongues, breath and need, into the rhythm, rhythm, rhythm, driving and relentless, rhythm and heat.

Then he clamped his mouth over mine and shouted down my throat, filling my lungs with his voice. Our tongues melted into each other, and we came. Soft and rising at first, then convulsing, hard, bursting, thrashing, thrusting, triumphant. One.

We lay unmoving for a while, before he pushed onto his elbows so we could look at each other. And it happened. Body to body, the liminal barriers of our skins melted, and we met in that field of wonder beyond our stories. I saw him. I felt tears building—no sting, only gratitude.

He knew it too. I could see the recognition in his eyes. His mouth moved as if he were going to speak, but made no sound. We stared into each other all the way.

Eventually, the world made our skins dense again, even though we still glowed.

He shifted a little. The movement caused his softening cock to slither out, and I made a little noise of complaint.

He laughed and collapsed back onto me, slack and deliciously heavy. "Don't worry," he whispered into my jaw. "There's plenty more where that came from. That was only story one, remember?"

I stroked his back slowly, needing the long lines of communion with his skin, still unable to speak.

MUCH LATER, after dinner cleanup, two more rounds of loving, dessert, and a very long shower, we lay in my bed, exhausted and ready for sleep. Marco spooned behind me, his arm hanging slack over my side, his hand curled and soft at my throat. I knew I'd never get to sleep this way, but it felt so good I didn't want to move.

I waited until his breathing told me he was asleep and drew away as gently as I could.

"Mmph. Where do you think you're going?" he mumbled.

I kissed his cheek. "I'm sorry, it's been a long time since I slept with anyone. I can't go to sleep when we're touching."

His voice immediately lost its sleepy fog. "You haven't? I find that hard to believe."

"Not *sleep* sleep. Not for a very long time." I doubted it was a good time to open another issue, but he deserved the truth. "Twenty years. Maybe a little less."

"You haven't spent the entire night with another human being in twenty years? That's impossible." He pulled me back against him again, but I rolled onto my back so I could see his face.

"It's neurotic, probably, but I've always felt that space for sleep is my private space. When someone is touching me, I stay hypervigilant. Can't relax."

He propped himself up on one elbow and leaned over me, his face an inch from mine. "Tell me his name. The last guy you slept with."

"Is this really a story you want to hear right now?"

"I wouldn't have asked if I didn't. It would've been easy to let it slide."

I rubbed my eyes and then turned into him. "His name was Danny. I told you about him the other day. We were teenagers, we'd been lovers. I still loved him, but he was infatuated with someone else. He let me sleep through the night with him sometimes. He killed himself a week after the last time we did." I smiled and stroked Marco's cheek. It felt bizarre, talking about Danny now. "He's the one who jumped off the tower at school."

"I remember," he said tenderly. He pulled in a deep breath, sighed it out. "I think there's part of you that is very lonely, Shepherd Bucknam." He dragged a finger across my lips. "So I can't touch you when you sleep?" He leaned in and kissed me so sweetly I wanted to cry.

I was a neurotic idiot, and embarrassment stung my cheeks. "Maybe once I'm asleep, if you still want to try. That might work."

"Okay." He kissed me again and rolled away. "Good night."

He was much too far away. I lay staring at the nearly invisible ceiling. I'd just spoiled a wonderful evening with an incredible man.

I AWOKE at first light, spooned in Marco's arms, his breath flowing down my neck in warm sleep-rhythm surges. I couldn't go back to sleep, but I didn't want to. This was perfect. The heavy caress of his breath on my skin, the hot animal mass of him behind me held me motionless, content. I could sleep anytime.

Later, while I made coffee, Marco went down to the street. He needed the *LA Times* for his morning ritual, he said, and the online version wouldn't do. He came back and settled in at the table, breaking the paper into sections, as if we'd done this forever.

I watched him read a while. "I've made an appointment tomorrow with Ramón Cruz of Off the Street. Do you know him?"

Marco didn't look up. "Not personally."

"I'm planning to make an annual gift to them in Stef's memory."

"Nice."

"When do you start on your new case?" I asked.

He lowered the paper enough to frown at me. "Already started." His face disappeared again.

I waited for more, but there wasn't more. Apparently, his morning ritual didn't include conversation. I supposed I could accept that, but right then, it didn't feel like it had room for me, either.

I tried to feel offended but simply couldn't work up the energy. After our intimacy the night before, I could still feel our connection singing inside me. From across the table, the nimbus of his raw male power enveloped me. No newspaper could prevent me from basking in it. I was content to give him an understanding space to read and drink his coffee, surprised that just watching felt so good.

Chapter Fifteen

Marco had gone, and I was just out of the shower when Juergen called saying he had the phone records and a progress report to deliver. I agreed to meet him for lunch, glad I had plenty of time for some yoga first. After last night, I needed it.

When I slid into the booth at Sandy's Kitchen, Juergen was already halfway through his hamburger.

"What have you got?" I asked and laughed. "That sounds like a line from a bad detective movie, doesn't it?"

He grunted and finished chewing. One of the things I really liked about him was that he was never in a hurry. He didn't wait for anybody, either. I was fifteen minutes late, and he'd ordered his lunch without me.

"The last activity on Lewis's phone was to and from one Walter Chisholm, Democratic candidate for California State Assembly." Juergen looked at me hard, his face blank. "Currently seeking reelection."

So that was who Stef had recognized. "Have the police talked to him?"

He nodded. "The cell number is tied to a phone bank. Several people have the ability to make and take calls or write text messages, even post to a Twitter account as if Chisholm's number had originated it."

He dipped a fry in the oasis of ketchup pooled at one end of his plate. "Your friend Fidanza and his partner interviewed everybody who had access to that number. Nobody knew anything, of course."

"And Chisholm?"

"They couldn't push him hard, but they had their five minutes with him," he said. "He didn't know anything either."

"But somebody knew something, because someone made an appointment with Stef. He must have known it was Chisholm, because he recognized him from the TV broadcast."

Juergen didn't even look up from his plate. "That's hearsay, not evidence," he said with a shrug. "Not enough to go after anybody, let alone a prominent public figure. With very powerful friends."

"But surely that's enough of a lead to investigate further," I said, unable to keep the impatience and frustration out of my voice. "It's all we have."

"It's a lead," he admitted, "but not a good one. Lewis could've been making stuff up, bragging." He stared at me, tired patience in his eyes. "You may not agree, but we'll never know for sure."

I waved the waitress away when she approached with a menu. I leaned forward. "I need you to investigate further," I said. "Find out more about the issues Chisholm is involved in, who's backing him, and what their agendas are. Even if it wasn't Chisholm himself, somebody connected to Chisholm's campaign called Stef, set an appointment with him, and then killed him. I'm going to find out who."

Juergen nodded slowly. "I thought you might say that. But you've run way ahead of the hard evidence. You say the phone exchange was to set an appointment. That's the key to the way you see it. Conceivably, it could have been to answer pollsters for Chisholm's campaign or pledge a donation, using that address." He held up a hand to hold off the protest he must have seen all over my face. "And I understand. I agree with you, actually."

He stared me down. "But you need to understand something else too. If you stir the mud around Chisholm's campaign, you may accomplish nothing more than warning off the killer. Worse, you could screw up the evidence that could put him away. Or her."

He returned to his fries. "Tainted evidence that could have nailed a conviction is a cop's worst nightmare. Better to go slow and get what you can, rather than charging in and stomping all over everything."

He looked at me, his pale blue eyes wise, weary. "I'm speaking from firsthand experience. Instead of catching the killer, you might give him a get out of jail free card. Just remember where good intentions usually lead."

I felt helpless in the face of such logic. "So Marco was right? I'm just supposed to be a good boy and leave this to the professionals?"

"So it's Marco, now, is it?" Juergen lifted one eyebrow, which was about as expressive as his face ever got. "I hope you're being careful, my friend."

I blushed. Juergen took a swig of coffee, clearly not needing more of an answer.

My promise to Stef sat heavy on my shoulders. "Still, I'd like you to look into a couple more things for me," I said. "The police investigation is already stalled, and I can't just do nothing. I can't."

He finished the last fry and a lone slice of pickle before wiping his lips with a crumpled napkin. "I heard that. What do you have in mind?"

"Gather as much background information about Chisholm's political landscape, his backers and their interests, whatever you can find without jeopardizing anything. And if you can, find out more about how that phone number integrates into the campaign phone bank. Not just who has access to it but some mechanics—how the calls are routed, who might have seen texts, or overheard calls between Chisholm and Stef."

Juergen nodded, signaled for the bill. "I can do that," he said. "But regardless of what I find, I'm telling you right now there will be nothing you can do about any of it." He looked at me deadpan. "Legally."

He handed me his blue folder. It was thicker than usual. "Here's a summary, plus the last three weeks of his phone activity. Don't flash that around, okay? That data could easily cause us both trouble we don't need."

"I'm not interested in breaking the law or even getting into trouble," I said. "I certainly don't want to screw up the official investigation. But I can't stop yet." I looked him in the eye with heat that surprised me. I could see it register. "I'll do everything I can to get Stef's killer. Everything."

JUERGEN'S WARNING that there wasn't more I could do legally to help Stef still sat like undigested food in my gut the next day as I met

Ramón Cruz, the director of Off the Street. At least this was something I *could* do—donate to an agency that helped kids in jeopardy and keep Stef's name alive.

Cruz was waiting for me in the nondescript restaurant he'd chosen on Western Avenue in Central LA. He was pleasantly tough looking and trim, probably forty, just starting to gray. Some old homemade arm and neck tattoos peeked out from under his short-sleeved shirt. He radiated a friendly but street-tough, no-bullshit atmosphere. I liked his energy. I'd made the right choice.

"I hope you don't mind meeting here," he said, all business, "but I have a court appearance in a couple of hours, and I have to go back to the office before that."

"I don't mind in the least. I appreciate you taking time to meet."

We glanced at the menus as soon as they arrived and ordered. He regarded me carefully, caution in his face. I was being evaluated. "So," he said. "You say you've done some research on us, so you know what we do. I'm hoping you want to give us money."

I smiled, nodding. Straight to the point. "I became friends with a kid from Oklahoma City a few months ago. He was an amazing young man. He was shot last month, and I'd like to set up something as a memorial to him."

"We can do that," he said softly, studying my face. "Unless you were exploiting him and now you're just feeling guilty."

That hurt so sharply I couldn't feel insulted. My mouth opened and eyebrows lifted all on their own. "No! I was trying to help him take care of himself. I was trying to keep him safe." I smiled to get rid of some pain, remembering Marco's cheap shot during my questioning. "I didn't do a great job."

"Forgive me for challenging you, but we've built our reputation on being extremely careful about where our money comes from, and about how we protect our kids."

"I understand completely." I pulled the envelope with a check from the inside pocket of my jacket. "This is for fifty thousand dollars. I'd like to make this an annual event in the memory of Steven Lewis. His details are in the envelope. I don't want any other kind of recognition."

"That's good," he said. "We're not a particularly high profile organization. We prefer to keep things simple."

"Is it possible to have his name visible somewhere, though? I do want that."

"Sure. If you'd like, we can allocate the funds to a particular program, so his name would appear on the information sheets and on the website."

"That's enough for me." Suddenly, I was on the edge of tears, because it wasn't anywhere near enough. I had to do more. "I'd also like to help out on some of your programs with the kids, if you can use a volunteer."

Cruz looked up from his plate, his forkful of salad frozen in midair. It took a long time for him to put it back down. "We are always desperate for funding, so please understand how serious I am when I say I may have to return your check now," he said slowly. "I can't possibly give you access like that."

"Why not?" I asked, stunned. Now I *was* insulted.

When he clamped his lips together, his jaw stuck out. He slowly pushed the envelope back toward me and made fists on the table. "Our staff goes through rigorous screening before they're allowed to interact with our kids at all," he said, his voice flat and hard. "Even then, we remain very, very careful. Alert."

He leaned forward, and his voice dropped to a rumble. "It's difficult to find people who don't want to get near the kids to use them for their own predatory agendas. Preaching, dealing, pimping, sex, whatever."

He sat back in his chair and stared at me. "Including rich people who want to buy their way to the kids. It happened once, but it'll never happen again on my watch. We're meeting here because I don't want you even scoping out the layout of our facilities."

I nodded, embarrassed. I should have thought of that myself. Marco was wrong—I could be naïve. I couldn't think of anything to say to explain. I pushed the envelope back toward him, and his face softened.

"You have to understand," he said, zeal relighting his face. "These kids have already survived all those forms of exploitation and abuse. And worse." His eyes blazed. "My job is to protect them long enough for them to rebuild, give them a fresh start."

"What I want," I said, my voice unsteady, "is to support your work. For Stef. For the kids who make it to your door." I swallowed, feeling helpless. "With hope for the kids who may not."

He picked up the check and tucked it away. "Thank you. And thank you for your good intentions. But this is delicate work. I ask you to leave it to those of us trained for the job."

My head snapped up. More echoes of Marco—he'd already taken up residence in my head. Leave this to the capable people. My money might be welcome, but I wasn't needed.

I wondered how often my mother had encountered the same humiliation: Give me your money, and then go away, play outside. Of course, it was likely she'd been barely sober enough to sign the check. What organization would have wanted her lurching around an office, making a fool of herself? But I wasn't like that.

He must have seen the hurt in my reaction. "Look," he said. "This really is work for specialists. I'm sorry if I insulted you—I talk too rough sometimes. But you have to understand that this is my life. It's what I do." He pulled his sleeve back to show more of the crude tat on his shoulder. I figured it was a gang mark.

"I survived the street," he said quietly. "Barely. I live to give others a chance to do the same."

"I won't pretend your comment didn't sting," I said, "but I'll deal with it. I understand better now why you have to be so careful." I weathered another pang of embarrassment. "I hadn't thought it through, really. It was an impulse offer—I just wanted to do more for Stef."

He glanced at his watch, then gave me a brusque smile. "You can tell I'm not strong on diplomacy, but I've got to get moving." He shrugged. "One of our kids is in custody, and his future is at stake. He needs me."

"No problem. I hope we can talk again under less pressured circumstances." Cruz's face didn't respond to the suggestion. I signaled for the check.

His handshake was warm and firm. Genuine. I looked him in the eye, letting him know I wasn't going to back off completely. "Until then," I said, "you've given me something to think about."

Chapter Sixteen

CRUZ'S REMARKS had hurt a lot more than I'd admitted to him. Being confronted with one's irrelevance was humiliating at the best of times, but in this case, when I'd really wanted to make a difference, it hurt. What right did he have to dismiss me like that? Was I supposed to just climb into my Maserati and drive away, leaving the operation of the real world to the skilled professionals?

The dove gray leather and bird's-eye maple luxury of my car mocked me. *Send all your good intentions to hell where they belong,* they said. *Go home to your tasteful Roche Bobois comfort and be irrelevant in style. Make another $50,000 donation, maybe two. Pour yourself a $200 bottle of wine—there's another bottle of that Barbaresco you opened for Marco. It's all yours. You bought it, after all. You don't need more relevance. You're rich. That's sufficient* raison d'être. *Your mother understood that. It's time you accepted it as well.*

I knew that was just a childish reaction to the rejection I'd felt. In any existential rant, irrelevance is the inevitable conclusion. But I wasn't my mother, this wasn't philosophy, and I didn't want to be existential. I wanted to make a difference, even though it was too late to make more of a difference to Stef.

I'd claimed I wanted to do more in Stef's name, but as I crawled through traffic on the way home, I wondered if all I really wanted was just to matter. I wanted to *be* a difference, not just to make one by spending money. To matter. To belong in the lives of others. Like Marco did in his family, a kind of belonging I'd never known. Might never know. Could self-interest always dress so easily in altruistic disguise? I knew it could, but I also knew there was more than selfishness in what I wanted.

Relationships mattered. Stef and I had mattered to each other, far more than either of us originally intended. I'd never really mattered to my mother, beyond being born and learning early to be a charming trophy child. But I'd made my peace with that long ago. I'd mattered to Danny, even if it hadn't been enough to save him. As for Stef, it hadn't been enough, either. Never would be.

Did I matter to my friends? I'd never asked the question before—I'd always assumed I did. I mattered to some of my clients. I made a lasting difference in the quality of their lives. I might eventually matter to Marco, but it was way too early to tell on that one.

The phone rang, and speaking of the handsome devil, there he was. "Hi, Marco."

"Hi." His voice was hushed. "I'm at work, can't take long. Have dinner with me tonight. Please."

The way my body responded told me Marco was taking up residence in more than my head. "Shall I make a reservation somewhere?"

"No. Come to my place at six." He gave me his address in Silverlake, and I repeated it directly into my GPS.

"Shall I bring food?"

He turned his head from the phone to shout, his voice curt and irritated, at somebody. It made me jump. When he spoke into the phone again, he was soft and inviting again. "You eat Chinese?"

"Sure."

"Then we'll get takeout." In the background, I could hear men calling his name impatiently.

"Well, what should I bring?" I asked, still sensitive about my relevance.

"Just show up," he growled. "Wear clothing that's easy to tear off."

I laughed. "I'll see what I can do." I understood that need very well. Leave the important work to the professionals, indeed. Well, I was a skilled professional too.

He grunted and hung up.

That gave me plenty of time for a few hours of research on Stef's phone records. Juergen had given me access to an online database that allowed me to look up who Stef had talked to. I'd set up an Excel pivot table to analyze numbers, names, lengths of time, and dates. I was a long way from being finished with it, but I was proud of what I was doing. I found it strange that I enjoyed the project but felt no urgency. There was something very satisfying about methodically plodding through the task. Logging each number was a step closer to Stef's killer.

THE AFTERNOON melted away as I worked, and I had to hurry my shower before heading to Marco's. I decided to take the Prius since I didn't know if I'd have to park on the street overnight. It certainly sounded as though I was going to be at Marco's overnight. I wanted that. The prospect made me feel much better.

Traffic was heavy, and it was a little after six when I rang the doorbell to his second-story apartment. The building was a standard U-shaped two-story built motel-style around the swimming pool, with stairs and a breezeway running in front of the entrances. Simple and utilitarian.

He answered the door shirtless and barefoot, wearing only a pair of boxers, holding a towel in one hand. He looked delicious.

He finished toweling his hair and grinned. "I was hoping you'd get here early so we could take a shower together." Ignoring the flowers and beer in my hands, he pulled me into him for a long, hungry kiss. My shirt started soaking up water droplets still caught in the hair on his chest.

I broke away. "You're getting me wet," I said, deliberately setting up the obvious joke.

He took the cue perfectly. "Isn't that supposed to be a good sign? All the books I've read say so."

I raised the bouquet and six-pack. "You mean I could have skipped the flowers and beer and cut right to the sex?"

His eyes glowed. "You're lucky I'm going to let you eat first," he said, and I could tell he was only partly joking.

"Welcome to my side of the tracks," he said, stepping back and spreading his arms.

I looked around. Very nice. Brown, black, and tan, with geometric cream accents. It felt like him—Spartan, but not ascetic. Open. The living room with the dining area to my right formed the long line of an L, which was completed by the kitchen beyond the dining table. Bathroom ahead, and opposite the bath to the left, around the corner, would be the bedroom.

Immediately in front of me on the far living room wall, a big flat-screen hung above a credenza arrayed in framed photos. Had to be family. With its back to the door, a comfortable-looking couch faced the TV. Matching armchairs sat on either side, facing in.

The wall to my left had more framed photos and a ceiling-high bookcase, packed full of books. A guitar rested on a stand next to the books. I could easily imagine him strumming a guitar. Still more sexiness. A small desk sat against the outer wall immediately to my left, looking out a window onto the breezeway.

"You'll give me the grand tour later, right?"

He shrugged, laughing. "You just took it!" Then he waggled his eyebrows. "Except for the bedroom, of course. I'll show you that a little later."

"Then can we take care of these, now?" I presented my offerings. "The flowers are wilting and the beer is getting warm."

He tilted his head toward the kitchen. "Help yourself to the fridge. I'll get something to put the flowers in."

While I floundered artlessly in an attempt to make the flowers look nice, Marco came up behind me and wrapped his arms around my chest, grinding into my ass. Inside his boxers, he was already firm.

"You okay on your own for fifteen minutes?" he murmured in my ear. "I've gotta go get the food."

I pushed back against him, and his arms tightened into a python's crush. "Sure. I promise not to get into trouble. In fact, I'll even set the table." He smacked me on the ass and went to get dressed.

After he left, I took the opportunity to examine his books. Nothing on police work. Nice boundary between home and work. Biographies, some political/spy thrillers. Two volumes of Wendell Berry poems, *Leaves of Grass*, a collection of Rilke in translation I'd never seen before. The bottom three shelves were all music. Theory, history, more biographies, mostly of opera stars. Collections of repertoire for baritone. I remembered his remark that horrible Saturday morning he'd come to my apartment after Stef's death, when I'd told him nobody walked out on Brahms's Requiem. "Not if they love music," he'd said. Now I understood. He did.

I laughed out loud when I came across one collection with Dmitri Hvorostovsky on the cover. No wonder I'd hit a nerve sparring with him during that interview. And since then, I'd learned just how well he could sing his sex.

I was still crouched at the bottom of the bookcase when the door opened and Marco came in with two white plastic bags showing the outlines of several containers. "Trying to learn all my secrets?" he asked. He sounded a little on edge.

"I want to hear you sing, sometime soon."

"I don't sing where I can be heard by others. Not anymore."

"Rubbish. You sang happy birthday to me in bed the other night, and then blew out all my candles. It was a dazzling performance."

He laughed. "Yeah, I sing," he said with a rueful smile. "I dreamed of singing professionally, long ago." He shrugged. "Then reality hit me over the head, and I became a cop."

"Didn't your family want you to become a singer?"

"No, I'm pretty sure they would have supported me in that," he said, sadness making his voice soft, distant. "I just wasn't good enough."

"Wow. I want to hear you sing more than ever. I want to experience that part of you. I don't care how good you are."

His jaw stuck out, hardening his face. "I said I don't sing for others."

"Not even in a chorus somewhere?"

"Not a chance. Even if my schedule allowed, which it doesn't." He walked into the kitchen and started unpacking the food, making it clear this line of conversation was closed. I'd ask again when the time was right, though. For the moment, I just floated in the thought of him playing his guitar and singing to me. Yes, in the moonlight, on a beach, next to a driftwood fire. Heady stuff.

An hour later, we'd polished off just about everything except for a small box of rice and a couple of the beers. "That was tasty," I said, rinsing my hands at the kitchen sink. "Was that a Marco-the-cop dinner?"

"When the cop is lucky and gets home before eleven, which is when the Number One closes," he answered with a shrug.

"That's the name of the restaurant?"

"Number One Chinese Restaurant." He nodded. "Yeah, I know. Sounds like it's from a B-movie, but that's the real name. I'm a regular, and now they usually throw in an egg roll, no charge. Except when Grandma is at the till. She never gives anything away."

We tossed out the containers and tidied up, navigating around each other with the same comfortable ease we'd had at my place. When we were done, we stood in the kitchen facing each other.

"So," I said, hooking my fingers inside the waistband of his jeans, just like he'd done to me at my place. "Take me on the grand tour now?"

THE BEDROOM was a shock. The floor was premium terra cotta tile laid at 45 degrees to the square of the room. By far the most carefully furnished room in the place, it was a minimalist sanctuary in mocha, cream, and brick, dominated by an enormous black-framed bed set on a raised platform and surrounded by a rectangle of lush red-brown carpet. An exquisite antique dresser stood opposite the foot of the bed, below a sleek, very modern mirror. From the ceiling, a modern art-glass chandelier spread its graceful asymmetrical arms out and down, its swirled cream and rust shades drooping like half-opened exotic flowers. There were few other furnishings apart from a lone art deco leather armchair with elegant wood arms, perfectly restored, and a matching period floor lamp next to it.

The statement was unmistakable. This was his sacred space. Nothing happened here except by his choice.

"Wow, Marco," I murmured. "This is stunning."

"Glad you like it. It's my secret indulgence." He pulled me to him. "Would you like to indulge with me here tonight?"

"Absolutely." I kissed him slow and deep, leaving us both breathing hard when we broke. "But I lead tonight. Seems only fair, after last time."

He started pulling at his clothes, but I pushed his hands back to his sides. "No," I whispered. "Let me."

I bent down and grabbed his T-shirt in my teeth, working it upward, back and forth until it rode his pecs, then returned to the taut flesh just above his jeans. I licked and nipped, sucking hard, enough to leave a mark or two, swirling my tongue along the lean wall of his belly.

"If you keep doing that," he groaned, "I'll shoot in my pants."

"That," I mumbled against his skin, "would be a terrible waste." I opened his jeans, let them sag to his hips, then drove my tongue through the fly of his boxers, maneuvering him into my mouth. He howled. I was barely in time, but didn't lose a drop.

We took our time getting naked and to the bed. By the time we got there, he was hard again. I pushed him onto his back and straddled his hips, leaned down for kisses. He clamped his arms across my back and pulled hard.

"I want inside *you* tonight," I whispered into his ear.

He tensed, hesitating a moment, before I felt his body relax under me. "It's been a long time since I've had a dick in my ass," he whispered back.

I chewed softly along his neck and jawline and pushed away until I could look into his eyes. "Mine's not that big. You'll barely feel it, I promise."

"Not that big?" he snorted. "Hard evidence previously gathered in this case directly contradicts your statement, Mr. Bucknam."

I laughed. "Evidence that hard probably shouldn't be contested." We rolled and played, licking and caressing until we were ready for more.

Something happens in a man's eyes when he welcomes another man into him. They widen slightly, and deepen with entry. Then a light comes up in them—some inner radiance is liberated, a wordless beauty, hant, sacred maleness.

I slid slowly in, and Marco's eyes ignited with that light, glowing as if to guide me all the way to his center, to the kind of homecoming that two men know when they consent to become lovers, even if lovers just for a moment. Only a lover enters into that kind of welcome, pushes home to that kind of light.

I knew he could see similar recognition in my face, his smile said so. "Oh, god," he moaned, "yes."

When he was relaxed enough for more, I turned him onto his side, hugging his left leg to my chest, pushing in all the way. Something melted in me, some distance-keeping barrier I hadn't noticed, and the heat of his body washed over me, claimed me. The coarse hair of his thigh scraping against my chest marked me, sparked me with every thrust.

He began to stroke his cock, but I pushed his hand away. "Not yet," I rasped.

He started to roll onto his back, and I eased away to let him, unsure of what he wanted. He grabbed a pillow and stuffed it under his butt for elevation, then grinned at me. "All ready. Get back in here."

Reentry was exquisite, and we both made guttural sounds of pleasure. It felt so right, so good. I bent forward to kiss him, and we became a pair of dolphins—arching, diving, playing, celebrating—rolling our jubilant dance in the incomprehensible vastness of ocean that held us, gave us this way of being together, wild and free.

Afterward, we lay together for a long time, nestled together but silent. He rolled onto his side and propped himself up on an elbow to stare down at me, trailing a finger down the side of my face and along my jaw to rest at the corner of my mouth.

"How much of me do you want, Shepherd?" he asked quietly. His dark eyes glowed. I recognized his demand for truth-telling.

My stomach tightened, as if I were looking over the edge of a high cliff. "What are you asking me?"

"Well," he said, dragging his finger slowly around my lips, "we can be fuck buddies until we decide not to be." He cupped my cheek in his hand and smiled, looking sad. "That's one possibility."

He drew a leg up over mine, until his thigh lay heavy and rough across my cock and balls. "Or we can see if there's more to us than that, in spite of whatever problems we might face." He ran his thumb across my lips, and I opened them to lick it as it passed. "I need to know, though. I don't want to invest in something built on wrong assumptions."

I knew he wanted more. I could see it in his face, feel it in his touch. This moment was far removed from any of the assumptions I was operating on the day I said good-bye to Stef at my studio's elevator. That day and all its assumptions belonged to a world that had disappeared. This was a new world. But I wasn't feeling very brave.

I stared up at him, frightened by the unexpected truth that I wanted more too. "I'd like to see if there's more to us. But no guarantees."

"Of course, no guarantees," he said curtly. "I'm not asking for any." He rolled on top of me, serious and tender. "I just needed to know if you were willing to explore the unknown. I figure this is territory that's a challenge for both of us, each for our own particular reasons."

I lifted my head to chew on his chin. "You're definitely a challenge to my assumptions, Marco Fidanza."

"Good." He pushed my head against the pillows and played his tongue all over my lips and then along my throat, stopping to lick each of my blood spots. "Good. Come to Sunday dinner with my family. Arrive at one, eat at two. No jeans, or my grandmother will call you a bum. I promise you that wouldn't be good."

I laughed, but I had to acknowledge the invitation. "That's a big step."

"Yes, it is," he said, dead serious. "An important one. Reserved for explorers only. I would never bring a fuck buddy to Sunday dinner."

And then we went exploring again.

Chapter Seventeen

The next morning, I sat at the table with Marco while we drank coffee and he read the newspaper. Maybe it was because I was in his apartment, or maybe because I knew better than to attempt conversation, but I didn't feel excluded like the last time. And after a while, I found myself unfolding the Opinion section to see what anyone had to say.

After I kissed Marco good-bye in the parking lot and watched him drive off, I climbed into my own car. I had plenty of time to get home, clean up, and get to my first appointment with Alana Phillips, the hypnotherapist Reggie had recommended. With Marco's taste still on my lips, I felt ready to slay dragons. Several, probably.

Alana's office was classy, professionally bland. She greeted me warmly at the door and invited me to sit in a big armchair that looked like it would recline when we got to work. After we got all the preliminaries out of the way, she put the completed forms on the couch next to her and folded her hands in her lap.

"Ready to get going?" she asked. I nodded.

"How are you feeling right now?"

"Ready. Strong, hopeful, a little nervous. How do we start?"

"Most clients," she said, "come to me for the first time with a fair amount of skepticism and some outright misconceptions about what hypnotherapy is."

She smiled as if we were sharing a private joke. "You can discard all your images about swinging pocket watches and people hopping around on stage as if they were chickens. You'll always be fully aware of yourself and will never be asked to do anything against your will. If for any reason our work begins to go in a direction that isn't appropriate or comfortable for you, you'll be able to stop what we're doing. I'm hoping that you'll be doing most of the talking."

"And I'll know what I'm saying, right?"

"Absolutely. When children daydream, they enter a perfectly natural altered state. I'm going to lead you into a very similar state of deep relaxation, which is an everyday occurrence. I want to reemphasize that you will be in complete control of yourself and the progress of the session at all times."

"All right. So I should fasten my seat belt now?"

She shook her head, laughter in her voice. "It's my job to maintain a safe space for you to access your subconscious in a way that is different, but as I say, perfectly natural. Your subconscious speaks most effectively in dreamlike images and metaphors, in subjective feelings. In your relaxed state, I hope to lead you on a little journey, but again, you'll be in complete charge of our expedition."

She waited for a moment, gazing at me. Her stillness was lovely, and I could feel myself relax in it. "Do you have any questions for me? You'll be able to direct our session in any way you wish, and ask questions at any time as well."

I tilted the recliner back. "No questions right now. I'm very comfortable with everything you've said. The application is different in my own work, but I think I understand. The altered states I encourage in my clients are usually entered through breathwork or meditation."

"Wonderful," she said. "So what I'd like you to do is just let your body relax. Let it sink down into the chair. Feel free to shift around to be more comfortable, just like you might do while you're going to sleep."

I closed my eyes and sighed out a deep breath.

"That's great. Just ride your breath, in and out, and open yourself to the images of your journey. Just before we set out, I want you to put your right hand on your breastbone. Let its warmth build until you feel it spreading outward."

I did as directed. When I felt my chest soften, I murmured, "Okay."

Her voice wafted across my body. "If the need ever arises, and you want to come to a calm, safe place, just put your hand where it is right now, all right?"

I nodded without opening my eyes, and we began. I felt myself sinking into a deep and comfortable state as I let her calm, encouraging voice wash over me.

She had me imagine I was setting out on a trail that led away into gentle but unknown territory. The path wasn't very wide; it was my path alone. After walking in the warm sunshine for a while, I came upon a stream. It was fast-flowing, but not so wide that I couldn't cross on some stones.

On the other side of the stream, the path began to climb up a mountainside. I looked back and felt satisfaction at the journey so far.

"What does the path ahead of you look like?" she asked.

"Much steeper. It's winding around some large boulders, and I have to hold on, pull myself up sometimes."

"What are you feeling as you climb?"

"I feel good. Confident. It's hard work, but I feel I'm on the right path even though I don't really know where I'm going."

"Are you carrying anything?"

"I have a backpack. It's pretty heavy. I don't know what's in it, but I know it's important."

"On a path like this, there's often a place where you can stop to rest a while. A pleasant, level spot where you can reflect on where you've been. If you come upon one of those places, let me know."

"I don't see one yet. I'm squeezing through a narrow place between several large rocks. I think they've fallen on the path from somewhere higher up. Oh. Now here's a ledge like that. Plenty big enough for me to stretch my legs out. This feels good, like I've accomplished something worthwhile."

"Well done. So when you feel like it, take off this heavy backpack and open it. What do you find inside?"

I laughed. "A kid's metal lunchbox. My God. Care Bears! This is really silly."

"How interesting. And what's inside the lunchbox?"

"A plastic bag of food I don't recognize. It looks like scrambled eggs, but it's delicious. And a bottle of mineral water." I laughed again. "Pellegrino."

"Is there anything else inside the backpack?"

"There's a big stone down at the bottom. It's very crumbly. It has pieces of seashell set in it, like fossils. That's what's heavy. It's got a lot of sadness in it. I have no idea where it came from."

"What do you want to do with it?"

"I want to throw it away. I think it belonged to me a long time ago, but I don't want it anymore."

"Okay. When you've finished eating and you're ready to move on, let me know."

"I'm done."

"Good. So you stand up. What do you see?"

"It's quite a view. I've climbed quite a long way. I'm surprised."

"So you can leave the backpack here if you want to, and pick it up some other time. What do you want to do about that crumbly stone?"

"I want to get rid of it now. I've taken it out of the backpack and pieces of grit break off it at the slightest touch. I dumped the bits out of the bottom of the backpack so there's none left in there. I want to throw this thing against a boulder. Smash it." Watching the stone shatter made me shiver. This was good. "I threw it as hard as I could at a rock below me, and it broke into pieces. I feel… oh no."

"What's going on?"

"The pieces of rock. They're turning into men, street thugs… they're armed… oh fuck, they're from my dream—they're going to kill me!"

Alana's voice cut through my panic, serene and strong. "The mountain might be able to protect you. Lean against the mountain, be a part of it for a moment. Do you feel its care and protection? What is the mountain saying to you?"

"It's saying…." I laughed, and I could taste a hideous bitterness in my mouth. "It's saying not to worry. But these guys are going to fucking kill me!"

"Can you listen to the mountain, trust it more?"

"No! I want to stop!"

"Okay. I want you to put your right hand on your chest, just like we practiced. Feel the warmth, and the protection of your hand. Let that bring you back into this room, to safety."

The vision faded, and I sat up. I'd failed. I was a coward, and I said so.

She'd have none of that, though. Her perspective was different, and strangely, I believed her. She made sense.

I told her I wanted another crack at this, and we made another appointment two weeks out.

She gave me a bottle of cold water from a tiny fridge, and we talked about the orchids she'd brought from home now that they were in bloom. When I left, I was still feeling a little disoriented, but definitely functional. I took my time driving home.

That night, my dreams were crazy, and I thrashed a lot. But somehow, it didn't feel wrong. In the morning I felt tired, as if I'd been working hard, but also that I'd done something really good for myself. Maybe next time, I'd get farther up the mountain, or wherever I was supposed to be going on my journey.

Chapter Eighteen

Sunday afternoon at the appointed time of 1:00—actually, fifteen minutes before the appointed time—I pulled to the curb in front of Marco's family home, a big white stucco ranch-style house on Berkeley Avenue. I'd wanted to be very sure I wasn't late.

The house and yard were immaculate. The yard and exterior were trimmed, tidy, and painted, surrounded by a white wrought iron fence with fleur-de-lis spikes on the top of each bar. There were already three other cars in the driveway, which sloped sharply up to the house, two of them minivans, one very upscale. I assumed those belonged to Marco's siblings and their families.

On the phone, Marco had briefed me on the family constellation. His grandmother, Marcella, was eighty-six and presided over every family event. Mike, Marco's father, was in his early sixties, recently retired, and the youngest surviving brother. There had been four brothers, but Alex had died in Vietnam. The other two uncles and their families wouldn't be coming today. There wasn't enough room for everyone.

Marco's mother, Cosima, had borne four children also, three boys and a girl. Don (Donato) was the oldest, an attorney, married to Francesca. They had four kids, eight to thirteen. I didn't even try to remember their names.

Marco was the second son, and had followed both his father and an uncle into a career in the LAPD. Marco's younger brother Ted (Taddeo) was a manager at Trader Joe's, and had defied his grandmother by marrying outside their parish. He and his wife, Jennifer, had three children, ranging from four to eight.

His youngest sibling, Arianna, was twenty-seven and unmarried, which was a source of repeated concern for the rest of the family. But she was in public relations and had announced she was too busy to marry.

I'd made notes from Marco's phone call and had gone through them several times. Big families were alien to me, and intimidating. I wanted to be prepared.

He met me at the door, looking a little anxious but happy. I was relieved when he hugged and kissed me openly. Clearly, whatever problems that might have arisen over his sexuality no longer existed in his immediate family.

Inside the house, I had no opportunity to look around as Marco hauled me into a vortex of noise and activity. Gaggles of children ran past me in one direction and then another. Everyone seemed to be talking at top volume and all at once, even the adults who sat next to each other. The racket rebounded off the walls with the intensity of a friendly riot.

Marco, who seemed oblivious to the chaos, kept his hand on my elbow and steered me directly to his grandmother, who sat in a rust-colored Queen Anne chair with her feet on a low matching footstool.

"Nonna," he said, bending down to her, "I'd like to introduce my friend Shepherd." He straightened again. "Shepherd, this is my grandmother Marcella Fidanza, our matriarch."

Pierced by her unwavering gaze, I stood grinning like the village idiot with my hand extended. She didn't move. I could feel her assessing me against her personal yardstick behind a polite but impassive mask.

After an eternity of nine or ten seconds, she extended a cool, blue-veined hand, which I took gently but with enormous relief.

"I'm glad to meet you, Shepherd," she said. "Welcome." Her voice was firm, in contrast to the fragility of her bird-boned hand.

Out of the corner of my eye, I could see Marco relax a little. I opened my mouth to reply, but before I had a chance to say anything besides a thank you, he steered me away. "Parents next," he murmured into my ear.

Cosima was striking. She wore very little makeup, made no effort to disguise her age, and offered not a hint of apology for it, as elegant as the graying hair she swept up in a classic French roll.

She radiated the kind of charismatic beauty that changes with age but never dims. Graceful, with the unhurried bearing of the self-possessed, she gazed at me with genteel welcome, but again, I felt an echo of the reserve that I'd felt from her mother-in-law. Maybe the track record of Marco's Sunday guests warranted the reserve. This time, I was allowed to make a minute of small talk before Marco took hold of my arm. I could only shrug apologetically to her as I was dragged away.

Mike, I thought, was what Marco would probably look like in thirty-five years—features roughened with age, but still handsome, solid, strong. He'd kept himself in good shape, and there was a grounded, weathered dignity about him that carried natural authority. His large square hand was warm when we shook, and I got the distinct impression that for reasons of his own he'd decided not to crush my hand in his grip, but instead to close on it firmly enough to let me know I should remember who he was. Not that I was likely to forget.

Again, I had only a short time for surface conversation before Marco pulled me away.

"We'll talk again later," Mike informed me with a blunt nod as he turned to scoop up one of his granddaughters.

"Did I pass muster?" I asked as Marco steered me toward the kitchen.

He poured two glasses of red wine from a carafe sitting on a side table "So far so good," he replied with a grin, "but you're far from done yet. Here," he said, handing me my wine, "brace yourself—you're on your own for a while."

Marco left me to meet his siblings on my own while he went to work in the kitchen. Don and Francesca were smart, smooth, and suburban. They lived in Orange County, and I discovered I needed to avoid talking politics with them after a brief and awkward exchange about funding for public education, precipitated by an innocent but ill-advised inquiry about their children's school. Seriously conservative.

Adventure travel proved a much safer topic, although the subtext of their one-upmanship when discussing exotic travel experiences lurked like a jagged reef dangerously close to the fragile hull of our first conversation. I avoided engaging at that level and let them score every point uncontested. Maybe that was what suburban competition sounded like—pushy, narrow, and predictable.

Ted and Jennifer were much more relaxed about life, more adventurous, less status conscious, but they grilled me about my relationship with Marco. I respected their protective interest and was careful to avoid any details of how Marco and I first met. Fortunately, they didn't push on that. We talked about music, art, and, of course, their children.

He'd called her a force of nature, but nothing in Marco's briefing could have prepared me for meeting Arianna. Armored in a sleek dark business suit and impossible platform heels, she barged into my conversation with Jennifer and Ted to offer refills of wine from the decanter she brandished.

"So you're Mr. Maserati," she said. Her tight smile told me she was looking for a fight.

"No," I said, trying to deflect her aggression with what I hoped was a friendlier smile. "I'm Shepherd Bucknam. I like my car, but I'm not married to it."

She stepped forward until she stood between Jennifer and me, much closer than was polite, clearly undeterred. She'd applied her perfume as an assault weapon. "My brother is a good man," she said without lowering her volume to match our proximity. "But he hasn't had it easy in the relationship department. If you hurt him, I'll personally rip your balls off."

She smiled sweetly and lifted the decanter, her long vermillion nails clacking against the crystal. I had no trouble imagining how they could make short work of any man's tender parts.

"More wine?" Without waiting for my reply, she filled my glass too full and breezed away.

Feeling a little dizzy, I made myself take a deep breath and let it out slowly.

"So now you've met Arianna," Ted chuckled. "Don't worry, her bark is worse than her bite." He guffawed, and added, "Most of the time." Jennifer made a face and slapped his shoulder in disapproval. I could tell he was speaking from experience.

"I'm very glad to hear that, even if it's only most of the time," I said, trying to sound nonchalant. But I noticed my hand felt a little unsteady lifting my overfull glass.

Was that what siblings did, stand up for each other like that? Having none, I had no way of knowing. No doubt they'd tormented each other as children, and then somehow united in mutual protection as adults.

I imagined Mike and Cosima twenty years ago, watching out for their kids until they could stand up for themselves and each other. What would it feel like to have that kind of protection from childhood on? I couldn't remember my mother ever being that protective.

WITHOUT ANY noticeable signal penetrating the din, the activity shifted. Three card tables were set up in the den for the children, and the adults slowly migrated to the dining room. The sideboard was laden with steaming dishes, filling the air with aromas that made my stomach rumble. Most of the vegetables were from one family garden or another, I was informed. Moms supervised kids as they worked their way along the food line first, carrying plates away to the other room.

In a wordless manifestation of family order, Mike stood at the head of the table, one hand on the back of his chair. Don seated Marcella to Mike's right and Arianna took the chair to her father's left. Cosima sat at the other end, opposite Mike, and motioned me to sit at her right, across from Marco. Ted sat next to me, across from Jennifer. When he was done getting his grandmother settled, Don sat next to Jennifer and Francesca next to Ted.

After Mike's brief prayer, Marco and Ted fetched the serving dishes from the sideboard, with Marco's starting with his grandmother, Ted's starting with his mother.

The placement of each person and the movement of each dish from the sideboard into its orbit around the table created a living ceremony of relationship, and it filled me with wonder. I couldn't remember feeling anything like it.

By comparison, memories of my own family Sunday dinners, with the three of us sitting in the big dining room at the long table, out of physical reach from each other, mostly silent, while Arabella served each of us, came back to me as barren and frigid. Lonely.

Was this what Marco had meant about how unthinkably horrible the prospect of banishment from his family would be, to have his photos disappear from every living room, to have his name never spoken and his place at this table removed forever? For the first time, I understood how that could be an unbearable loss.

The last dishes entered the table circuit, and as Marco sat down, he caught my eye and grinned. The belonging that clearly had coursed through his heart since birth, since before birth, flooded over me.

Envy seized me, and fear. "You need to know that I become part of the people I love, and they become part of me," he'd said. He'd given me fair warning—he meant it. Did I want those layers of obligation, as attractive as they might feel right now?

I smiled back at him, awkward and intimidated.

Cosima was the consummate hostess, engaging me in conversation while probing deep enough to learn what she wanted to know without breaching social boundaries. Marco had already told her I was independently wealthy, so the question of my work never arose.

But with graceful efficiency, she collected all she needed to know about my family, education, travel, artistic and musical taste, political and religious views, even my philanthropic work. She was utterly charming and surgically relentless. It was clear Marco came by his detective skills honestly.

In turn, I learned about Marco's childhood, her life as a policeman's wife, and what it was like to have Mike home all the time now that he'd retired. Ted chipped in frequently, as did Jennifer, while Don and Francesca's conversation oriented more to their father and grandmother, as did Arianna's.

Even so, I felt Marcella's gaze land on me every now and then. I felt fortunate I wasn't in Arianna's line of sight unless she leaned forward to get around Francesca and Ted. Which she did a couple of times.

Once was to cut through at least two other conversations to ask me, "How did you and Marco meet, anyway? He said it was during the course of an investigation, but that's all." The table went silent.

"I don't discuss my cases with family, Arianna," Marco shot back. "Especially you, for reasons you already know."

"It's okay," I said to Marco, clearing my throat and leaning forward to meet her eyes. "A close friend of mine was murdered, and Marco and Detective Alvarez were assigned to the case. He interviewed me as part of the investigation."

"So you're a murder suspect?"

I saw a hard glint appear in Mike's eyes. It didn't look like he approved of where this was going.

"Everyone connected to the victim is a suspect to begin with, I've learned." I forced a smile, trying to keep it light. "I'm afraid I didn't make the cut after the first round."

"And what—" She stopped. Mike's hand had come to rest lightly on her forearm. There was a heartbeat of complete silence at the table before the previously interrupted conversations resumed as if nothing had intervened.

"I'm sorry about your friend," Cosima murmured. "A terrible loss, I'm sure."

"Thank you," I replied, missing Stef's easy laughter again. "Yes, it was a horrible shock, and still very painful."

After dinner, Marcella was installed in the living room, the women and older kids started work in the kitchen, and the brothers cleared the table. I asked to help, but I wasn't allowed. I didn't belong enough for that yet—I was still a guest. Mike motioned me over, and we strolled together out onto the back patio.

"Your house is wonderful," I said. "Everything is so well maintained. Cared for, I mean. I can feel the care."

He grunted. "That's what retirement does for a man. But it'll take me another twenty years to work through the honey-do list I was given as a retirement gift." He rubbed his jaw, looking resigned. "Cosi's informed me she's working on a new one in case I speed up."

I laughed. "Even so"—I nodded—"the place looks great. Must have been a big change from police work."

"Yup." He didn't elaborate. I waited for him to take the lead.

After a while, he spoke quietly. "It's not an easy life, being attached to a cop. Stress and frustration. Danger. Crazy schedules, and a shitload of waiting."

I met his eyes, acknowledging what he was saying to me, and then looked away, following the line of half-buried bricks that separated the lawn from the shrubs against the fence.

"Yeah. I've already got some of those. It could take some getting used to." I grinned. "Fortunately, I've got things to keep me busy."

"Huh. Marco said you support some charities."

I nodded. "I just set up an annuity in Stef's memory—my dead friend. Off the Street. I met the director, Ramón Cruz. He runs a solid operation on almost nothing. Seemed like a good choice."

"You ever hear about LAPD's Jeopardy Program?"

"Absolutely. They came up high in my research results too. And the Police Activity League. But for Stef, I wanted to focus less on gang intervention and drugs, and more on kids who are essentially homeless. Kids kicked out of their homes because they're gay, maybe. Physically or sexually abused. That kind of focus."

He looked at me sideways. "Abused. That a big deal for you?"

"Everyone's got scars, Mike," I said, turning to face him. "Nobody gets a free ride. Not even the rich."

He looked away and nodded, a half-inch motion marking solid understanding and acknowledgement. "I helped out in PAL a fair amount over the years," he said after a little while. "Made a difference, I think, as much as anything can."

"That's all we can do—try to make a difference."

"Yup." He adjusted a tendril of rose climbing a trellis, his big fingers moving with care and a delicacy I found unnerving. It spoke of a complexity in him I hadn't touched yet.

Mike's three sons drifted out of the house, arguing about something, and joined us.

"We've got to get going, Dad," Don said. "Chrissy's got soccer tonight." They embraced and kissed each other on the cheek.

He stuck out his hand to me. "Good to meet you, Shepherd. Look forward to next time."

"Me too," I said as we shook.

Marco sidled up to me. "We should probably head out pretty quick as well."

I nodded. "Thanks for everything, Mike," I said, as his hand took charge of mine again. "It was an honor to be in your home."

He nodded slightly, meeting my eyes, and released my hand.

Ted and I shook. Taking my elbow again, Marco guided me back into the house.

"I need to say good-bye to the others," I whispered.

"Oh, yes. On pain of death," he chuckled.

I paid my respects to Marcella and Cosima and exchanged cautiously civil farewells with Arianna. Then we stood outside the front door.

"So," I said with a heavy sigh. "My place or yours?"

"Mine's a lot closer, but I need to stay here just a little longer. Give me half an hour to get there."

"See you there." I headed for my car.

Chapter Nineteen

I'D DELIBERATELY left my phone in the car because I didn't want to be disturbed while I was with Marco's family. When I turned on the ignition, I saw that had been a good decision. I had two voice messages from Carol, my real estate agent, wanting me to take a look at some new studio possibilities.

The truth was I was nowhere near ready to get serious about a new place. Every time I thought about it, I fell into my ache at having failed Stef, who I was convinced would have grown into the most wonderful Daka I could imagine. Without doubt, he was more naturally gifted than I was. With time, maybe he would have been even more wonderful than Peter Karspek, who had taught me so much. All those gifts lost to a couple of bullets. That ache rose like a wall against my own return to coaching.

Besides, I reminded myself, I'd originally told all my clients I wouldn't be taking appointments for two months, and I was well within that window.

Still, I made a voice note to send out an update, saying it would be even longer than two months. I needed time. That understanding landed in me with physical force, knitting together disparate fragments of what I wanted, making me stronger.

In our sessions, Reggie kept asking me what I wanted, and I'd had trouble telling him. Now as I slowly drove to Marco's, what I wanted had distilled into clarity. I wanted time to heal, to get over losing Stef. In theory, I knew I wasn't responsible for his death, but I felt I'd failed him. It gnawed at me.

The first step in getting over all that was to do everything in my power to catch his killer. Whether I succeeded or not, I needed to know—with certainty—that I'd done everything I possibly could. I needed that closure. Then maybe I could process my grief with a clear conscience.

Realistically, I had so much boiling around in me that I wasn't in any condition to coach a client even if I did have a studio. Hell, I couldn't even finish a hypnotherapy session about my own issues. I was the one who needed help.

I called Carol back and let her know I was going slower on a new studio than I first expected. She knew me well enough from our other transactions that I wouldn't bail on her, so she agreed to back off, as long as she could keep sending me listings. I said sure, and five minutes after we hung up, I heard the clink of some arriving in my e-mail.

While I was in business mode, I called Juergen for an update. He said he was putting together his report, and would call me in a day or two to brief me fully.

I was impatient to learn what he'd found, although I didn't say so. It wouldn't have made any difference to Juergen. He had one speed only—his own.

It's odd, how memory works. As soon as I pulled into Marco's parking lot, I thought of our first sex at my place, which led me to the farmers' market where we'd bought food for the dinner, and the fat woman there who had pressed her card into my hand.

In a jolt of surprise, I knew I wanted an appointment with her. "Find past-life lady," I said into the hands-free, grateful I'd bothered to enter her into my phone. I had to smile at myself for listing her that way. Up came her number.

"Call," I instructed.

It took several rings for her to answer. When I identified myself, her voice rose almost an octave. "Oh, I'm so glad you called!" she gushed. "Do you want to make an appointment?"

I did, and we set it up for Wednesday. When I was finished, Marco was standing beside the car, dressed in jeans and T-shirt, with a backpack slung over one shoulder. I climbed out.

"What do you think about going over to the Chavez Ravine Arboretum with a couple of beers? It's too nice an evening to stay inside." He leered. "Unless, of course, you want to go straight to bed."

"It would be nice to be outside for a while," I said, "but I don't have a change of clothes."

"We're about the same size. You can wear some of mine." He laughed a jeering, high-school locker-room-jock-competitive laugh. "Although I really am much bigger than you where it counts. You'll get lost in my jeans."

I'd have snapped him with a wet towel if I'd had one handy. "That's not what I heard you say last time I had you speared to the bed, my man." It felt good to be teenager-stupid for a moment. "You were begging for mercy."

We both laughed and headed upstairs. It took us half an hour to get out of the bedroom, and that's only because there was no foreplay.

AT MARCO'S suggestion, I left my car in his parking lot and rode with him to Chavez Ravine in his unmarked car, complete with the sinister war-wagon bumper. I'd never ridden in a police car before, and it wasn't a particularly pleasant experience. Sitting in the front seat with the utilitarian array of computer screen and radios between us was an unwelcome visual of what his daily work was really like. I wanted to say something, anything, just to pay respect to his job, but I knew whatever I said would be inadequate. The car's interior was scarred with use—hard-edged and unbeautiful. Dangerous. I didn't want to look through the mesh into the backseat, let alone the trunk.

On the arboretum grounds, we pulled onto the shoulder of a side road and hiked up a hill into the trees. I just followed Marco, who seemed sure of where he was going. He picked a stand where the ground cover was less brown, which in LA qualified it as lawn.

"You come here often?" I asked.

He gave me a wicked grin. "This is within spitting distance of the police academy. These woods are filled with generations of horny cadet pranks and encounters you don't want to know anything about."

"Any involving you?"

"You do not want to know," he said, separating each word, grinning and shaking his head firmly. "Trust me, I'm a peace officer."

He sat, pulled out our beers, and stuffed the backpack between him and the tree as a cushion. "C'mere, babe," he said, patting his lap. "Put your head right here. Facing out, though, this time."

I laughed. "Okay, but just this once." I stretched out perpendicular to him and let my head rest against his thigh. The warm dry air flowed slowly down through the trees and over us in a fragrant, peaceful river.

He turned my face toward his. "So how was meeting the family?"

"Good," I said, immediately regretting how lame that sounded, once the word was out.

"Good?" He trailed a thumb between my parted lips. "That's it?"

"No, there's lots more," I said. "Give me a chance to not be distracted by your thumb in my mouth."

He pulled away but left his hand resting on my chest. Its delicious warmth and weight pushed into me. An urge blossomed through me to open my chest and let him all the way in, let him physically hold my heart while it beat. That scared me.

I sat up a little and took a pull on my beer before lying back down and gazing up into his face. Truth-telling with Marco felt really good, even if it was scary.

"I envy you," I said quietly, letting the words out. "Even now, I can't really imagine what it would be like, growing up in a big, high-energy family like yours, with so much connectedness, both for good and bad, being part of each other in ways I can't imagine. I found myself wanting what you have but knowing I never will. Sitting at that table made me feel poor for the first time in my life."

He said nothing, but stroked his hand up my throat to cradle the side of my head, pulling the back of my head firmly against his crotch. It felt like a gesture of acknowledgment, of intimate inclusion.

It had changed my line of sight, though, and I gazed down the hill. Everything that was not us felt very far away.

"I finally understood what you meant about family tradition and belonging. About what being shunned would mean." I turned into him to see his face again. "And what you said about becoming part of those you love. It's very powerful."

He lifted me from his lap and crushed me into a kiss, which lasted a long time as his tongue plundered my mouth. He didn't say anything as he lowered me into his lap again, but his eyes glowed with emotion.

His hand pinned me to his body by my throat, his thumb scraping against the roughness of my birthmarks.

His touch there made me queasy, so I moved his thumb off them as gently as I could. "I feel like I'm dragging a lot of baggage around with me right now, Marco," I said, suddenly feeling embarrassed and discouraged. "I'm beating my head against my issues with violence, trying some hypnotherapy, but I couldn't even finish the first session. I was a basket case for hours afterward. I've made another appointment, though."

I smiled, bitter and defensive at the caution I saw in his face. But I figured he might as well know the whole shit list of things I was trying. "There's more to it than just my reaction to violence, though. I can feel it. I have to crack open whatever that is. I even made an appointment with that past-life lady we bumped into at the farmers' market. Her name's Lorena."

He snorted in disgust. "Great—nothing like paying good money to a charlatan to complicate your life. Why are you telling me this? You know how I feel about frauds."

"Because you deserve to know who you're getting involved with. When Stef was killed, something in me changed, and I'm trying to make sense of it. You should also know I have a PI looking into his murder." His body tensed under my head.

"Damn it, Shepherd—I can't talk to you about that. You're not a suspect, but you're still a person of interest. That means not a word. Just back off for both our sakes, will you?"

I looked up at him, aching for understanding. His face had hardened into a mask. "I'm not doing this because I question your work," I said, trying to escape his disapproval, "or even because I think I'll find anything useful to you. I just have to know for myself that the trail ends in a blank, if that's what it does."

I lifted a hand to hold his arm. "You have to understand I couldn't live with myself if I quit before I'd done everything I could to find Stef's killer. And I will never ask you to violate your rules regarding the case. I promise."

He looked away and said nothing. Eventually, I broke the silence that had settled between us. "I'm getting a report in the next day or so.

I'll tell you whatever you want to know about it. I'll show you everything I've got, if you want."

"Who's your investigator?"

"Juergen Hostler."

He grunted. "At least he's one of the good guys. I can trust him to brief me if he finds anything I can use." He stared down at me hard. "I hope to god you don't screw up the investigation, babe. You'd be hurting Stef, yourself, me—everyone connected."

Gazing up from his lap, I watched his Adam's apple rise and fall as he swallowed. "It would be the end of our exploring together too," he said quietly, stroking my cheek with his thumb. "I don't think you have any idea how much I don't want that to happen."

The pain in his eyes told me how serious he was, and a sickening dread wormed through me. I didn't want to have to choose between my commitment to Stef and what was growing between Marco and me. That was completely unfair.

"Believe me, I don't want that to happen, either," I said, trying to project confidence I didn't really feel.

Neither of us spoke for a long time, and in the hot, dry silence, darkness fell around us.

Chapter Twenty

THE WAITRESS at Sandy's Kitchen recognized me as soon as I got through the front door and pointed toward the booth where Juergen sat, cheerfully snatched up a menu and place setting, and followed me there.

Juergen had already ordered, so I just asked for a dinner salad and bowl of soup. I wasn't particularly hungry anyway, except for the information inside the blue folder that sat on the table waiting for me.

"Thanks, Juergen," I said, after the waitress had left. "I appreciate you going the extra distance on this."

Juergen fixed me with those ice-blue eyes and shrugged. "Worth a try. But there is no more distance, at least that can lead the police anywhere," he said. "Your buddy Fidanza ran up against the same wall, I'm pretty sure."

"Then what's our next step?"

He shook his head. I knew I was about to get bad news. "I put all the pieces I've got into a plausible scenario—my best guess." He paused. "This is as far as I go with you on this, my friend. It's the best I can give you."

A wall. He was giving up. I tried to be angry with him for abandoning the most important job I'd ever given him, but I couldn't. I knew him too well. He'd never even hinted about quitting before—on anything—in the five or six years he'd worked for me. I didn't reply, and he didn't say more. It was an uncomfortably long moment—for me, at least. Juergen's face gave away nothing of what he felt.

We sat back as our food landed in front of us. What little appetite I had before was gone. The oversalted smell of the cheese and broccoli soup made my stomach promise revolt if I ate it.

"That's not the good news I'd been hoping for."

He shrugged again, carving up his open-face roast beef sandwich. "It's not good news," he agreed. "But it's as good as we're going to get."

I slumped back on the bench, resigned. "Whenever you're ready."

"First the data," he said around a mouthful of roast beef. "Walter Chisholm, Democrat, is running for reelection to the state assembly. You knew that already, but if he's elected, this would be his last, due to term limits. He won by a hefty margin in his previous two campaigns, but this time, he's barely ahead of his opponent. He's got a young law-and-order Republican contender who's shaking the money tree, even among donors who've supported Chisholm in the past."

"Money problems?" I asked.

Juergen shook his head. "Not directly, at least not yet. It's something of an open secret that Chisholm is gay, but he's well established so it's old news. The press isn't eager to make it an issue. But according to my sources, a sex scandal would change the rules, make his sexuality fair game. Strategists on both sides believe that would cost Chisholm several points. Donors could run away."

"You've talked to both campaigns?"

He stared hard at me, like I'd insulted him. "According to my sources." He repeated the words with more precision, took another mouthful, and chewed for a minute.

"Chisholm's biggest backer is a company called Staviscor, a small but very successful defense contractor. They're what I'd call a jackal company. They stay out of the spotlight, never put themselves in position for much public scrutiny, and hunt down juicy contracts that other companies might not want to touch for public image reasons. Or they wait for the big lions to take what they want and then subcontract to clean up what's left of the carcass."

"Lovely."

"Not my word for it," he said, his voice cold with disgust. "Example. They caused a stir a couple of years ago when they partnered with a private prison in Chisholm's district to test their new pain-inducing weapons on prisoners." He grimaced, showing teeth. "In the land of the free, pioneers of crowd control at its finest." He must have been outraged, to show that much emotion. He was silent for a moment.

"At any rate," he said, mopping up the last of the gravy from his sandwich, "as part of their support for Chisholm's campaign, they provided all the communications equipment for the headquarters and loaned one of their IT honchos to run it for them. It's a pretty sophisticated operation. The phone banks are tied directly into the central computer system where a small team can manage the phone calls as well as all the new social media stuff. Robocalls, texts, Twitter, Facebook, other platforms I'd never heard of before. StumbleUpon. Instagram. Reddit," he snorted. "Did you even know there was a Triberr?" He shook his head in disbelief.

"Chisholm's personal cell phone is plugged into that whole system. Messages can be sent out by anyone on that team as if they came from Chisholm himself. To say nothing of calls and texts received on his number."

He put his fork down and looked me in the eye, telling me this was important. "What this means to our investigation is that Lewis's text messages to Chisholm setting up their appointment and Chisholm's reply could have been seen by several people besides Chisholm himself. Particularly Corey Robbins, the IT guy from Staviscor who runs the shop and can watch everything. There is no way to identify who arranged the fatal meeting with Lewis."

"No identification that would stand up in court," I said.

Juergen nodded. "That's all that counts, ultimately."

It was true. I had to accept what all the law enforcement professionals like Marco and Juergen had known for years. This was part of why Marco didn't want a dilettante like me to get involved with the investigation. I poked at my salad.

"It's a pretty efficient way to keep a thumb on Chisholm's campaign," he said with grudging respect. "Donate a small fortune in sophisticated communications equipment and then provide the key manager to run it. I can imagine that Robbins reports to his real boss two or three times a day." He smiled, cynical. "On a phone that doesn't go through the campaign office, I have no doubt."

"Elegant, in its own way."

He grunted his agreement. "The bottom line is that Staviscor has a lot to lose if their boy doesn't win back his seat one more time. Chisholm is on several committees that have direct influence over the supervision of Staviscor's California playground."

He stopped and pushed the folder toward me. "Those are the bones of what's in here," he said, tapping the folder. "What's not in there is my best guess as to what happened. Which is raw speculation and not to be relied upon. Not to be shared with anyone else. At all."

The waitress came to clear away our plates. "You've barely touched your food, hon," she chided. "You not feeling well?"

"Actually, no, I'm not," I said. "I just can't eat. I'm sorry."

She stacked everything, full bowl of soup and all, along her arm and dropped the check between us. "Well, I hope you feel better soon, dear. That soup would have helped," she said as she wheeled away.

I looked at Juergen. "This is where we hit rough water, isn't it?"

He gave me a blunt nod. "I have a strict rule against sharing speculation with my clients," he said. "I like hard facts." He held my gaze for a moment, as if reconsidering his decision to tell me anything more. "I'm making an exception in this case because I want to give you as much as I possibly can. Here is everything I've got, speculation included."

He leaned forward again and dropped his voice as if confiding a secret. "I think Staviscor pretty much owns Chisholm. There are a couple of pretty young assistants on his staff, and they usually go wherever Chisholm goes. Males, I mean. I suspect their job is to answer Chisholm's booty calls, keep his sexual activities in-house during the campaign. I think Chisholm bumped into Lewis somewhere and decided to go grazing in unauthorized pastures."

I rubbed my eyes, glad I hadn't eaten anything. I could feel worse news coming.

Juergen dropped a fist heavily on the back of my hand. Not hard enough to hurt, but enough to startle me. When I looked up, he met my gaze and held it. "Rumor from more than one source says Staviscor has used unpleasant and drastic measures, let's say, to protect their interests in the past. They're dangerous folks."

He took a sip of coffee. "My best guess is that they were willing to let Chisholm stray once with Lewis, but when he made a second appointment, they saw a problem. Someone on Chisholm's communications team, probably Robbins himself, intercepted the exchange setting up Lewis's second appointment and reported it to whoever was in charge of Chisolm back at Staviscor.

"Robbins would never have heard back as to what anyone decided to do with the information until the police showed up asking questions. I figure someone at Staviscor dispatched a professional cleanup guy to take care of Lewis after Chisholm left. He surprised Lewis, taped him to the chair, and waited until Chisholm was at the fundraiser he attended that night, so there could be no logistical connection to Lewis's death. He could easily have scrubbed the place clean while he waited, and then shot your friend."

"But the killer couldn't have got into the complex where my studio is without someone opening the door for him," I protested.

Juergen snorted. "Do you know how easy that is, especially for a professional? Chisholm could've opened the door for him on his way out without ever knowing who he was. More likely, Mr. Cleanup waited for someone else to open the door and seized his opportunity. He just waited for Chisholm to leave, then tidied up unwanted loose ends."

I stared at the scarred Formica of the tabletop, horrified at how easy killing Stef must have been for a professional. "And all the information like the suite number would've been in the exchanges between Stef and Chisholm."

"Bingo. End of story."

"Is it really?" I asked.

His nod said it was. "I believe the people behind Lewis's death are quite prepared to repeat their actions if they feel threatened. I'm not going further on anything that involves Chisholm or Staviscor."

He shrugged a little apology and smiled. "I'm done being a hero, my friend. I've got two sweet little granddaughters, and no one in the world can pay me enough money to jeopardize their health and happiness. Fire me if you want, but I get off this bus now."

"Of course I'm not going to fire you," I said, a little insulted that he thought I might. "I understand. And I respect your decision." I looked down at the folder. "You say there's no mention of this scenario in the report."

"Nope. Nothing written down. This is strictly between you and me and only verbal. I won't even discuss this over the phone with you. Any more discussion of this has to be face-to-face."

"Do you think the police got this far?"

"Oh, yeah. They knew it was a professional job right away. The bedding was gone, all the surfaces cleaned. Not even a used tissue in the trash. I'm pretty sure they put it together this way too."

"Wait a minute." I stared at Juergen while my thoughts rearranged. "The police would have shown Chisholm a photo of Stef. Even though he denied recognizing him, that makes him complicit in Stef's murder. That and the appointment data on Stef's phone should have been enough to push further."

Juergen's shrug told me he was trying to be patient. "Not if Lewis's phone messages disappeared into the campaign system. There's no proof Chisholm met with Lewis and no way to prove that Chisholm was lying about the photo short of a lie detector. The police couldn't possibly make an elected government official sit for that without a helluva lot more evidence. And without causing a serious shitstorm."

Juergen's smile was laced with disgust. "Just hooking a politician like Chisholm to a lie detector probably would have made it explode, anyway."

I nodded, defeated. The police had stopped, and now the best private investigator I could hire had stopped. I knew Juergen wasn't a coward. Long ago, he'd earned the right to choose his battles.

If he'd found something viable, he'd have given it to Marco, but all he had was his own hunch. Marco and Alvarez had hunches of their own, and none of them could put anything together that would stand up against the rules of evidence.

Very wisely, Juergen wasn't going to pursue a conjecture that could endanger his family. It was time for me to face the reality that Stef's killer would probably never be arrested, let alone convicted.

I picked up the folder. It was too light, too thin. "I really appreciate you staying on the bus this long, Juergen. Thank you."

I looked at him and fought the lump growing in my throat. "I've done everything I can think of for Stef, and it feels like pathetic failure."

"Hey, bucko." Juergen leaned across the table to swat my shoulder. "I've run into more dead ends than you ever will. It's always a rotten feeling. We did the best we could for him but came up empty."

"Well, almost empty," I said. "I got your expert opinion. For what it's worth, I think you're right about what happened. I wish I could think of something more to do about that, but I can't." I just couldn't let it stop there. "Not yet, anyway."

"Stubborn bastard, aren't you?" Juergen stared hard at me. "Something else you should know, something your buddy Marco would be too proud to tell you."

My head snapped up. "What?"

"It's not as blatant as you see in the movies, but word is they were *encouraged* to accept the dead end—which was very real, by the way." Juergen's smile was tight, bitter. "Further investigation of Chisholm or Staviscor on such slim evidence would have met with... difficulty."

I had to defend Marco's honor. "Marco would never cave to that!"

Juergen's voice hardened. "It's not caving. Don't you *ever* think of it that way. For a detective like him, it's the dark side of being realistic."

He sighed, and in that tired breath, I could hear his confession that in his time on the force he'd faced the same dark reality himself. "He loves his job, my friend. And he is as loyal as they come. True blue. It would have torn him up, but yes, he would have accepted his superior's guidance on that."

Marco had been so angry the night he'd told me he was off the case, and I'd said I didn't understand his being reassigned. He'd said I couldn't understand, because I wasn't a cop. He'd said he couldn't explain. Now I understood, and I ached for him.

"Well, they can't pressure me like that. I'm not giving up, even if I don't know what to do next."

Juergen's eyes hardened into ice. "For god's sake, don't get yourself in more trouble than you can get out of in one piece. I promise, it would be very easy to do here. If you blunder into Staviscor's crosshairs, you sure as hell wouldn't be doing Lewis any favors. Or anyone else, either."

"I don't want to die," I said defensively. I knew he was right, but something in me pushed back. "But neither did Stef. I can't explain it, but I owe Stef more than this."

"Like I said, Lewis wouldn't want you to get killed too." He slid heavily out of the booth looking like a gruff, sensible grandfather. "It's hard to admit there's nothing more you can do. Believe me, I know. Sometimes it takes more courage to admit you're licked than it does to keep going."

I hated that he was right. I didn't have the courage to admit I was licked.

Chapter Twenty-One

THE NEXT morning was my appointment with Lorena, the past-life lady. From the scant provable facts of Juergen's last report to the completely unprovable insights into my problems arising from a past life was a pretty spectacular leap. Or maybe a journey through hyperspace. Either way, my head took a while to make the shift.

Lorena's apartment was on Fifth Avenue, just a few blocks from Venice Beach. I parked on the street behind a battered Chevy pickup with planks and a cement-encrusted wheelbarrow poking out of the bed. The whole street snoozed in funky, laid-back, Venice Beach decay. Between the sidewalk and the curb, a giant agave spread its thick leaves in a voluptuous hazard to any passersby. A bougainvillea that hadn't been pruned in years sprawled along the fence and littered the sidewalk with blossoms that had fallen anytime from five minutes to weeks ago. Some were now no more than broken brown flakes. Dusty purple zinnias straggled upward between a couple of young volunteer palms. Unwatered grass and weeds, long and brown, appeared to have given up trying to accomplish anything until rain arrived. I smiled at what I imagined Mike Fidanza's opinion of this landscaping might be.

The gray, maybe-it-was-once-a-shade-of-green stucco apartment building offered an intercom with twelve buttons. I pushed the buzzer for apartment 103, and the door buzzed open without anyone asking who I was. The worn, narrow lobby had a half-full bin for unwanted junk mail, a bank of scarred mailboxes, and an archway to a stairwell and hall. The hall ran in only one direction. Although it was eleven o'clock in the morning, the thick air still smelled of someone's breakfast fried in bacon fat.

I knocked on the door, and Lorena opened it right away, her face bright with excitement and perspiration. "I can't tell you how glad I am that you're here, Shepherd," she enthused, dabbing at her forehead with a tissue. "All I can do is follow Guidance and let people decide for themselves what to do." She waved me in, but there was no room to get past her, so I just waited.

"But you," she said, fixing me with her ecstatic gaze, "are ready to pop. So ready for your next step. Congratulations. I'm very happy for you." She turned and stumped past the half-open bathroom door into the tiny living room, and I followed.

Even though she was obviously pleased about it, being ready to pop didn't sound like a good thing to me—but I was way out of my element here.

She headed directly to an ancient brownish plaid recliner partially covered with a bright turquoise throw, settled in with a whoosh of relief, and levered the footrest up until her thick, blotchy ankles were horizontal.

"Please make yourself comfortable in that chair," she said, pointing to a wooden armchair, the only other place in the cluttered room where a human being could sit. She gazed at me for a while, beaming and dabbing her throat with a tissue, and then closed her eyes, taking some deep, noisy breaths.

"Just sit back and make yourself comfortable, dear," she said. "Just relax and let Guidance give you the information you need for your next step."

Apparently, that was all the introduction to her work that I was going to get. I looked around the dim room. Almost all the wall space was covered in erratically hung swaths of fabric, some depicting Buddhas or temples. One large maroon one, strung across a rubber-footed white curtain rod, served as a partially drawn divider for the kitchen and I supposed the bedroom beyond it. I didn't really want to think about her bedroom.

Stuff was piled haphazardly on every horizontal surface in the room—books; stacks of mail sliding sideways, some of it unopened; tchotchkes; a beautiful conch; a couple of framed photographs perched on whatever had happened to accumulate underneath them. Nothing looked like it had been dusted recently, maybe in a long time. The air was heavy with patchouli or incense, and I became a little claustrophobic. Fighting it, I took a deep breath of what air was available and relaxed as instructed. And waited.

Lorena's eyes popped open. "This isn't why you're here today," she said cheerfully, "but I'm instructed to tell you that there's something coming to you soon from your mother. It's very important, and can change your life."

"My mother's been dead for several years and can't give me anything she hasn't already," I said. Marco had dismissed her as a charlatan. This was a discouraging start to proving otherwise.

"Doesn't matter," she said, completely unconcerned. "The doors between life and death, between spirit and form, are opening for you. They're opening for everybody in this challenging and exciting new age, but for you, it's particularly important. This is a powerful gift from your mother, and it will change how you feel about her."

I smiled, suddenly sorry for Lorena. There was nothing my mother could give me that would change how I felt about her. Coming here had been a stupid thing to do. Was I really this desperate for help? Maybe I was. It was embarrassing to admit that possibility.

She closed her eyes again, and her mouth began to move without making any sound, as if she were praying or speaking to people inside her head. I decided it was the latter.

"You are here today, Shepherd," she began in a heavy voice that startled me, "to take your next step. We are pleased."

This new voice was easily an octave lower than she'd sounded just seconds ago. Her face had become Buddha-like, knowing and calm, as if the world and all its plants, animals, and people, even all the stars and planets, moved inside her mind in untroubled beauty and serene wisdom. My skin prickled.

"We ask that you not be afraid, but listen calmly to us," she said in her new mannish voice. "We need to talk to you about death. We know you're afraid of dying and have unhappy dreams about it. You think that your fearful vision lies ahead of you, yet to occur, but in reality, it is already in your past. This death offers you a key to understanding what lies ahead."

How could she have known that I was so afraid? Of course. She could have seen my reaction when she was talking to me at the market, when she told me death followed me. But my dream? There was no way she'd have known that.

"You think you are already open enough, connected enough, love enough, and within the confines of your current state, you've done well. But there is much more for you to do in this incarnation. It is because of this that we asked you to come here."

Lorena was silent for a moment; I had no idea how long. Her lips began moving again. This silent conversation was a long one.

"You feel caution about becoming deeply involved with a lover. And you believe that you have not been loved enough. This is a frequent perception on your plane. It's time for you to leave that belief behind. You are loved more than you know, and you are called to accept that. Let love change you. Then you, too, will have new power to love.

"Your work with others is good; you increase their experience of light. We approve. But now you come to a frontier of your own, and to enter your new dimension, you must enter a new life. Beginning with this old death. Unfinished business." Lorena scratched her jaw, never opening her eyes.

"In an earlier life, you loved completely, with your heart wide open. Too open. But your love was not returned in kind. In fact, you were betrayed into violence. This is what you feel and fear, that love will kill you."

I wanted to think about that for a while, but Lorena, or whoever was speaking through her, was on a roll.

"Sometime soon you will have opportunity to revisit this sad moment, this sad moment when part of you closed in betrayal. Take action when the moment comes. You must not be afraid to go deep. Behind what seems like pain and tragedy lies freedom to reclaim your full power.

"We urge you to be courageous and follow every opportunity to grow, as strange or as frightening as it may appear to be on the surface. Even if growth means leaving your present work. This is a turning time for you. Fulfillment and happiness lie along one path, isolation and loneliness along the other. You must soon choose which path to follow."

Lorena shifted her bulk and belched without apology. "Do you have any questions for us?"

What the hell. If this was a séance, or whatever it was, why not try? It's not like I'd been briefed on what I was expected to do. "I want to ask about Steven Lewis. Do you know of him?" I felt like I'd paid the gypsy at the carnival, and I might as well get my money's worth.

There was a long silence. "Usually, we do not discuss those who have passed, but you—" Lorena's brows knit together as if she were puzzled, or couldn't hear something clearly.

Her lips resumed her silent conversation for a while. "This is good," she continued. "You and the One you called Stef have shared many lifetimes. Father and son, brothers, sometimes lovers. Mostly brothers. It could have been much more this time, but warmongers killed him, men in love with violence, for whom the death of others means nothing. Still, he is content with what he shared with you. You will see him again, when the time comes. Your karma together is lovely. Very bright."

Goosebumps. She could never have known that I called Steven Lewis Stef. There was no way. I forced myself to ignore the chills skittering across my skin. "What more can you say about my past death, the unfinished business?"

"You are on the right path. Be courageous. Love and death are often mixed wrongly on your plane. Reclaiming your power to love regardless of death will be a great gift in your life, and in the lives of those you love."

Reclaim the power to love? Before I could ask anything more—and I wasn't even sure I had more to ask—Lorena gave out a long moaning sigh and her head dropped back against the back of her chair, mouth agape. It wasn't the loveliest sight in the world, but as I sat gazing at her, I filled with some strange kind of happiness or gratitude, a new sense of possibility, weird as the situation was.

Then she opened her eyes and smiled like a happy schoolgirl. "Guidance is very pleased for you, dear. You've done well."

Then why did I feel so unsure? At least I hadn't thrown up when whoever had been speaking through Lorena had mentioned my death. Maybe it did make a difference if what I'd been struggling with was already in the past.

Still in a daze, I declined a glass of water, placed my donation, as she called it, on a little altar I hadn't noticed among the clutter until she pointed it out, and wandered back out to the car. Even if Los Angeles doesn't have fresh air often, by comparison to the apartment this qualified, and I was grateful. It helped me come back to earth.

What do I do with this bizarre information? In the car, I strapped myself in and turned the key. I had no idea, but in spite of my expectations and cynicism, I felt like the session had given me direction. Sort of. "Guidance," whatever that was, had told me to take action, go deep and be courageous, whatever that meant. I hoped I'd be courageous. I would do my best to go deep. At least that was a metaphor I understood.

And it sounded like Juergen's hunch was right. Staviscor was probably full of warmongers, for whom the death of others meant little. But a psychic speaking in a trance wasn't evidence for anyone but me.

I called Marco, inviting myself to his place for dinner, promising to fix dinner for him. He agreed enthusiastically. He'd already had Chinese twice this week and was ready for a change.

"You can't take her seriously, babe."

I lay against Marco, who had propped himself up against his headboard. I shivered, feeling his voice rumble through his bare chest and into the back of my head. I liked hearing his voice that way. I let my eyes roam the bedroom floor, littered with our clothes where we had tossed them in our haste to get naked. I was having trouble deciding whether or not to take Lorena seriously. Part of me certainly didn't want to, but it was running into some surprising resistance.

"I honestly don't know. She spoke about things she couldn't have known unless she were the real thing. It doesn't fit into my personal version of reality, but that's true for a long list of ideas."

"Like what?"

"Think of the millions of people who take the idea of a virgin birth seriously," I said, instantly regretting my choice of example. "I'm not passing judgment on anyone else," I said in a hurry to control the possible damage. "I'm just saying that idea doesn't fit into my personal version of reality. It clearly fits just fine with a lot of other people."

"Yes, well. Don't volunteer that opinion at a Fidanza family dinner." We'd never discussed it, but his Catholic roots were inescapable. After a moment, he said, "But that's religion. That's different." He sounded defensive.

I twisted around so I could look directly at him. "Why is it different? Do you think Lorena believes in what she calls her 'Guidance' any less completely than the most devout monk believes in his god?" I wanted to get away from religion, but cosmology was exactly what we were talking about. "Whatever that is, it possesses her, speaks through her. She might be deluded, but I saw her in action. Her belief in what she does is absolute."

Marco grunted but didn't say anything more. I leaned in for a kiss.

"Frankly," I said, "I sometimes envy the certainty I see in others. Your grandmother. Lorena. It would be simpler to be guided by that kind of certainty. Doubt makes things complicated. But when I get close to someone else's certainty, I can tell it's not for me. It's for them."

I gave him another kiss, sloppier and slower. "Maybe I'm still just stumbling toward my own. One thing I am certain of—I like kissing you." Which I did again.

He held back until we came up for air. "But seriously—learning from death in a past life? That's just New Age bullshit."

"Is it? Don't tell a Hindu that, or maybe even a Buddhist."

"Okay, okay," he said, laughing in defeat. "Take your vacation into woo-woo land, but don't forget where reality lies." He pointed to his lips. "Right here. Kiss me again."

I did. He pushed me backward and climbed on top of me.

THE NEXT morning, Marco had to be at work for an eight o'clock meeting, and we were both still deeply asleep when the alarm went off. I made coffee while he took a shower, wishing there had been time for a quick frolic before we took off. But there wasn't even time for a glance at the newspaper, let alone sex.

I handed him his coffee when he came out fully dressed. "You are one of the few men I know who looks sexy in a white shirt and tie. How do you do it?"

"Maybe it's because I hate wearing them—the rebellious captive-in-chains look."

I laughed, but he was right. He looked sexy in them precisely because they carried his energy of unwilling submission behind them.

I ran an appreciative finger down the length of his tie, stopping at its point just above his belt. "I think you're on to something with that rebellious captive-in-chains thing. It bears some exploration one day. Neckties can make fun restraints in other ways."

"Don't start," he said, looking more than a little interested. "At least not when I have to leave for work in fifteen minutes."

"A safer topic, then. I'd love it if you came with me to the outdoor concert Friday. It's at the Levitt Pavilion in MacArthur Park. Dustbowl Revival is playing—they're kind of crazy and fun. A few of us thought to make it a potluck picnic too. Are you game?"

"Who is 'us'?" he asked, his face guarded as he shrugged on his jacket.

"Peter Karspek and a couple of the other guys from my concert-going group. It will be a nice, relaxed way for you to get to know Peter better."

"Relaxed? Maybe not. Why do you want me to know Peter better?"

"Peter is my oldest friend. He's an interesting, intelligent, gentle man. He's generous, and widely traveled. I thought you might enjoy conversing with him outside official roles."

"I doubt it. He's had you for fifteen years. I'd probably just stew in my jealousy."

"He's been a mentor and a friend for fifteen years. He's never *had* me, never tried to." I searched Marco's face for any sign of understanding. "And when it comes right down to it, he's the closest to family that I have, at least that I can introduce you to."

Marco's jaw told me I wasn't making much progress. I changed tactics. "You invited me to meet your family, and I said yes."

"That's not—" He stopped himself.

"I know it's not the same thing," I said softly. "But it's the best I have to offer. Please come. I'll fix the picnic. I can even pick you up at the station, if you want. It's not that far from the park."

"You won't have to. Alvarez can drop me off if I'm running late." He kissed me. "I need to get going."

"Thank you. I really mean that. I know it might not be easy for you." I scooped up my courier bag and followed him out, waiting for him to lock the door.

"I'll do my best to be civil," he said. "But if Karspek so much as flirts with you, all bets are off."

Chapter Twenty-Two

I ENJOYED myself at the picnic more than Marco did, but I'd expected that. From the moment he arrived directly from work and pulled off his tie, I could tell he wasn't in a party mood. The music was fun and rambunctious, and the potluck was suitably fabulous for five gay men who loved to eat good food. The evening was perfect, except for Marco's discomfort.

Peter seemed to have picked up on Marco's state, and made real effort to include Marco in conversation, often directing his comments to me as half of a couple with Marco.

To Marco's credit, he'd been warmer than civil, but he'd seemed preoccupied, like he wanted to be somewhere else. Which he probably did. Still, I considered the evening a success, even if not a spectacular one.

As soon as he got into the car, he closed his eyes and let his head sag back into the seat. At one point, I thought he'd gone to sleep.

"Thank you for coming tonight," I said as we pulled into my garage. "It meant a lot to me."

"I did my best, but it's pretty clear I have almost nothing in common with them apart from liking food and music."

I shook my head. "I know they're not your first choice of acquaintances, and they certainly have their flaws, but you have me in common with them too. For better or worse, they're the best friends I have."

"No wonder you latched on to Lewis," he said as we got out of the car. "You must have been very lonely before he showed up."

Was that true? I thought about it for a moment on our way to the elevator. "I don't think so. Stef wasn't a substitute for anyone. More like a little brother that I didn't know I had, and then lost before I could even—" I swallowed my grief. I didn't want to visit that place right now.

Marco put his arm around my shoulders. "Hey. I'm being unfair," he said. "Karspek was a perfect gentleman, and the rest were too. I'm sure I'll learn to like them well enough."

The elevator opened, and as we rode up, I kissed him. "You seem very tired tonight. You can take a hot shower, then let me give you a neck massage and put you to bed."

He laughed. "After the noble sacrifice I've made, being so good?" He shook his head. "You're not getting off that easily. No sleeping until I get my reward."

Chapter Twenty-Three

In the morning I brought him coffee in bed, but the sight of him sprawled facedown across the rumpled bed made me set the tray down on the dresser and climb in next to him.

He'd arranged to go in to work later than usual, and the luxury of him not having to go anywhere right away felt like we were on vacation. We were timeless. If this coffee got cold, I'd be content to make him another.

The sound of his deep, rhythmic breathing, the raw male heat radiating from his skin, the sweet randomness in the way his muscular limbs lay sprawled slack on the bed turned his body into a living sculpture. I had to touch him, tracing his spine down to the firm rise of his ass.

He grunted and rolled into my hand, and I softly raked through the crisp hair around his navel. "Morning," he croaked.

"Yeah, it is. And we don't have to go anywhere for three hours. Isn't that great?"

"Mmpf. Correction—two immediate destinations. Bathroom, then breakfast. I'm starving." He rubbed his eyes, stretched, and shambled away like a zombie to pee. I picked up the tray and headed for the kitchen to start breakfast, glowing inside. I loved making him breakfast.

When he emerged from the bedroom in a pair of sweats looking damp and adorable, his hair still wild from the shower, I had fresh coffee waiting for him as well as the *LA Times* broken out in his order of preference.

He looked at the table and came into the kitchen for a slow kiss. "You know, I could get used to this," he said.

"Me too. Pretty fine, isn't it?" I went back to cutting fresh fruit while he tackled the paper.

We ate in comfortable silence. I was used to reading the news on my tablet, having compiled a range of feeds and blogs that I was interested in, which included local and entertainment news from the *Times* online. But there was something different about sharing the physical paper with this man. It was part of his tradition. I'd begun a delivered subscription so he'd have a paper whenever he stayed over.

Maybe it was still the novelty of it, but I loved entering into a ritual that was distinctly his when we unfolded the paper and broke it into sections. He started with news, and I took editorial or business. I became part of his tradition when we did. I could share so few of his other daily activities, and I was grateful for this one. I didn't even mind the grimy ink on my fingers afterward.

Eventually he put the paper down and finished his coffee. It had to be cold by now, but he never seemed to mind. Maybe it was a cop thing. "What's on your docket today?" he asked.

"You, until you have to go. Then the gym. This afternoon I'm going to look at studio spaces. Carol's got four possibilities lined up today." As soon as I'd said it, I swore at myself. I was stupid to have been so blunt about it.

He stared at me for a moment, not saying anything. Not moving at all.

"Your call, of course," he said finally, his voice flat. "I don't want you to have another place like that, though."

I held his eyes, now unable to retreat. "Who was the guy who told me on our very first date, 'Don't make my job an issue. That's a deal-breaker for me'?" I said as gently as I could.

"It drives me crazy thinking of you doing the same things we do in bed with other men. Even Peter. Especially Peter."

"I don't do what we do with anyone else," I said. "It's a little like a handshake. The mechanics stay the same while the meaning changes completely with context." I smiled, feeling a little hope. "Believe me, no client is ever going to mean what being with you does."

"I get the logic. Logic isn't the problem. One of my many flaws is that I'm old-school possessive. You already know that, though. I told you I was greedy and wanted all of you. I still do."

He started to say something and stopped, making a wry smile instead. "This is an argument I don't really want to have today. Are you okay postponing it?"

I caressed his hand, and suddenly, that wasn't enough. I half-rose from my chair, leaned across the table, and kissed him. He responded, tentative. Better than no response at all. I touched his cheek, hoping my fingers told him how sad I felt.

"We might as well have it now, don't you think? It's been waiting for its moment center stage since we agreed to be more than fuck buddies. Part of the looming disaster we both toasted on our first date."

"No. I can't do it now. You made me breakfast and gave me a newspaper, for god's sake. I'm sorry I opened my mouth."

"Here we are arguing about scheduling an argument." I laughed, discouraged. Neither of us wanted to attack this radioactive monster. I picked up his empty coffee cup. "Want more coffee?"

"No, thanks."

"We'll have to have it soon, you know."

"I know." His voice was laced with regret. He was in no hurry. Neither was I.

A brusque knock at my door diverted our attention. It was a courier. I signed and took the envelope. It was from the attorneys who managed the family trust. I was intrigued, as I had almost nothing to do with them other than the quarterly meetings to go over the financials.

I tore it open and began to read the cover letter, and everything stopped.

"What's wrong?" Marco's voice cut through my shock. "You look like someone just ran over your dog."

"I...." I started, but I couldn't stop reading. Sweat began to drip from my armpits, and my mouth kept sagging open. When I'd finished the letter, I looked up at him, numb. "You'll never believe this, but it's from my mother."

"You're shitting me," he said, his eyes wide and disbelieving. "That is way too weird."

I turned back to the letter. "Huh-uh. Not shitting you. She wrote the enclosed letter to me, then gave it to her attorney with the instruction that it be delivered five years after her death."

I began to shiver. "Christ, today is the anniversary. I'd completely lost track." I sagged into the chair and pushed away the newspapers. Marco scooped up the debris from our breakfast to make space for the packet.

"It's a gift from my mother. Just like Lorena said."

"Do you want me to go? You might want to do this alone."

"Oh, god no, anything but alone. Please stay." I headed toward the living room, my eyes still fixed on the letter. "In fact, can we sit together? I'm feeling very scared right now."

HE SAT at the end of the couch and stretched out his legs, patting the space between them, and pulled me back into his arms when I parked. I set the enclosure letter aside and stared for a while at the sealed envelope addressed to me. It was spooky, seeing my mother's handwriting. It was smooth and legible, so she must've been relatively sober when she wrote it.

After a while, Marco murmured into my ear. "Eventually, you're gonna have to open that."

"I know." I took a deep breath, stuck a finger inside the flap, and tore. The letter inside was also handwritten, on the heavy vellum my mother had always used. For a second, I thought I could smell her perfume on the paper, but that had to be my imagination.

"Can you read this over my shoulder?" I asked. "I want you to know what it says."

"I'm not going to read it, babe," Marco murmured into my ear. "If you want me to know what it says, you're going to have to read it aloud."

I began to read aloud.

> *Dear Shepherd,*
>
> *It's not news that I haven't been a perfect mother to you, but it might come as a surprise to you that I did try as hard as I could, and tried to protect you, even when I didn't.*

I've done many stupid and terrible things in my life, and when I review them all, the worst—without question—was failing to protect you from your Uncle George. I hope you can believe that if I'd known what he was doing to you whenever he could, I would have killed him sooner.

As it happened, I didn't find out until after your father and I had shipped you off to school in Switzerland. After your father died, George would come to visit every now and then. I didn't really understand why, since he and I had so little in common besides our love of a steady stream of martinis. He would show up and we would mix up some drinks, talking about nothing important. After a while, he would usually beg off to lie down in one of the spare bedrooms.

Then one day, thinking he was in a different bedroom, I walked in on him. He was masturbating into one of your soccer jerseys. At once, I understood perfectly why he came to visit.

Predictably, I went to the bar and mixed up a fresh pitcher of martinis. George came out of the bedroom, his face ashen. I stopped all his horrible explanations and excuses—I couldn't bear to hear him talk—and handed him another martini. And then another, and another.

He was pathetic. He knelt in front of me, whining and moaning about how sorry he was while I made peace with this discovery that my brother was the worst possible kind of monster. I excused myself for a moment and went to my bedroom. I fetched the gun from my bedside table and collected all the barbiturates I had in my medicine cabinet. I had plenty.

I made him write a note of apology, saying how sorry he was. That came easy for him. Then I forced him at gunpoint back to the bedroom and made him lie down where he had been molesting you yet again in his mind. I gave him the bottles, one by one, making him swallow the pills until they were all gone. I gave him a couple more drinks and then sat down to wait. He passed out soon enough, but he kept breathing for a horribly long time. I was quite surprised at that. At least he didn't throw up, which I've heard can happen.

When I was certain he was dead, I called our attorney and then the police. Because of the note and his fingerprints on the pill bottles, it was easy for them to conclude that George had taken his own life. As far as I was concerned, he had.

I would like to say that somehow I killed George to avenge what he had done to you, but I don't think I'm really that noble. In fact, I have always suspected that I killed him to avenge what he had done to me. Selfish, as always, to the very last—that's me.

I have always loved you more than anyone else I've ever known. More than your father, more than anyone. I realize now that because I adored you, and was so proud of your intelligence, your beauty, your social elegance, I groomed you into a kind of performing pet. I regret that more than I can possibly tell you now. I am so very, very sorry.

For whatever reason, I have always been awkward in sharing how I truly felt about you and I have left you to piece together an understanding of our relationship all on your own. I am certain it isn't a pretty picture, but ugly as I expect it is, I deserve it. Unfortunately, it's too late to change.

So I've instructed Tom Richardson to deliver this letter to you five years after my death, which I pray will be soon. God knows I work toward it every day. I'm eager to make my exit through the bitter mercy of juniper berries.

There are so many things I would do over in my life if I had the chance. The one thing that I know I would never ever change is having you. For what it's worth, I think you've turned out extremely well, in spite of my colossal failures.

I love you, and I am so sorry.
Mother

I dropped the letter in my lap and sagged back against Marco, pulling his arms tighter around me. The past I thought had been mine seethed and roiled around me, shapeshifting into a different one. Another past life I had no idea existed.

AFTER YEARS of believing my vision of my early life, I'd just discovered I'd been wrong. Cognitive dissonance, Reggie called it in some of our sessions, when the discovery that something believed with certainty proves to be otherwise.

Disoriented, I could feel memories shifting around deep inside like unsecured cargo on a ship in heavy seas. No clear design or meaning, but movement that couldn't be stopped.

Neither of us spoke for a long time.

"Well. I think that qualifies as a gift from my mother," I said, still slightly seasick.

"No shit. But I don't even want to guess at how the fat lady knew it was coming." He pressed his cheek against the side of my head.

"The fat lady just sang, and I'm busy suspending disbelief," I said. "About Mother, Lorena, about death and life. The whole nine yards. Christ. Or whatever I mean by Christ. What else have I been missing?"

Marco didn't answer, and I didn't expect him to. He just held me, his cheek against the side of my head.

"Tell me about Uncle George," he said after a while.

"We had sex. A lot. Ancient history." I stroked his hand, grateful to be reeled back from gazing into my unexamined and insufficient worldview. "Long ago and far away."

"It's just come back to visit, babe. It's right here in the room with us. Tell me." His voice was firm and gentle, and I let go into it.

"I've helped at least two therapists retire in comfort by talking about this. I'm over it now. Really." I reached up to stroke his face. "I'll be merciful and give you the condensed version."

I opened my memory box for Uncle George. "When I was about nine, my mother told me that if I learned to provide a service people needed, I'd never be out of a job. It was one of the few pieces of useful advice she managed to give me, and the moment she said it, I knew it was true.

"The first irony is that both she and my father made sure I'd never have to work a day in my life. They weren't just well off. They were rich. Dad had set up my trust fund when I was born, and everything they had ended up in it. Even the house, after Mother died. So livelihood would never be my problem.

"The second irony in this vignette is that by the time she gave me this piece of wisdom, Uncle George had already taught me the lesson about providing a valuable service—in a way that made complete sense to me, even as a little boy.

"One day when I was taking a bath, he came in and sat on the edge of the tub. He asked if he could wash my back, and I said yes. He got me to stand up, then soaped up and fondled my little boy parts until his hands were shaking so bad that he couldn't hold on to my stiff little penis. Then he bolted from the bathroom.

"The second time Uncle George wanted to play with me, I understood him perfectly. I knew I could give him what he wanted… not only what, but how. I can't explain it very clearly, but it was a kind of complete understanding. A revelation.

"Somehow, he became transparent to me. Intuitively, I knew what would make him happy. I could feel his need like a solid thing inside him. I could feel his terrible shame, and what he was afraid of, but I knew what he wanted without him saying a thing. I felt nothing but compassion for him, although I didn't even know that word then.

"I knew I could lead him into what he longed for, and I was proud—happy—to do it. I gave him what he needed. I felt peaceful and strong and happy when I did. I could use my body to provide a valuable service. Somehow, I also knew I was destined to become skilled in that service, and I was actually grateful to him for showing it to me.

"We played often, Uncle George and I, until I went to school in Switzerland. He was my very first client."

I kissed Marco's hand that held me against his chest. "So that's the story of Uncle George. By the time I got back from Europe, he was long dead. Suicide, my mother said. He'd taken pills. I suspected it might be linked to his taste for little boys, but at worst, I figured maybe someone was blackmailing him. I certainly wouldn't have. As I said, I was grateful to him, even though I also understood that what he'd done with me was wrong. Wrong for him to do, not so much wrong for me. I would never have guessed Mother made him swallow those pills. Not in a million years."

Marco wrapped his arms around me tighter but didn't say anything. His heart hammered against the back of my head.

"Jesus, Shepherd." Marco kissed the top of my ear. "You never had a fucking chance. Right now, Uncle George is very lucky he's already dead."

I squeezed his hand, telling him it was really okay. "A chance at what?"

"To be—and don't take this wrong—to be normal. To fall in love like you could have—in the right time, with a peer. You've always had men wanting something from you, taking from you. I'm sure you've always given them more than they'd hoped for. But that's not love."

"Not always," I said. "I loved Danny. And I wanted to give him way more than he wanted from me."

"Fair enough. But still, George robbed you of your childhood."

"Maybe. But I'm not really looking for a better past anymore. I've had good therapy. Tons of it. I don't work with clients out of that old place. I've grown, a lot."

I twisted around to face him. "Strange thing is, I just found out my past is better—and worse—than I thought. That's even scarier, in some ways. It even feels like it's changed my future, and I don't know how."

Marco pulled me to him, pressing my cheek against his chest. His heartbeat thundered in my ear. Its steady rush and thump was the most comforting sound I could imagine.

"What scares me is how bad I want you to have a happy future." His lips brushed the top of my head. "And I'm pretty sure it's completely selfish. I'm feeling a heavily vested interest at the moment."

His protectiveness washed over me like a river flooding its banks, lifting me, carrying me away. I surrendered to it. There was no shore, only his wild, fierce current enveloping me, taking me somewhere new and strange.

"Thank you," I whispered.

I lay curled against him for a long time. I'd never felt so safe, so complete. I felt a tear trickle along the side of my nose. I didn't want to move, even to wipe it away. He did, with his thumb.

Eventually, I had to touch him. As I reached up to caress his face, I had a startling revelation. "My god, I need to get rid of the house."

His eyebrows shot up. "The house?"

I could understand his surprise. I was surprised too. "My parents' place in Laurel Canyon. It's been sitting empty since Mother died. I haven't had the stomach to do anything about it. For the last five years, I've just pretended it didn't exist."

I couldn't just sell it, though, without seeing it again. Now that I knew. "I ought to go check the place out before I put it on the market. Say good-bye. Would you come with me? I don't want to go there alone."

Marco nodded slowly. "Sure. But I won't get more time off for a few days at least. Can it wait that long?"

"Of course. It's waited for five years already." The decision filled me with excitement. "I'll set things in motion in the meantime."

"Thank you," I said. Looking up into his eyes, I saw nothing but care and affection. Marco wasn't just a great lover, but a real friend. I was incredibly lucky.

Our looming argument over the new studio came back to me, but right then, it seemed easy to solve. I couldn't give up my work any more than he could give up his. We'd have to find a way. I was sure we could.

CAROL, MY real estate agent, was thrilled to have a two-million-dollar listing drop into her lap. It more than made up for my delay in buying studio space.

The trust had retained a property manager to check the place weekly and have it cleaned monthly. Even the structural and soil engineering reports were current. Carol assured me that she didn't mind at all having to coordinate with the property manager in arranging to prep the house for sale.

Fortunately, the trust had drawn up a complete inventory of the contents, from major furnishings to artwork, clothing, and personal effects. From the list, I could get an idea of what to keep, what to sell, and what to give away. I already knew the safe was empty. Shortly after Mother's funeral, I'd moved the contents to a safe deposit box—mostly just her antique jewelry. I was glad I hadn't sold the jewelry. Now it was more valuable to me than it would be to anyone else. Ever.

Still, I had to go see the place again for myself. I hated the prospect, but with Marco beside me, I knew I'd get through it just fine.

Chapter Twenty-Four

In the days before Marco and I could visit the house, I had plenty to do. I put out discreet feelers to board members of the Bucknam Trust and some of my social contacts, mostly my concert and art gallery set, about Walter Chisholm and his campaign. Not much came back except general gossip about his opportunistic political style and sexual escapades, but it had been worth a try.

And I had my second appointment with Alana Phillips.

She welcomed me warmly when I arrived at her office. "It takes courage to revisit a disturbing place. I respect your determination."

I shrugged. "I don't feel like I've got a choice. My life seems to be shifting around a lot, and now seems a good time to try again." We locked eyes, and my resolve surprised me. "I've got to get to the bottom of this dream. I'm tired of it haunting me, and I think this is the way to beat it."

She nodded. "I understand, and I'm glad to be your ally in that."

We got settled, I did my breathing. When I let her know I was ready, Alana spoke again. "Before we get going, I want you to put your right hand on your sternum, like we did before. Let its warmth build until you feel it spreading outward across your chest. This is the way you can bring yourself back to the here and now, grounded in the everyday."

I did and instantly felt more secure. I let the feeling spread. "Got it," I said. And off we went.

The path I followed was rougher this time. Sharp brambles hung over it, and I had to push them away in order to pass. When I got to the stream, the stones I had used before were gone and the water was cold and swift. It looked dangerous, forbidding. There was nowhere to cross.

"Are you sure you want to go on?" Alana asked.

"Absolutely. I've got to."

"Then maybe somewhere along the stream there's a better place to cross. Can you find it?"

I turned upstream, keeping as close to the bank as I could. There wasn't really a path, but as I wove in and out of bushes and around trees, a quiet happiness began to build in me. This was an adventure. I was going into the unknown. There wasn't even a path.

The forest became thicker, and after a sharp turn, I saw a spruce had fallen across the stream just where it had narrowed into fierce rapids. That would be my bridge.

I climbed up over the exposed wall of roots, inching along around the sharp stumps of limbs, and through the thicket of upper branches. To my surprise, I quickly scrambled to the other side, proud of having found a way.

I looked up at the mountain. Like the water behind me, it seemed colder and more forbidding than last time. As I pushed through dense brush, I eventually found a deer trail leading up the slope. I could tell it was a deer trail because their dark round droppings lay here and there along it. I imagined them walking along this trail, stopping to graze, a gentle unseen presence. I pushed on, and the brush thinned as boulders became more frequent.

"The wind is cold," I said.

"Colder than you can bear?" came Alana's voice whispering between the rocks.

"No, I can do this." I pushed on and began to climb. The trail began to feel familiar, as if I were on track again.

"Now it feels like I'm on the same path as before," I said. I climbed. The wind stiffened as I approached the ledge marking the place I'd stopped last time.

"I'm here," I said. "On the ledge like before. The backpack is gone, but that soft rock is sitting right in front of me. It seems larger. I think it's grown since last time."

"And what do you want to do with it now?"

I stared at it for a while, unsure. I leaned down to touch it. My hand, my whole arm burned at the contact, bringing with it a rage that consumed me. "I'm really angry again. I want to destroy it. I'm going to smash it again. I don't care if the thugs come. This thing deserves to be destroyed."

"Before you do anything to the rock, lean against the mountain for a moment. See if you can draw strength from it."

I leaned against the slab of rock behind me, still angry from touching the ugly stone. The mountain, massive and timeless, seemed to reach into me. So calm.

Maybe I could just move on. After all, the stone would break down on its own. But that wasn't what I wanted. It sat there like an enormous rough egg, daring me to ignore it.

My rage melted into disgust. "I still want to destroy it," I said, grinding my teeth. "There's something despicable inside it. It deserves to be shattered."

"What does the mountain say about it?"

It hadn't occurred to me to ask, but it suddenly seemed like a very important thing to do. I turned my back on the ugly stone and pressed my forehead against the rock face of the mountain.

"What do you think I should do?" I asked. Strength flowed into me, washing away both anger and disgust. I could feel something voiceless telling me it was my choice, that whatever the rock contained, I would have to face it should I choose to break it. And I knew I had to.

"I'm picking up the rotten stone. There. It's done, and I'm glad." An icy gust of wind curled around me. I already knew what would happen next. From the scattered pieces of the stone, six young men emerged. Lean, Latino. Five of them were the ones I knew would kill me. The sixth, standing farther away, seemed intensely familiar, as if we'd known each other a long time. He carried no weapon but stood at a distance with his hands shoved in his jeans pockets, looking helpless and sad.

"They're back. One of them has a piece of pipe. They're closing in, and I don't know what to do." The man with the pipe began to laugh, slapping the pipe against his hand.

"Can you ask the mountain for help?"

I could feel the mountainside behind me, hard and sharp. But surprisingly warm. The man with the pipe raised his arm, ready to strike. I pushed my back against the mountain, calling to it for help. As my attacker's arm swung down, the mountain swallowed me.

"The mountain just opened up," I said in amazement. "I'm falling. I can't see anything—it's completely dark, but the mountain has taken me."

"Are you willing to see where you go?" Alana's voice was faint and far away.

"I have no choice," I laughed, amazed. "There's nothing to hang onto." Then I was no longer falling, but floating. Although I could feel light around me, I still couldn't see anything.

"Do you want to see?" asked a new voice, without using words.

Before I could form the word "yes," I felt my answer shine out of me into wherever I was.

I was on a street walking. I was somebody else. "I'm, I don't know how I know, but I'm in Brooklyn. My name is Felipe Morales. This is like my dream. No, this *is* my dream, I recognize the street. I'm happy. I'm going to see my lover. He's at the bar. El Flamboyán. He doesn't know I'm coming. I'm going to surprise him. I love him so much, and he loves me."

"How old are you, Felipe?"

"I'm 17. I'm going to see Luis."

"I'm so happy I could sing at the top of my lungs. He is so handsome, so good to me. I love him with my whole heart, with everything I have."

I laugh, euphoric. "I'm standing across the street from the bar, waiting for a break in the traffic. I jog across, past a group of guys clustered around a shiny car parked in front. It's beautiful, but I'm on my way to see my boyfriend. My love.

"My eyes adjust to the dim light inside the bar. I see Luis with some of his friends. I know they don't like me and don't like me being with him.

"I don't care, because he always says he's proud to love me. I greet him—everyone is speaking Spanish, including me. It's my language. We're Puerto Rican. Everyone here is. This is our place.

"Luis is angry and embarrassed to see me here in the bar," I said. "He doesn't like me touching his arm. His buddies push me away, cursing, and Luis doesn't stop them. He stares at me, angry and cold, and then turns his back on me.

"He pretends I mean nothing to him. I can't bear it. I'm alone, so embarrassed. I'm afraid. I turn and run from the bar, into the alley behind it. I'm crying. Luis wouldn't stand up for me, I'm so humiliated.

"I'm wiping my eyes on my sleeve. I hear something behind me. It's two of his buddies plus three others. I don't know their names, but I know who they are.

"They're calling me pretty faggot boy, prettiest little faggot in Williamsburg. One of them has a piece of pipe. I can tell he's going to kill me with it.

"Luis is standing off at a distance behind them, just at the corner of the building, hands shoved in the pockets of his jeans. Now I understand that he's afraid too. For a moment, I feel sorry for him. His eyes are wide—full of pain—but he doesn't say anything. He's not going to stop them.

"I have nowhere to run. I give up. I just give up. It's the only thing I can do. Here they come." There was no pain this time when the pipe broke my arm, and then again, when it smashed into my neck.

The vision continued, but it fragmented, then blurred. It was a while before I could speak. It seemed like forever before I had anything to say. "I'm floating. I'm looking down at my body, feeling very sad. More like disappointment than grief. I watch my killers melt away into the street traffic. Luis is the last to leave. He's crying. I can tell he wants to touch me, but he's too afraid.

"I'm floating up, farther away. I can't see anything, but I know I'm going home. Not to my house, but really home. It's strange. I'm happy, angry, and sad at the same time. Mostly I'm angry. Luis did nothing. He let me die without saying a fucking word."

I could feel my body sobbing in a soft chair, but I was somewhere else, far away. "I'm somewhere I don't understand.

"Someone I can't see is asking what I've learned. He's very kind, and wise. I tell him love will get you killed."

Then there wasn't any more to see. I knew that was the end of my journey.

I followed my sobbing until I was back in my body. Suddenly I weighed too much, didn't want to open my eyes. Eventually I had to, so I stared at the ceiling of Alana's office, unable to do much else. She'd put some music on, very low. Vague synth washes, slowly shifting chords. Comforting. My arm weighed thirty pounds as I pulled some tissues from a box next to me. I wiped the tears and snot from my face and stared at the ceiling some more, letting the music flow over me in gentle waves.

I HAD no idea how long I stayed stretched out in that chair—not moving, not talking, feeling the music caress me. When I was ready, Alana and I talked a long time, especially about the images, and I had to admit that helped. She suggested I take some time to myself, go somewhere I could reflect and integrate, she called it, and to phone her in twenty-four hours to let her know how I was doing.

I drove home, taking extra care, still disoriented. Was this really a vision of a past life, or just a strange way of making sense of my recurring nightmare? Alana refused to advise me on what my session journey meant. She said it didn't matter whether it was historically true or not, what mattered was how the metaphors of the session were meaningful to me in my life now. And I had to figure that out.

Her work was to support my journey, not to interpret it, Alana said with a warm smile. I understood, but squashed a worm of irritation. I didn't want more questions to hold. I wanted some answers.

The only meaning that stayed with me was my lesson at the end of the journey—love would get me killed. But there was more to it than that, I knew.

That yet-undiscovered message of this journey had huge meaning for me. I could feel it, large and strange, patient, looming near me, still shapeless. Somehow I'd find out what that meaning was.

FOR ONE thing, I didn't agree with Alana's view that it didn't matter whether my experience was historically real or not. It might not be essential to know, but it mattered to me. A lot.

I decided to corroborate its historical authenticity if I could. If I couldn't, no problem, I still had the metaphorical significance, whatever that turned out to be.

After I'd thought about how to frame my request so I didn't sound like a lunatic, I gave Maddie, my virtual assistant, a call.

"Make It So Services—good afternoon, Mr. Bucknam," she chirped. "How can I help you today?"

"Hi, Maddie. Do you have a way of researching something on the East Coast? New York?"

"Sure. I have Internet, of course—news services, university libraries, and some other resources I can contact directly if need be. What can I do for you?"

"I saw a picture of a bar in Williamsburg, which I think is part of Brooklyn. I'm pretty sure it was called El Flamboyán. What I'm looking for is any information concerning the death of someone named Felipe Morales nearby." A chill skittered down my spine as I spoke the name aloud.

"I believe he was beaten to death in the alley next to the bar. In the picture, there were several young guys admiring a new car. It had hips over the rear wheels and a long boxy front, and the guys had longish hair. Some of them had sideburns and mustaches, so I'm guessing the picture is from the 1970s. Does that give you enough to start with?"

"Sure does. How soon do you need what I can find?"

"I'd mark this one urgent, Maddie, so soon as you can. I'm happy to cover any extra expense to expedite it. That would include, of course, any third parties you need to use in New York."

"I'll get right on it then," Maddie said with her unflappable good cheer. "I'll give you a progress report tomorrow afternoon. Anything else?"

"As a matter of fact, there is. Will you put together anything you can find in the news archives that mentions Walter Chisholm or a California company called Staviscor? Then make a separate file for the mentions where they're actually linked. Staviscor has been a regular contributor to Chisholm's campaigns. There ought to be public records about that."

"Right. Is that urgent too?"

"Not really. Do that after you've got the New York information."

"Got it. Anything else?"

I laughed. "That should keep us both busy for a while, I think."

"Okay, then. Thanks, and you have a great day, Mr. Bucknam."

"Thanks, Maddie. Talk to you later."

For some odd reason, I felt like immersing myself in water. Although it wasn't part of my regular routine, I decided to use the lap pool at the gym. I dug out my trunks and goggles, threw them in my bag, and headed out.

MY LONG swim, followed by a couple of rounds in the sauna, had done me in. The physical exhaustion felt terrific. I sat sagged into the sofa's cushions after supper, while Kiri Te Kanawa's recording of Richard Strauss's *Four Last Songs*, cranked up high, crashed over me in transcendental waves. She sang each song with depth and dignity, surrendering to Death fearlessly, with real beauty, but it was "Beim Schlafengehen" that I was playing for the third time. Her voice soared above the orchestra as I thought about Hermann Hesse's lyrics and stared at the urn of Stef's ashes.

I wondered whether Stef would ever need to revisit our brief, powerful friendship in some future past-life therapy.

I laughed at myself. I knew that wouldn't make much sense to others, but in my current state, it seemed a perfectly reasonable question to ask. It was a good thing I hadn't had anything to drink.

My phone rang—it was Marco. I turned down the music and sank back into the couch with a smile, opening myself to his heat, his intense aliveness.

"I've got the whole weekend off," he crowed. "It's all organized, so all you have to do is say yes. I'll come to your place Friday night. We can go up to your house in Laurel Canyon Saturday morning—late," he said with a husky purr, "after I finally let you out of bed. Then I've got great tickets to the Dodgers-Padres twilight game—should be another highly charged one, after that incident with Greinke at the beginning of the season. After the game, we end up at my place. Sunday afternoon, we have another quiet dinner with *la famiglia Fidanza,* and you can defend your manhood again from my overprotective sister. How does that sound?"

Before I could answer, he growled softly into the phone. "I've missed you. Seems like ages since I saw you. Be prepared to make up for lost time."

I laughed. We hadn't seen each other for four days, but suddenly, it did seem like way too long. "That sounds perfect." I made my own noises into the phone. "I've missed you too. Lots of catching up to do."

Chapter Twenty-Five

Marco's promise about not letting me out of bed wasn't an empty one. We romped most of Saturday morning, happy, affectionate, and wild. But as we drove up to Laurel Canyon, I lost that glow, and tension about where we were headed took its place. It was pushing noon by the time we turned onto the drive lined with Mediterranean cypress and pulled up in front of the ranch-style house where I'd survived childhood.

I got out of the car and immediately missed its air conditioning. Quiet heat shimmered all around us and dug into my skin. I gave Marco a resigned smile and pulled out the house keys.

The house would have been leading-edge chic when it was built in the late fifties. Square, flat lines made the house look vaguely industrial in spite of the surrounding landscaping that was still perfect. My parents had bought it around 1970 and added a second wing to form a U-shape around the pool. Even so, the place looked small now—a little sad too. It seemed to pine for half a dozen big-finned cars from its original era, turquoise and white, or black and pink, with lots of chrome, and maybe Louis Prima's band on the record player to cheer it up.

Inside, it was cooler. The property manager had taken the dust covers off all the furniture. All the really valuable art had been removed right after Mother's death. I'd had it all sold at auction since there was nothing I'd wanted to keep. There were still more than enough decent pieces left to show the place for sale. The hardwood floors gleamed. Now it seemed like the house was lonely, waiting for people to show up. People who had left a long time ago and never returned. Never would.

"So this is where you grew up," said Marco as he looked around with a policeman's detached efficiency. "Not sure I would've wanted to come to Sunday dinner here very often."

"I can promise you they were too quiet for your taste," I replied. "Strained and tedious are words that leap to mind."

I shivered, remembering standing in this doorway on my return from Europe. My mother breezed in wearing something expensive and beige, martini glass in hand, to give me an air kiss on each cheek before leading me out to the patio by the pool.

I was too tired to object. I hadn't really wanted to come back at all, but I was only eighteen. Switzerland had been a welcome escape for me. An escape from this house. In spite of Danny's death earlier that year, I'd been happier in Europe than I'd ever been here.

I had the same hollow feeling now, standing in this foyer, that I'd had then, being pulled into the swirl of my mother's circle of friends, three of whom were waiting to greet me on the patio. No doubt Mother had summoned them, the especially favored few, to be on hand to welcome her trophy son back from his European polishing. Immediately, I was on display again.

But now I understood what I hadn't then—she'd been hiding behind her martini shaker, keeping herself occupied with her friends, unable to forget her secret—that a year earlier she had sat in one of her guest bedrooms aiming a gun at her own brother, forcing him to empty another pill bottle, watching him die.

I swallowed against rising bile. I'd been right to stay away from this place. It was hollow and unhappy, even darker now that I knew what had happened.

I turned to Marco. He was watching me. "Traveling back in time?" he asked.

I nodded. "This place has always felt empty to me, even when I lived here. Hollow. Sad."

"Want to give me the grand tour? I want to see where you lived."

We started with the original wing, passing the library now empty of books, the office with no business to conduct, a couple of guest rooms that looked out onto the pool, and finally my parents' suite. It had its own wood-paneled sitting room, complete with fireplace. And a bar, of course. Then the big bathroom with an extravagant hydro jet tub Mom had installed while I was at USC.

Marco's eyes flicked from detail to detail, his jaw set. We went back toward the foyer and then through the living room, dining room, kitchen, and finally down the newer wing past two more guest suites to mine, on the opposite side of the pool from my parents. I opened the door.

"Pretty snazzy for a young boy," Marco observed. "I would have killed for this much space to myself."

I stood in the middle of my old bedroom, feeling claustrophobic. For all its rambling square footage, this house had been my mother's prison. I realized with a start that maybe she'd hated it even more than I had. She must have, but she had nowhere else to go. How desolate.

Marco strode over to my bathroom door and opened it. "Is this where your uncle first molested you?"

"No. My bedroom was on the other side then. I didn't move in here until I was twelve."

"But he was using you then, too, wasn't he?"

I nodded. "Until I left for Switzerland. I was nearly fifteen."

"So he did you in here too," he said, cocking his head toward the bathroom.

"No. By then we just used the bed."

"And you lived in this house for how many years after you came back from Europe?"

"Just one. I went off to college as soon as I could. I didn't like staying here. Moved out as soon as I could."

Marco clenched his hands into fists, tight as his voice. "I want to see the other bathroom. Where he did it the first time."

I numbed myself down as we went back to the guest bedrooms in the other wing and entered the second. "This used to be my room."

I pointed to the door. "That's the bathroom in there."

Marco walked over and pushed the door open, scowling at the fixtures as if they had been complicit in Uncle George's behavior.

"Same tub?"

"Same tub."

I walked up to stand behind him, resting my chin on his shoulder and hugging him around the waist. "It's an old, old story, Marco. No one escapes childhood without injury. Life goes on. I've moved on."

He twisted in my arms and pinned me against the wall with his body. He kissed me, infinitely tender, and stroked my cheek, but his eyes burned with rage.

"I know it's stupid," he said. "But I wish I could've been here to protect you."

I smiled and kissed him back, suddenly hurting and feeling lost, on the verge of tears. "No, babe," I replied. "That was my mother's job, and she pretty much blew it."

As soon as the words were out of my mouth, I gagged. That was a lie. She hadn't been able to protect me, and I was wrong to blame her for what Uncle George had done. Moreover, when she'd found out what happened, she killed her own brother.

"I take that back," I said, as my tears began to spill. I slid down the wall into a squat. "I have to forgive her. She wasn't a perfect mother, but I've hated her for not protecting me. She did the best she could. And when she found out, she did far more than most mothers ever would. She was so much stronger than I thought."

I covered my eyes so I wouldn't see Marco crouching beside me as I sobbed. I was too ashamed to look at him. I had been relentlessly cruel to my mother, believing something that wasn't true.

"Forgive me, Mom," I sobbed. "Please, let's just forgive each other."

The moment I said the words, something melted in me. Quietly, without theatrics. It didn't even feel like forgiveness, because suddenly there was nothing to forgive. She'd been waiting all this time for me to see. She—and all that stood behind her, a kind of graceful, fragile ancestry connected in me, opening me to her. Through them flowed a river of compassion and love, watering some parched place in my heart.

I was so taken that I stopped breathing, my mouth half open until I could let out a soft groan of release.

"Hey." Marco pulled me into his arms and rocked me as we sat on the bathroom floor. He just held me until I could look at him again.

I laughed shakily. "You must think I'm a nut case. Maybe I am. I certainly feel like one at the moment, but I needed that."

He didn't say anything, but waited with his arm around my shoulders until I could stand and kept an arm around me as I said goodbye to the house. It felt good to lock the door and walk away.

Marco took me back to his apartment, stretched me out on his couch, and covered me with a blanket. I don't know how long I slept.

"WHAT A great evening for baseball," Marco said, stretching back so far his knit shirt rode up to reveal a swath of his ridged, olive-skinned abs and the thick treasure trail I'd come to know so well. "Perfect seats, the setting sun behind us, and a clear evening in the low eighties. Perfect. You want a hot dog?"

Only hours earlier, my tongue had been roaming that delicious territory, and I wanted it again. I tried not to be distracted by the lean, exposed flesh.

He caught me staring and grinned. "Not that hot dog."

I laughed. "Then no, thanks—that's the only one I want. I'm afraid of what they put in the other ones."

"Come on," he coaxed, pushing his Dodgers cap up his forehead. "You can't go to a baseball game and not have a hot dog. Not saying you have to have two like I will, but at least one."

His face was so full of boyish enthusiasm I had to relent. "Okay, one. Mustard and ketchup both, sauerkraut if they have it, and onions, but no relish."

Marco shook his head in mock dismay. "No relish? Skimping on your green vegetables again, I see. Well, I'll let you get away with it this time. Be right back."

Kershaw had already retired the Padres' first three batters by the time Marco returned, and the first LA hitter was up.

"I was about to send out the St. Bernards to rescue you," I joked, holding the hot dogs and beer while he got himself settled.

"Are you kidding?" He unwrapped his first dog in a hurry and took a big bite. "That was fast. Short lines today," he mumbled around his mouthful.

I pulled mine out of the foil and took a bite. I had to admit, in this setting, it tasted fantastic.

Somewhere in the middle of the fourth inning, my phone rang. It was Maddie. "I've got to take this," I said to Marco. "Sorry." I got up and walked away.

"I think I found what you are looking for, Mr. Bucknam," she said. "I pulled in two other researchers to help me since you said this was urgent. We found a news clipping from a Williamsburg neighborhood paper, then double-checked it against police records. It seems the person you are looking for, Felipe Morales, was beaten to death next to the bar you mentioned on May 12, 1976. The police record indicates that his assailant was never identified." Her voice softened. "The kid was only seventeen years old."

Then she was all business again. "I'm drawing up a full report, and I can e-mail it to you by tomorrow morning."

A shiver of triumph raced through me. What I'd experienced in my session hadn't been mere imagination. But had I just made it up some other way? Was it really from a previous life of mine? How else would I have come up with that information? Did I really want to know? Yes, I did. That was certain. I had to find out.

Through the phone, Maddie's concerned voice pulled me back. "Mr. Bucknam, are you still there?"

"Still here, Maddie," I said. "I just started thinking about what your news might mean. I just thought of something else—can you also check to see if the name Luis Santiago comes up anywhere around this incident? Same general area."

"Sure will, Mr. Bucknam. I'll get right on it." Maddie's voice was brisk and efficient as ever. "Is there anything else?"

"Yes. Book a flight for me to New York on Monday and put me in a decent hotel somewhere in Brooklyn, close to that Williamsburg area. Just two or three days is all I need. I think. You still have my credit card on file?"

"Certainly do. I'm assuming you want first class seats on the plane?"

"Yes, please." I took a deep breath and let it out, trying to manage my climbing excitement. Maybe I was getting ahead of myself, but I felt on the brink of something wonderful. "Thanks, Maddie. You did a great job, and I appreciate it a lot."

"My pleasure, Mr. Bucknam. I may not be able to get more information on this new person tonight, but I'm sure we'll track him down quickly enough. I'll send you this first report in the meantime, and your flight info. You have yourself a great evening."

When I got back to Marco, he was watching Yonder Alonso fly out to center field for the second out. "It looks like I'm going to New York for two or three days next week. I want to tell you a weird story that just got stranger."

Marco didn't take his eyes off the field. "Can it wait until the end of the inning?" Blanks, who according to the program, was playing left field instead of first, was coming to the plate.

"Sure. It can wait until after the game if you'd prefer." I laughed, a little giddy. "The way Kershaw is mowing them down that won't be long at all."

"No need. Let's just get this guy out first, though. He's dangerous."

I glanced at the program again. "Anyone holding a bat who stands six foot six and weighs two fifty is definitely dangerous."

Blanks swung hard at the first pitch, looking for a home run, and after another slider, it was 0-2. Kershaw made him look bad as he stood motionless for the next pitch, a slow rainbow curve for a called strike three.

As the Padres took the field, Marco swung around to me. "So. What's going on?"

I filled him in on my hypnotherapy session and what Maddie had found. By the time I was done, he was staring out at the field again.

"Too weird for you, isn't it?" I asked. "It's too weird for me too. But I'm like a fish on a hook, Marco. I've got to follow this pull."

"You're talking to a guy who makes a living from focusing on hard, provable facts." Marco shrugged. "You had that fat lady, and now this. You're in territory I don't understand and don't want to explore."

He turned to me, his face clouded. "And yeah, it does make me a little twitchy. I don't mind the reincarnation theory, but the idea of being saddled with past-life shit that you have to clean up in this one seems really unfair to me."

"Unfair?" That had never occurred to me as an issue. "Why?"

"Because there's no reliable way to take care of what you're supposed to clean up." He polished off his beer. "I'm sure I'd have all kinds of shit to clean up from past lives, but until someone lets me know what that shit is and what I need to do about it, I don't feel the least responsible for taking care of it."

"What if you don't have to? I mean, what if not everyone has to do it consciously?"

"Just special people?" He was smiling, but I could tell he was irritated. He didn't like that kind of special.

I laughed. "Or just those like me who need the extra help. Maybe especially slow learners. That's what I'm feeling like at the moment."

After a silence that lasted two outs, he shook his head. "I dunno. Maybe it's right for you, but I can't hike out too far into that. Do what you have to do, babe, but please don't go all woo-woo on me and start stringing moonbeam crystals around your neck." He rubbed his eyes. "I don't think I'd handle that very well."

I put my arm around his shoulder and squeezed. "I don't think that's a risk. Besides, I've got my own built-in crystals." I pulled my collar open and back. "They're what I've been trying to figure out. I'm trying to understand something that seems very real to me. Apparently there's some historical basis. I've got to find out what that is."

He ran a finger along the marks on my neck, looking resigned. "If that's what you've got to do." He turned back toward the field, his voice tight. "Meanwhile, I'm on the outside looking in. Just remember I love you in this life. Not some other."

He'd never used the L word before. The instant weight of obligation it carried was crushing—a responsibility bigger than I could meet. I swallowed against my fear, remembering what I'd told the wise presence at the end of my journey as Felipe: *Love will get you killed.* I couldn't bear to say it aloud.

I had to acknowledge what he'd said, though. I squeezed his thigh and leaned over to kiss his shoulder. It was the best I could do for now.

Chapter Twenty-Six

Sunday dinner with Marco's family had gone well enough, although I couldn't shake the feeling that all afternoon he'd wanted something from me but wouldn't tell me what it was. Worse, everyone in his family seemed to be half expecting something too—some kind of gesture or statement I hadn't made. I felt guilty for my failure, even if I didn't know what it was. Cradled in my arms, the container of leftover roast and vegetables Cosima insisted we take back to Marco's sent up its own fragrant reproach.

Even now, as Marco unlocked his front door, led me in, and dropped his keys in the dish on his desk, I felt like he was still waiting for this unspecified event to occur.

"It was good to see your family again, get to know them a little better," I said, putting the leftovers on the kitchen counter.

He came up behind me and wrapped his arms around my waist, pulling me to him and nuzzling my neck. "They like you. Even Arianna, in her own way. My grandmother approves of you. I promise you, that's a real accomplishment."

I had to confess. "I kept getting the feeling that they were waiting for something from me, but I couldn't figure out what it was. It was like being in a stressful dream."

"They're still wondering who you really are, I think." He chewed on my ear, and his hands roamed up my chest. "Can't blame them really. You're still something of a mystery to me too."

"What?" I turned in his arms, wanting to see if he was serious. He was. "I can understand that I'm an unknown to them, but how can I be a mystery to you? Starting with our first date two months ago, we've told each other our most private thoughts. You've seen me at my worst, hanging my head over a toilet. Bawling like a baby, just yesterday. We've made love more times than I can count. You know all my secrets."

He pulled away and went into the kitchen, carrying the leftovers. "There's much more to you than your past. And the fantastic sex we have."

"Still, I can't possibly be much of a mystery to you." I tried a joke. "You're a detective, after all."

He didn't laugh. He closed the refrigerator door too hard. "Arianna put her finger on something when we were talking. She's usually a pain in the ass, but she's also perceptive. She said you're always a facilitator and never a participant, engaged but separate. She figures you're too used to being alone, that you don't think you need anybody else."

"What a terrible thing to say about anyone," I said, stung. "Everybody needs someone else—even Arianna." She certainly didn't know me well enough to make a pronouncement like that. She couldn't be right. She was just poisoning the well.

I put my arms around Marco. "I feel like I'm most alive around you. I love that. Seems to me I've spent far too much of our time focused on my personal issues—about my mother, about Stef, even about a past life and the metaphysical questions it raises. You've put up with all of that. My closet has no more skeletons."

"There's way more to you than that." He smiled, looking a little sad. "I said last night that I loved you. I wasn't fishing for you to say the same to me, although I hope you will, sometime soon."

His smile got sadder. "It's just that sometimes I feel like I can't reach you, that you're holding something back, like you're facilitating our intimacy. I hate that feeling. I want us to be full and equal participants."

I kissed him again. "I've had to be self-reliant, and I have no big family to belong to. You've told me much less about your past than I've told you about mine." I tried not to make it sound like an accusation. "I want to hear those stories too."

And then there was the lurking issue of our work. "Maybe the problem is that we've both removed our professional lives from our equation. We don't talk about what we do. By your insistence, and my agreement."

He shook his head. "That's probably part of it, but not the core." He took my face in both his hands. "I want you, Shepherd. I'm greedy. I want all of you, and I know there's more. I won't be satisfied until I find the rest of you. Once in a while, just like you described, it feels like I get all the way through to you, past the self-sufficiency, or whatever that barrier is. I connect with the one who tells your stories. I love that man. I want him in my life so bad I can taste it. But most of the time, it's like he lives behind a glass wall. I know he's there, I can see him, but I can't touch him, and that drives me crazy." He stared at me hard, as if trying to see into my flesh. "Just knowing he's there is not enough."

A wave of helplessness washed over me. "How does anyone share everything in just two months? It's impossible. Have you? You haven't even told me about your music, let alone sing for me. Have I made that an issue? No. I'm giving you everything I can, Marco. I don't think there's anything more for me to give right now."

He shook his head, an emphatic no. "Yes, there is. There's lots more." He pushed his thumb against my lips, and I let him push it in, rough and bitter in my mouth. And hot. It pushed down on my tongue and my whole mouth yielded to it. "I want it all. I won't settle for less."

I pushed his thumb out with my tongue, although what I really wanted was to swallow his whole hand. "Nobody can give all he is to another. Will you give me all of you? It's not possible."

"That's not what I mean."

"What do you mean, then?"

That stopped him. "I'm not sure, but whatever it is, it's there." He held the sides of my head and pulled me to him.

When we finished kissing, I said, "I'm sorry. Maybe I'm just preoccupied by all my recent turmoil." I hoped I was right. "I hope I'll be more accessible when that gets settled. But right now, I honestly don't know what else I have to give you."

I kissed him again, this time slow and tender. "I want to give you what you're asking for. I don't want to hold anything back, believe me."

"I do believe you. That's the scariest part. What if it turns out you can't?" He swallowed hard. "Just remember, that behind your beauty, your body, your brains, even your money, there's someone I want to be with. It's him I'm in love with, and I want him to open himself to me so I can love him more. Notice is served, my prisoner prince in the glass tower—I intend to lay siege."

"Give me a little more time. Please," I begged. "I'm in chaos right now, still sorting through Stef's death. Let me validate or throw out this past life question that's got me so off-balance. I want to give you what you're asking for. Maybe I'm not doing that yet, but I'll keep trying."

"Just remember who's willing to share your life without being paid to, babe." Marco began to unbutton my shirt.

"I can't stay tonight, remember?" I felt embarrassed reminding him, as if it proved how I wouldn't let him in. "I've got to pack for an early flight to New York."

"Then stay as long as you can," he growled against my skin. "I'll take what I can get, for now. Just remember I want the rest of you too."

I was happy to give him what I could. He wasn't gentle taking it.

Chapter Twenty-Seven

After a restless night, I didn't feel any clearer about last night's frustrating exchange with Marco. Apparently I was stymied, unable to grasp what he'd been getting at, so I turned my attention to the trip ahead of me. Whatever I couldn't grasp would still be waiting for me when I got back from New York.

During the limo ride to the airport, I called Laurie in Oklahoma City. I hadn't found the right place for Stef's ashes yet, but didn't want her to think I'd been neglecting it—after all, the urn was sitting in my living room. It was good to hear her voice—smart, grounded, humorous, good-natured.

When she said she figured Stef was still happy to hang out with me, I had to wipe my eyes even though I was smiling. I also told her that as a gift from Stef I wanted to set her up in her own salon. Laurie was Stef's family. Isn't that what family did, help each other? He would have easily earned the money to do it himself if he'd lived, and I simply wanted to finish that project on his behalf. She said she liked the idea but needed to think about it, and that was all I needed to feel like I was doing more for Stef. Still not enough yet, but something.

I'd been wanting to do something for Marco, too, and last night's exchange stirred me to action. I phoned Bucknam Trust's manager and told him to buy Marco's mortgage. I knew I'd pay a premium for it since it wouldn't be bundled, but that didn't matter to me. I'd make him a present of his clear title at Christmas, or maybe his birthday, coming up in August.

Finally I called my attorney to change my will. It seemed kind of melodramatic, but witnessing what seemed to be the end of my previous life had changed the way I felt about dying—to say nothing of reminding me that I could die at any time. I'd never had such a clear sense of living on the crumbling brink of the unknown, and it brought with it a new sense of nakedness and urgency.

I didn't want to die without providing for the people I cared about. And I did care about Marco. Dammit, even if he thought there was more to me than I was giving him, I loved him as well as I could. I'd tell him so again, when I got back.

I'd decided to make him my principal beneficiary—he wouldn't get everything because the Trust had mandatory bequests and established commitments, but I'd make sure he'd get far more than enough to retire on comfortably whenever he wanted. Not that he'd want to let go of his career if I died tomorrow. I knew him better than that.

By the time I got on the airplane, I felt much more at peace, as if I'd taken care of a few more things that had been waiting for my attention.

I imagined Stef smiling at what I'd done as I settled into my seat and prepared for whatever I was going to find in New York. When the flight attendant came by to offer me champagne, I toasted Stef with it. And Felipe.

I wanted to toast Marco and me, but I was afraid to. I didn't know if I could be what he wanted. His intense connection—with his family, his work, his ideas—shone through everything he did with an immediacy that I envied. He poured his energy through everything he did. Whatever that vibrant ability was in him, it seemed stunted, maybe even deformed, in me. How could I connect to the world with the same intensity he did?

Chapter Twenty-Eight

By the time I got to the hotel in Brooklyn, the sun had set, and I didn't want to go to the site in the dark. Instead, I went for a long swim in the sports club adjacent to the hotel and took a late dinner in my room. While I was waiting for it to arrive, I went through Maddie's final report, which as promised, was printed, bound, and waiting at the desk for my arrival.

The new information was that one Luis Santiago, nineteen, whose family lived on the same block as Felipe's, had fallen in front of an afternoon rush-hour J train at the Marcy Avenue Station on June 2, 1976. Exactly three weeks after Felipe Morales had died. According to entries from the parish record, a mass was held in memory of each of them on the first anniversary of their deaths, and there were announcements in the church bulletin.

As I read, I knew for certain Luis hadn't fallen. He'd jumped. I remembered how he'd looked in my vision, hands stuffed in his pockets as if they were trapped there against his will, his face blank with horror—and despair. I tried to imagine the shame and torment that had chewed at his insides those three weeks after Felipe's death. Not a long-term option.

Another dam-burst of compassion like the one I'd felt for my mother surged up and poured through me again, this time to Luis, wherever—and whoever—he was now.

"I forgive you, Luis," I whispered to him. "You didn't know how to stop them. I understand. I didn't know how, either. I forgive you."

I don't know if I was expecting some dramatic voice to answer, but it didn't happen. Instead, I felt my own insides relax, open toward something new.

The next morning after meditation and a late breakfast, the doorman hailed a cab for me. As I gave the driver the address that used to be El

Flamboyán, my heart raced. I stared out at the storefronts passing in a jumble of colors and offerings, rubbing my palms dry against my jeans more than once. I was nervous. No, I was scared stiff—of something, of what I might encounter, maybe even afraid of what I might not. Either way, I had no choice. I had to see for myself.

Ten minutes later, I was standing on the busy sidewalk of a perfectly ordinary Brooklyn street. Encroaching gentrification had produced a trendy teahouse immediately beside a timeworn Laundromat, with its accordion security grating, once painted white, pushed back just enough to allow access to the scarred wooden doorway. The rest of the street looked like the same mix of old and new, electric with the raw vitality of the neighborhood.

There it was—still a bar, but now an Irish pub, with its current name *Céilí* painted in big gold Gaelic script across a green background. I stuck my head in. The bitterness of stale beer assaulted me, but I felt nothing. This wasn't what I'd come to see.

I went around back, and there was the dead-end alley, stinking of garbage and urine. I wanted to go deeper, but my feet didn't want to move. I pulled in a long breath, blew it out, and started walking. Nothing.

Maybe I should just go home, a voice whispered. I must have made this into more than it really was, just imagination tapped in a therapy session. No. I had names. Felipe, Luis, the bar. I couldn't have made them up if I'd tried. They were real. Or had been real.

My eyes wandered along the brick wall opposite the bar's back door, toward where it joined the next building. My vision rippled.

I began to feel queasy, off-balance. There I was, lying on my back, my broken arm bent sideways as if I had an extra elbow, head turned away from the blow that had crushed my neck and collarbone, eyes still open. Empty. Nobody else around. Blood puddled beneath my mouth and nose, but I'd stopped bleeding. I'd died right here.

My killers were right. I'd been a pretty little faggot.

Heat burned up through me, firing every nerve in my body. My whole chest fried, my breath rasped in shallow gasps. Shivering and sweating, I stood as if electrocuted, unable to move.

Stop fighting it, a voice from somewhere said gently. *Let go. Let it all go.*

So I did, as if I were Felipe giving up all over again. I sobbed through an aching throat. My shoulders dropped. The burning current gathered like a thunderstorm behind my eyes, hovered, spun, and plunged, swirling down through my body, down my legs, and through the stinging soles of my feet into the cratered asphalt of the alley, as if flushed down a toilet.

It was gone. Where I expected emptiness inside, I was full of stillness—exactly where something hard and angry had occupied so much space. In the wake of its passing, the vision of my broken Felipe body lying in front of me faded.

My lungs started working right again, and I could walk—shakily, but one foot in front of the other, until I got to the sidewalk in front of the bar. I felt something newborn in me, fragile, fresh. The dumpsters and scattered garbage sparkled in the sunlight.

As I stood on the sidewalk, the city's raucous life grabbed me and swept me into its tumult. The sudden crush of people, cars, horns, a bus belching diesel fumes pulling into traffic with a grinding roar, the morning sunlight falling angled and fresh against every building, every person, every scrap of litter on the sidewalk, the smells—everything, including me, danced. Every motion was graceful and had meaning. Every noise was a welcome contribution to the flow.

My heart ached with the beauty of that dance of uncompromising racket, a dance I shared, giddy with pleasure. So many lives colliding or intersecting, I had no idea which. It didn't matter which. I knew it all belonged together. None of it was wrong. I was held in all of it.

A strange wholeness—so dense, so deep it couldn't be disrupted—held me buoyant in its impossible arms. It held the cab I flagged down; held the big-bellied cabbie swearing at a kid darting in front of us on his skateboard, and held the kid as he surfed between cars, skinny, pimpled, defiant; held the doorman at my hotel; held the airline agent as I changed my flight home to tomorrow; held me as I showered, then stood staring out my window for hours, not caring I was naked to the world.

My body still floated, weightless. Timeless. Eventually, it occurred to me I was hungry.

As I pulled on pants, I caught the red spots on my neck in the mirror, and saw them as if for the first time. They were exquisite. I caressed them with powerful tenderness. Just as I'd always intuited, they were a true part of me, and now I loved them for it. They were my bridge between lives, and they'd driven me into a new kind of self-understanding. I was grateful beyond words for their gift. I finished dressing and reentered the world.

Chapter Twenty-Nine

It felt good to be home. Whatever happened to me in that alley in New York had stayed with me since. Some kind of openness infused the way I saw things. I felt lighter somehow. Happier, in fact. I often surprised myself, noticing I was smiling for no conscious reason.

Marco had been tied up with work for the two days since I'd returned, and that night would be the first time we could get together. In the meantime, I'd been busy too.

On the flight home, I'd realized Marco would be deeply offended if I bought his mortgage without his consent. I'd just be making my money an issue between us, which was the last thing I wanted. I was relieved, catching my tone deafness in time. Instead, I'd had the provision put into my new will, which I'd signed the day before. I'd also got things lined up for Laurie's salon acquisition should she say yes to my proposal.

Maddie's report on Chisholm and Staviscor had arrived yesterday—nothing in it caught my attention. She'd been characteristically thorough, with scanned newspaper articles going back over ten years. The four years of campaign contribution records looked extensive too. Staviscor had begun funding him during his first campaign. They had a long-term relationship—mutually very beneficial, I had no doubt. If elected, this might be Chisholm's last term in office, but it was going to be a big one. After leaving office, Chisholm would likely become a lobbyist for Staviscor, continuing the relationship. I thought of him glancing at Stef's photo and shaking his head, as if he'd never seen him, let alone touched him, and ground my teeth.

While the data in Maddie's report was relevant information, I saw nothing that struck me as a key to Stef's death. But then, I wasn't Juergen. I had no real idea what to look for.

Juergen had refused to go further in the investigation of Stef's murder, and I understood his reasons—agreed with them. But I wasn't going to give up yet. With the questions about my past life laid to rest, and I laughed when I had that thought, I had more energy to devote to my investigation.

I pulled out all of Juergen's reports and the other data he'd collected, including the phone records, and added it to Maddie's files. Combined, they made a hefty stack.

Marco wasn't going to arrive until around seven, and he was bringing takeout. I had the whole afternoon free. I spent most of it on the living room couch combing through everything Juergen had put together relating to Stef's death. Every now and then, I'd look up at his ashes, just ten feet away, patiently waiting for me to bring them closure.

Closure still looked like putting Stef's killer in prison. As I thumbed through Juergen's reports, I had to admit I hadn't the foggiest idea of how to achieve that. It was dismal, feeling this stymied.

Stef deserved more, but I was beginning to doubt I could give it to him. Both Juergen and Marco, the two men I'd hoped would solve this, had turned away from the investigation. I knew their reasons for doing so were perfectly appropriate, but that didn't make me feel any better. I felt ashamed that I couldn't do any more on my own.

"I'm sorry, Stef," I said softly, gazing at the urn. "I'm not giving up, but I'm stuck. I just don't know what else to do."

I gathered up all the papers, put the blue report folders on top, and set everything in a pile on the table next to the urn. Hefty as it was, that stack of paper wasn't much to show for his life and death, I thought. He was so much more than that.

He was an animating force, lifting the people around him more vibrantly to life. Without doubt, he'd had that effect on me. A month after I began to mentor him, he badgered me into taking him to Knott's Berry Farm because, he said, too much meditation wasn't good for me and I needed some roller-coaster rides to loosen me up.

I'd scoffed at first, but he shamed me into it with his enthusiasm, his sweet love of adventure. In the face of it, I couldn't say no without feeling stuffy and dull. I still couldn't believe I'd said yes two hours later when the ride attendant checked to make sure we were secured into our seats on something ominously called the Ghostrider.

He gripped my hand the whole ride, lifting our arms for each drop, screaming and laughing, his eyes glassy with happiness. It was the longest two minutes of my life.

The next time—yes, we got right back in line—we were both screaming and laughing. On the Boomerang, too, although I had to close my eyes when we started going backward. When we wobbled across the platform to get in line for the next ride, he grabbed my face in both hands and kissed me as if my lips were his only source of oxygen and he hadn't had any recently.

For the rest of the afternoon, he vibrated with a six-year-old's Christmas-morning excitement I couldn't remember seeing in an adult before, and I fell under its spell. I even ate the ominously blue snow cone he bought me without a murmur of protest.

When we got in the car to come home, he leaned over to kiss my cheek, murmuring, "That was a fine thing to do with you, Shepherd. Every damn bit as good as sex. Or near enough." He looked me in the eye as if I'd just given him a fabulous gift. "Thank you."

Then he sank back into the seat and was asleep before we got out of the parking lot, his face glowing, heartbreakingly soft, angelic. His contentment filled the car, and I drove back happy—grateful—to be wrapped in it.

I rubbed my forehead and eyes, suddenly feeling very tired. I needed to shower before Marco arrived.

The phone rang. It was Carol, letting me know she had a good offer on my old studio, and to ask if I was ready to get serious about a new one. I said I thought maybe, although I didn't feel very enthusiastic about it. We arranged to meet tomorrow for lunch to go over the offer and look at the new possibilities she'd found.

I'D SHOWERED and changed, and set the table for two before Marco arrived. He was late, held up at work, but I didn't mind. On a romantic whim, I'd put out a bunch of candles. I wanted this evening to be special, to show him that my trip to New York had changed me in a way that mattered to us.

He had takeout from Number One, holding up the bags like a triumphant hunter carrying a brace of pheasants. When we hugged, I could tell he'd had a hard day—he smelled like stale office air, sweat, mountains of paper, and lunch eaten at his desk. On him, it smelled great.

"Hey. Really good to see you again. I missed you." I kissed him again.

"You were gone only two and a half days, babe," he said laughing. "You're going to have to be a little more self-reliant."

I punched him softly in the shoulder. "Take me as I am, *babe*. You wanted more of me, this is it. I'm thinking I should be less self-reliant, not more."

He laughed. "Point taken."

I took the takeout bags from his hands. "I'll put these in warming dishes for the oven if you want to take a shower first."

He feigned horror. "Are you kidding? Takeout doesn't taste right unless you eat it out of the cartons. The cardboard is an essential flavor of the cuisine." He wrapped his arms around me from behind and ground up against me. "I'll shower later, if you catch my drift."

I pushed back against him. "I understand your drift very well by now. I'm in favor of it. In fact, I'm a big fan." I pulled his arms tighter around me. "In that case, light the candles, because we're ready to eat."

I watched the candlelight play across the planes of Marco's face as he moved and ate. He was beautiful. He never said much about the cases he was working on, but his anecdotes about the people in his work-life ranged from horrifying to hilarious. His intelligence, his dedication, and his love for his work gave each one of them color and dimension.

His stories were never about his partner Tomás, though, as if what happened between the two of them was off-limits for storytelling, protected by loyalty. That made Marco beautiful to me too.

I waited until he had finished one about a court appearance that morning, and covered his hand with mine. "I love you," I said quietly. "Just wanted you to know."

He stopped chewing, and in the candlelight, his eyes went darker still. When he had finished his bite, he didn't pick up another. "That's not something you say easily, is it?"

"It's not something I've said often, that's for sure, but you already know that. Actually, it was pretty easy to say right now. I do love you, and it's never been so clear to me as it is right now."

His jaw clenched and relaxed as he brushed his napkin across his lips. "I think we can reheat the rest of this later, if we work up an appetite again. What do you think?"

"I think that's a terrific suggestion." I said, laughing. I pushed my chair back and stood without letting go of his hand. "I'm glad you feel that way."

We made our way to the bedroom without letting go of each other and undressed in a hurry.

On the bed, he rolled on top of me, taking charge as he usually did. This time, I pushed back and rolled over him. "Let me, this time," I said, staring down at him. "Let me."

I needed him, but even more, I needed to show him how I needed, how I had to love him, had to pour out my love to him or explode. I could see in his eyes that he understood.

A heavy river of hunger, passion, of tenderness, of ferocity, of longing to hold, to cherish, to infuse him with everything soft in me crested my heart and came flooding out, swirling us together in a hot, drowning ecstasy of blending, pushing us out into an undulating sea more vast than anything possible but love itself.

When we'd come back into our own bodies, I rolled off with a groan and lay beside him, giddy and spent. I started to laugh. I couldn't help myself. I stared at the ceiling.

"At the risk of repeating myself, I love you, Marco Fidanza."

Without a word, he pulled me into a spoon, wrapped me in a crushing embrace and held me there. I couldn't remember ever being so content, so happy.

MARCO WAS in the shower when I padded out to the kitchen for a glass of water, humming tunelessly. I was cleaning up the dinner leftovers, still warm and fuzzy from our lovemaking, when Marco stalked in with the sheaf of papers and reports about Stef in his fist.

"What are you doing with these?" Marco asked, his face and voice dropping the temperature in the room from postcoital warm and fuzzy to just above freezing.

I put down the carton of rice, not bothering to disguise my irritation. "Those are my reports from Juergen about his investigation of Stef's murder, plus some related documents and notes I've made along the way."

"How the hell did you get these?" he demanded, holding up Stef's phone records. "If anyone at the department finds out you have these, I'll be up for dismissal."

He glowered at me. "I told you to back off and leave this to the people who know what they're doing. You've put a lot of good people at risk of serious trouble."

I had to protect myself from his anger, and I closed down. If he wanted an argument, I'd give him one. "Why should anyone get in trouble? You're not even investigating this anymore."

I walked over to him. "Look, you heard me, at the morgue, promise that I would get to the bottom of this. Do you think I said that for your benefit? Did you really think that I would stop just because you guys had to? I've never kept what I was doing a secret from you. In fact, I offered to show you everything I had. You weren't interested, as I recall."

He slammed the papers down on the dining table. "I'm telling you again. Leave this to professional law enforcement."

"I have. Juergen is every bit as professional as you. I hired him. He investigated. He gave me his findings, and they're in those reports. He told me your department was encouraged to accept that the case was at a dead end. I understand that. He also gave me his guess about Staviscor and what happened, even though he wouldn't write it down. He thinks you suspect the same scenario he does. I understand why he's backed off too. But without help from the police or from him, I decided to keep going—because Stef deserves it."

Marco stepped back, ran a hand through his hair, still damp from the shower. I'd never seen him so angry. "And you would burn down my career simply because Stef deserves '*it*,' whatever the fuck '*it*' means? He's dead! Is he really that much more important to you than I am?"

"Oh, that's not fair, Marco." I held out my hands to him, pleading. "What if you were shunned by your family? What if you'd been rejected by your parents for being gay, beaten by your father, declared dead by all your family except for a sister? Who would be your ally then? Not every family is as tight-knit and loving as yours. Stef's sure wasn't.

"It's turned out that I became that ally for Stef, and I'm not going to turn my back on him. I'm going to do everything in my power to find out who killed him."

"And you're leaving all this shit around in the open. Right on your coffee table. Christ, Shepherd, this case is still open—it will never close, don't you get that? The second we have new information, we'll be right on it. On top of that, you're involved in the case. You're a person of interest. If anyone from work found this stuff here, I'd be canned."

I couldn't keep the sarcasm out of my voice. "What, you think I have a parade of police officers coming through my apartment to bonk? Who else from your work is going to see this here?"

"Don't be naïve. If someone from the department heard even a whisper that you have Lewis's phone records, they'd get a warrant to search this place." He glowered at me. "In a heartbeat."

"I'd make it clear I got them from Juergen and not from you."

"Do you think they would take the word of a high-priced prostitute on that? They would take one look at how much time we've spent together over the last six weeks and tear my life apart."

And there it was. The argument we'd postponed. I stood there for a moment with my mouth open, until the shock wore off. "A high-priced prostitute. Thank you very much."

"I'm just telling you how the department would see you."

Well, I could be just as cruel. "Sure—because that's never been an issue for you. But then, you couldn't really mean that as an insult, since you're a high-priced prostitute too."

Marco's head jerked, his voice dropped into menace. "What the fuck do you mean?"

"It's pretty simple, but I'll connect the dots for you anyway. A prostitute is someone who has sex for money. It's their job. You befriended and seduced a suspect for your job. I have no doubt that you fucked him because it was your job. That makes you," I said slowly, "like me." I leaned forward on the counter, hurting him with his own prejudice. "Just. Like. Me."

Marco stared at me for a moment, not moving. I could feel him pulling away fast. Maybe I'd gone too far. I tried to break the spell with a joke. "But still, this can't be a real fight. We're both stark naked, and nobody gets into a serious fight when they're naked."

He stared at the papers on the counter and turned away. "I've got to get dressed."

"What for? For God's sake, Marco, it's 10:30 at night. We love each other. You're not going to leave just because we've had a squabble, are you?"

He wheeled on me. "You think that's what this is, just a squabble?" He nodded slowly, as if suddenly comprehending.

"A squabble. You know what? You're a spoiled brat. You jeopardize everything I've worked years for, fought and bled for, and when I get angry about that, it's just a squabble. Arianna was right. You must be so fucking used to getting your own way you probably don't even think about the damage you cause others as you march over them to get what you want."

He turned away. "Yes, I'm leaving. I think we should call things off for a while. I'm risking everything being here, and you, as usual, risk nothing."

Stunned, I followed him into the bedroom. I didn't even know where to start. "That's not fair!"

"Not fair, maybe, but true," he said pulling on his socks. "You've got no skin in this game. If this blows up, I lose my career, everything I've made of my life. But you?" His scorn was acid. "You lose nothing. Your biggest problem is still which restaurant to call for dinner reservations."

"That is *not* true. I risk losing you, and I risk failing Stef. Those may not seem to be big to you, but they are huge to me."

"You'll do fine. You sure as hell won't be a disgraced ex-cop scraping out a new life as a security guard in some godforsaken warehouse at two o'clock in the morning."

"Marco, what the hell is happening? You told me early on that you become a part of the people you love. You told me you love me. Can you really turn that off just like a faucet?"

He didn't even look at me as he pulled on his pants. "I can't just turn off my feelings, no. But I do have to figure out how serious a mistake I've made in feeling about you the way I do. I need time apart to do that."

"And I just hang out while you decided that? We don't get to talk about this more, try to work out the problem?"

He shrugged into his jacket, leaving his shirt half buttoned, and snatched up his keys. "Not until I figure some things out. In the meantime, you do whatever you need to. Go to a concert with your *club*."

"For god's sake, Marco! We love each other—we just... just... consummated it. We can get through this. Please stay," I begged.

"If I stay, I'll say something even more damaging. So I need to leave. Right now." He loped to the door and slammed it behind him.

His absence folded itself around me, cold and hideous, the invisible outline of a thing, a negative image of what used to be present, as if I'd suddenly lost an arm and only the pain of its loss remained.

Chapter Thirty

I STUMBLED through the next morning, dislocated and numb. I'd dozed during the night but couldn't really sleep after Marco left, starting wide-awake over and over, aching with despair. The towel he'd used still hung damp on the shower door. I couldn't bear to throw it in the laundry. I made coffee, made myself drink it, and then dragged myself off to meet with Carol.

Carol carried on in her high-energy cheerfulness even though she could tell I wasn't focusing well. I agreed to the offer on the old studio. It was good enough, and I didn't have the energy to negotiate further. Then we walked through three properties that might serve as a new one, and I told her to make an offer on the second. It would do. I'd have it gutted and refinished anyway, and add more security than I'd had at the last one.

But it all seemed so unimportant compared to missing Marco. He'd taken a huge piece of my life with him, and the hole he'd left showed no signs of filling in. Worse, I didn't want to fill it with anything but him. Without any warning, I'd slip and fall into it. Whenever I did, it took me a long time to climb out again.

I went home, wishing Marco would call. I called him. And got sent to voice mail.

I made myself eat the rest of Marco's and my takeout leftovers from the night before, crying as I ate because it might be the last thing we'd share.

I couldn't stay in my apartment—I needed an escape. Maybe a few days in Mexico or the Caribbean would help. Stupid idea. Maybe I should go to Puerto Rico, see where Felipe's family came from. Stupid idea. I plunked down on my sofa and stared at Stef's ashes. They told me I wasn't going to vacation anywhere until I could let go of them.

Besides, at that moment, I didn't have the heart to pull out a suitcase, let alone fly to the Caribbean. I did manage to pour myself a glass of wine, though. Several, actually. Two bottles' worth.

From my window, I watched the sun set, watched the traffic's lights snaking along on Wilshire below me, watched the world carry on as if nothing was wrong, until I staggered to bed.

I WOKE up with my first hangover in years. I had to summon all my energy to shower and make coffee, which felt like major accomplishments. Every movement took so much effort, I was ready to go back to bed, even after three cups of coffee.

My phone clinked, informing me of a new e-mail message. I pulled it out of my pocket to take a look. It was from Marco. Hope engulfed me, hot and sudden as a brush fire. My hands shook as I tapped the message open.

> *I apologize for leaving like I did night before last. I do love you, but I fell too hard and too fast. You're the best at physical intimacy, but I'm not sure how much you know about love, which is intimacy and vulnerability.*
>
> *I realized that what's been bothering me is your invulnerability. You're like a castle I can't storm. You told me about a fear of yours that love will get you killed. Maybe that's what this is really about. I don't want to be the only one in this relationship with his whole life on the line, taking risks. I need some time to think about all that. Marco.*

Invulnerable? If I'd only been able to share what had happened in New York with him, or how I felt right in this moment. I was as far from invulnerable as I could possibly get.

Marco was being unfair. *But what if he's right?* a quiet voice asked, making me squirm. *What if you've held yourself back from him precisely because you're afraid? What if you really have believed love will get you killed?*

I opened my laptop to send a reply.

> *I miss you so much I hurt all over. I sure as hell don't feel invulnerable. I know I want us to keep going, and I'll risk anything to hang on to what we have. On our last night, I felt more love for you, felt more at one with you than I can say. We can't end like this—you haven't sung for me yet. Please, can we get together and talk? Please....*
>
> *I love you. Shepherd*

I stared at the screen for a moment and then deleted the line about hearing him sing. I certainly meant it—it was just another part of what we hadn't shared yet, a deep part of him I wanted to experience. But the way I'd said it, it was too easy to misunderstand in an e-mail, and I didn't know how to make it sound better. He'd think I was just being a spoiled smart-ass. Again.

Before I hit send, I knew he wouldn't answer. I knew him well enough to understand that. I imagined his face as he recognized a message from me—sad, stubborn, and hard, deleting it without reading, and turning back to his desk.

What would life without Marco be like? Well, I'd still have my work, just as Marco would have his. Maybe it really was time for me to start seeing clients again. Even if I didn't have a studio at the moment, there were a few I'd be comfortable seeing in their homes.

With a resigned sigh, I set up a fresh calendar on my computer, preparing to get back to work. I wasn't at all excited at the prospect, but I couldn't sit around drumming my fingers while Marco made up his mind about me. Life goes on.

Chapter Thirty-One

I'D NEVER felt so alone. No Stef, no Marco, no real work to do. I floundered, trying to find something to hang on to, something that gave me a sense of direction. Even Peter and the rest of the concert club had made other plans for the weekend. It made sense, as I hadn't called them since the picnic concert.

Out of desperation, I called Lorena, the past-life lady who had pressed her card into my hand at the farmers' market weeks ago. Over two months ago now. She answered before I had figured out exactly what to say.

I started to explain who I was, but she recognized me right away. I didn't ask her how. Instead, I asked for an appointment as soon as she could fit me in.

"Oh no, dear," she said, wheezing into the phone. "You don't need another reading. You're well on your way." She seemed quite happy about that, and content to let me stew.

"But my life is falling apart. I need help understanding what's happening." I could hear the little-boy fear in my voice, and it embarrassed me.

She giggled as she agreed that my life seemed in chaos at the moment but it was good. Concentrate on the new spaces, she said. Ask yourself what's in them. Whatever or whoever it was she called Guidance was very pleased for me. Whatever that was worth.

She laughed herself into a coughing fit when I told her Marco didn't think I loved enough or was vulnerable enough, and that I was afraid it might be true. It took a moment before she could speak again.

"Nobody ever loves enough," she said grandly, "as long as they're breathing. Sit in the empty places, see what comes to you."

"Oh," she exclaimed. "One more thing. You were somewhere good a while ago. Somewhere green. Eating outdoors. Yes, a picnic. Do more of that. More time outside in nature somewhere."

It didn't seem at all strange to me anymore that she knew I'd been somewhere green and good without me mentioning the outdoor concert. My sense of what was normal had taken major direct hits recently.

Her voice rose in pitch, wobbling a little in her excitement. "What's happening to you really is all uncharted, dear. You're breaking open, and it's going to be wonderful, I can tell. But this is something you can't prepare for. Even though you and Luis have such a strong connection, he can't help you—"

I interrupted, even though I'd stopped breathing. "Who's Luis?"

"Your lover. Wait, no, that's not his name. I got mixed up."

"You mean Marco?" I began to shiver. I must have turned the AC down too far.

"Yes, Marco. He can't help you with your next step. You just have to let go and let it happen. Open yourself to it and trust."

I couldn't let it go. "Are you saying Marco is a reincarnation of Luis Santiago?"

"That's not for me to say," she said airily. "Pay no attention to that. I just got confused for a moment and forgot Marco's name."

As if I could actually ignore what she'd said. It took me several heartbeats to shape a one-syllable word. "Thanks." I hung up, stunned, sweating. Too dizzy to stand. I pulled on a jacket and sat on the couch, hugging myself.

Was it possible that Marco could be Luis reincarnated? I decided I didn't really want to know—the knowledge was too dangerous either way. If he was, Marco's accusation that I risked nothing was a hideous projection. That would drive me crazy. A soft voice came from somewhere: *They both put duty and tradition over love.* I couldn't think about it.

IT TOOK me a couple of hours to calm down. I tried reading the newspaper, but there was no Marco sitting across from me. I canceled the delivery.

When I could, I called Laurie to see if she'd come to any decision about her hair salon. She said she was grateful for the offer, and that she would take the money as a loan but not as a gift. After some haggling, because I didn't want to charge any interest and she insisted on it, we agreed on terms as low as she let me make them.

We talked for a while about where she might set herself up in business and her thought was to buy into the business where she was presently working. She got along well with the owner, and it was a pretty good location. She laughed when I said it looked like she'd got all the business smarts and Stef had got none of them. She agreed.

The next day I made an appointment with a client. Although he was pleased with the session, I found it empty and strangely uncomfortable. I didn't feel like I'd really been fully present for him—distracted or disconnected, somehow. The truth was I didn't enjoy the session as I always had before, but I chose to ignore that.

At one point, I felt Marco sitting in the corner scowling at me. Not really scowling, just watching, judgmental but impassive—which was even worse. He'd managed to disrupt all my carefully built professional boundaries. Making the appointment had been a mistake. It was clear I still needed more time before I could return to work.

As we'd agreed at my last appointment, I called Alana to let her know how I was doing. She said sometimes it took months to integrate a past life experience. She was warm and supportive when I told her about my trip to New York, but surprisingly noncommittal about my conclusions. How was I going to integrate that into the way I experience the world now was the question she kept returning to. And she was right, of course—otherwise, what was the point?

That was exactly the question I had no answer for. I'd thought it would make a difference for Marco and me. Apparently, I'd been wrong. Or simply too late. And I'd probably never find out which.

A FEW days later—I'm really not sure how many, all I was sure of was that Marco hadn't called or answered my messages—I stood in front of my window staring out toward UCLA, and a patch of green caught my attention.

That would be the botanical gardens. They weren't big, but the place was beautiful. Just the kind of place I needed to think, to feel, and probably to cry. A lot.

I grabbed my car keys and stopped. Driving there suddenly seemed silly. Inappropriate. It couldn't be more than a mile away—I'd walk. I tucked the keys in my pocket anyway, to get back into the apartment.

When was the last time I'd walked anywhere? Maybe I needed something that different. Walking in Los Angeles. Who would have thought?

It was hot outside on the street, but I didn't care. I crossed Wilshire and headed up Selby feeling like a rebel, defiant and free. For the first time since Marco cut me out, I felt a flicker of happiness. It felt awfully good.

I wandered in the garden all afternoon. I couldn't remember the last time I'd been so wonderfully enveloped in living things, immersed in the sweet, wise quiet they created. Somehow, I'd lost touch with the green part of me. Maybe I'd been too busy to even notice that I'd lost touch with it. I had to do more of this.

I walked slowly, or sat and stared, submerged in a different way of seeing, of being alive and beautiful. Strange or familiar, every plant was beautiful without artifice, all the way through.

The hours passed. I could feel the knots in my heart soften a little. I still hurt, but the pain became natural or found context somehow. As I sat on the bank of the little creek, no more than a skinny pond, really, I realized the asphyxiating pain I felt in my nightmares—the pain in my throat and chest—was not the pain of injury or even imminent death. It was the pain of loss.

It was Felipe's pain. He'd already lost everything before he was killed. That's what really hurt. I remembered feeling him just giving up—the pain of his broken arm was nothing compared to his ache for what he'd already lost. That's why he gave up before that pipe crashed into his neck. My neck.

Wandering in the garden helped me sort through that. I decided it was true—I'd become preoccupied with myself, trying to avoid the panic of feeling vulnerable. In my mantra, I'd thought of it as being safe, but right then, it felt like cowardice—an attempt to avoid being hurt. I possessed no special exemption, no entitlement, no get-out-of-pain-free card. I could never protect myself completely. Nobody could. Life was like that.

When the five o'clock closing time came, I headed out and walked home, mindful of taking with me some of the quiet strength of the garden. Yes, I needed to grow my own, but until I got better at that, I'd draw on places like this.

I called Reggie, I guess as a kind of confession that all this time I thought I'd been open enough, and that I was beginning to see that I hadn't. He laughed. "There's always more, that's the beauty of it, old son."

I asked him if I could set an appointment. To my surprise, he said he'd talked with Alana and agreed with her that I needed some time on my own. To integrate, he said. He reassured me he was available if I ran into trouble, but wished me a good time and hung up. For a moment, I was angry at him for just hanging up like that, but I knew he was right. Whatever came next, it was mine to find.

CHAPTER THIRTY-TWO

THE NEXT morning, I woke up to a new sense of direction. That felt good. Viable.

I wasn't looking to fix the pain of Marco's absence—I knew there was nothing anyone could do to fix that for me, especially if in his last life he'd been Luis. He'd be the last person to help me now. Or would he? I couldn't count on it.

Besides, I didn't need rescuing from my misery. This felt more like I had to find a missing piece of a puzzle and I had no idea what it looked like—the piece or the puzzle it belonged to.

I stood at my window again, looking out toward the UCLA campus, and the botanical garden called to me again. Maybe I needed another dose of nature. It was ironic, I thought, that the next step I needed to take in my life, a life centered in such a nature-unfriendly city as Los Angeles, should require that I go to a quiet green place, the kind of place made rare by the city itself. I grabbed my keys and a bottle of water and headed out the door.

As I walked, I thought maybe I should do more for green spaces in LA. They seemed fragile, needing as much human protection and support as they could get simply to stay alive. I snorted at the thought. That was just a learned response, to pour money into some cause, telling myself I was actually doing something. Philanthropy wasn't a bad thing, but for me right then, it was nothing but evasion.

Once I was inside, I began to see the garden differently. The life there was not fragile at all. Yes, there were plenty of plants and trees that wouldn't be growing here without human effort and protection, but what was actually happening inside the garden *because* of the plants had nothing to do with anything other than the living things themselves. It was electrifying. Plants simply grew—flourishing or not, reproducing and dying. And it wasn't just the plant life. Butterflies, insects, and the birds drawn to feed on them were there too. All these life forms, interacting in an intricate reciprocity, did so without the slightest sense of entitlement or demand for safety.

Fire, drought, urban planning, city politics, earthquakes, pollution—any combination of those could wipe this entire garden out in an hour or over years. Regardless of any event, everything left alive would continue to grow as it could. Each plant, each creature simply did what it did, taking, giving, breathing in, breathing out in the most primal patterns of exchange possible.

It was what I told my clients in our first session. Our breath was our first and most fundamental experience of intimacy, of intercourse. Taking in, breathing out.

Something shifted in me. I could feel the entire world around me breathing in, breathing out, in gracefully synchronized giving and taking. Here in this garden, the scenery was beautiful, but I saw seagulls at landfills, my mother holding a martini, whole forests of coral dying in toxic waters, weeds alongside roads shriveling, sprayed with poison, Danny shivering in my arms, crying and bleeding, Marco, Peter, Uncle George, people in absurd luxury, and people in squalor—all born, breathing in, breathing out, living, and dying.

My vision shifted again, or maybe the spectrum of what I could see expanded. From one vast undifferentiated ground of being, there emerged countless distinct forms of life, each with its own nature, its own language—existing, giving and taking, reproducing or not, and returning to the unlimited ground of being again, putting aside its temporary differences to return home.

As I would, in my time. I saw all life as already one thing—there was nothing I couldn't accept as myself, nothing I couldn't love.

The living earth under me rose up, undulating in kundalini ecstasy, flinging off the unresponsive, gathering it back as compost, unrelenting in its pulsing dance. I was part of everything, or rather I was everything contained in one human skin that I could barely feel. I loved my flimsy body with the same love I felt for the ant crawling across my leg.

I was a fountain, no, *the* fountain out of which all life sprang and the bottomless pool beneath it into which all life returned. I was the one wail of grief from countless mouths, the one scream of pain; I was the howl of empty hunger that drove men's greed—all of it flowed through me, belonging, and I held it. And let it go. It was all one thing. There was nothing but oneness.

I was no longer breathing. I became ecstatic as all life blew its breath into me. That universal breath was mine for a moment, and then I became an exhalation and breathed life into everything else. My little life form, no more significant than the dragonfly or a tree, and no less significant than any other, radiated the same life. One life in many forms, *I* was one life in many forms, not only universal, but eternal.

Every death was mine, every birth, every blossom, every seed. There was nothing that was not me, and I spun wide as a galaxy to let each spiraling life find its place in me, for its own time, in its own beauty.

My vision retracted, and I saw myself as a solitary little man again, sitting by a small bridge in a tiny garden that most people in the world would never hear of, let alone visit. And yet the invisible wholeness of life remained inside, pulsing, nourishing me, generously letting me nourish it.

My hands shook as I opened my bottle of water, water that had traveled farther and shared more life forms than my Shepherd body ever would. I swore I could hear it offering me its stories, like meeting an old friend after many adventures—a sacred friend, offering me the gift of life. I drank deeply, felt it flowing into me, happy to be me for a while before moving to another me.

I stayed until closing again. But this time, I walked the paths, pouring myself out to each form of my life, feeling that life pour itself into my current form in reply. I had never had such an intimate conversation. I had never blessed or been blessed so passionately, laughing, touching, knowing. I was a vast family reunion of one.

I don't remember much about the walk home. I do remember that I made a salad for supper. Washing, loving, thanking, and cutting the vegetables was a new experience for me, sacred and happy.

Chapter Thirty-Three

THE NEXT few days tumbled in a kaleidoscope of mystical amazement and mundane plodding, happiness and desolation. I ate and slept; I ached for Marco. I wrote checks, I even went to the gym, but nothing seemed to matter the way it used to. Not to me, not to anything. Yet somehow, it all mattered more than it had before.

I was tripping, although I'd never done acid. The vast dance of life unfolded and flowed around me, subtle and brash, loud and silent, ugly and beautiful. Often, it was more than I could bear, and I would have to stop and cry.

My new vision of oneness persisted, but it began to ask a question: Now that I knew this, what difference did it really make? Marco's dismissal of metaphysical issues came back to me, and I had to admit he had a point. What should I *do* with this experience? Why was it important?

It changed nothing outside me, even though it had changed everything inside. It didn't fix suffering, mine or anyone else's. It didn't solve anything, so what was it for?

It wasn't *for* anything, I decided, especially solving problems. It just *was*. Maybe it merely meant that what I did mattered, that I didn't have to *make* myself matter. I was already part of the dance of life. My little Shepherd part. A tenant in this temporary body, I would be part of the dance whether I did well or not, shared openly or not, was kind or not. I would dance in this Shepherd form for a while, and then life would go on. I, life, would dance on. What kind of dance I danced mattered to me and to all that danced with me. How others danced was not mine to change. Life would go on regardless, because that's what life did. It *always* would go on.

Maybe Marco would eventually let me back into his part of the dance. I wanted that, a lot. But that was his to decide, not mine. In the meantime, I mostly stayed in my apartment as if it were my chrysalis. I had changed, but I wasn't done with some transformation that required solitude to complete. I had to learn about the fluid person I was becoming.

One morning, I sat in my living room, unwashed and unshaven, drinking coffee, reflecting on the turbulent dreams I'd awakened from, and my gaze landed on Stef's ashes. Something slid into place inside me, and I saw exactly where to release them back into the dance.

Laughing, I put down my coffee and picked up the urn, kissed it and held it in my arms like a baby, giddily humming "Va, pensiero." I didn't know how my subconscious picked that melody, but at that moment, it was the only one that would do.

"Your ashes go free today, Stef," I crooned. "Today is the day. Thank you for being patient with me." I set them down and headed to the shower, brutalizing Verdi's exquisite music without a shred of regret.

AN HOUR later, I was headed along the Pacific Coast Highway, Verdi's chorus cranked all the way up, Stef's ashes belted into the seat next to me, and my backpack and his cowboy boots on the floor in front of them. In no time at all, we were winding along Old Topanga Canyon Road toward Red Rock Canyon Park.

There was only one other car in the parking lot. I parked on the opposite side, facing the canyon, lowered the windows, turned off the music and the engine. I just sat for a moment, letting the silence and hot pungent air of the canyon wash through the car, banishing the last of the air-conditioned comfort. I patted the urn, still cool under my fingers. This was perfect.

"Time to return your ashes to the dance, Stef," I whispered, indescribably happy. I put the urn in my backpack, raised the windows and got out. The air was full of tiny noises—insects, breeze, life.

A knife-slice of grief cut through me as I picked up the boots and slung the backpack over my shoulder, but it faded as I locked the car and headed down Red Rock Road. In a hundred yards or so, I peeled off to the south along a wash, down into a deeper arroyo lined with trees.

Flowing through the scrub oak and juniper, the air hummed and whispered with life. I brushed off a spot to sit beneath a pine tree and breathed in the rich, dry scent of the earth. Yes, this was the place. I took the urn out and set it beside me to lean against the trunk.

"This feels like the right place to me, Stef," I said, wishing we could have one more conversation. "Even though we came here just that one time. You liked it, said it reminded you a little of home. It's wild and rough, like parts of Oklahoma must be, but it's California too. As you said, coyotes and rattlesnakes in common, for sure."

My recollection of what he'd said startled me with insight I hadn't understood consciously. Stef hadn't had a trace of rattlesnake in him. Stef's spirit was pure coyote, adapting swiftly to his new habitat in LA. California had been the promised land for him, holding promises of freedom and excitement, yes, and money as well. Just as he was getting to know the territory, a rattlesnake had got him.

Stef knew what rattlesnakes looked and sounded like back home, of course, and to be wary of them. He was far from stupid, just naïve. It was the artifice of the city that had got him, where rattlesnakes often wore convincing disguises. One could even look like a repeat client.

I propped the boots next to the urn, feeling a little guilty, as if I should keep them even though I knew I'd never wear them. No. They couldn't just molder in my closet. I let my fingers trace their bumpy decorative stitching for a while, cherishing all the times he'd worn them, recording the feel of the design.

"So your boots stay here too," I whispered, making my caress part of saying good-bye.

I hadn't noticed I'd been crying. I wiped my eyes and squinted out at the steep slope, followed the scrub oak that thickened as it descended. Maybe there was a little stream at the bottom, at least when it rained.

A sudden breeze pushed at the branches above me, making them dance. "Is that you telling me to get on with it? Okay, then!"

I stood up and took some photos of the urn and boots against the tree for Laurie and for myself. Then I opened the urn and poured out the ashes over the toes of the boots, took more pictures of the mound of gray, black, and white. A gust of wind burst up the slope, lithe and quick, and the finer ashes blew away into the tree, dusting the trunk as well as the boots.

"There you go, Stef. Steven Lewis. Friend." Tears burned my eyes with the tender finality of the moment. "I know we've been together in other lives. Nothing else could explain our connection. I'll see you again sometime. As you would say, that's a sure thing."

I took more photos of the vista and of the ashes as they blew around. Some of them wouldn't turn out because I couldn't focus well through the tears, so I took lots. I put the camera away and stuffed the empty urn into the backpack. Stef was moving on.

For the first time in I don't know how long, I had nothing more to do, nowhere else I had to be, so I just stood there, drinking my water and memorizing the view, feeling the life of the canyon include me, letting it flow through me. It whispered of movement. Change. I peed on the ground next to the boots, a ceremony of contributing to life here, as Stef's ashes would.

Time for you to move on too, a voice said, but my heart rebelled. "No," I said aloud, surprised at my vehemence. "Not yet. I'm not ready."

Stay here as long as you like. You can't go backward into your old life, your old work. You're released too. Move forward.

This was supposed to be about Stef, not me. I forced myself to refocus on why I was there and the magic of Stef's release, but I couldn't. I should be feeling triumphant and happy for Stef. Instead, I shivered, as if someone I couldn't see was watching me.

The thought of giving up my work charged me with fear of the loss for a moment, but I already knew the insight was true. I'd changed. My recent client session had shown me how much.

You did well, working to rescue men who'd lost touch with the beauty of their bodies. They were grateful, and you enjoyed their gratitude. But you don't need to rescue anyone ever again. It's not your job. You don't need to learn their stories, either.

It was true. I'd loved men's gratitude—basked in it in the afterglow of every session. Was that merely rationalized narcissism? No. I'd loved the beauty and magic of my healing service. But I could feel in my gut that's what it would become if I kept on seeing clients. I couldn't let that happen.

It really was time to move on. I slung the backpack over one shoulder, waved at Stef's boots, and headed up the slope. At the parking lot, I dropped the urn into the trash barrel—just another empty container, no longer needed.

Everything that used to be Stef was moving on. In my own way, I was too. I was trying to rebuild my life post-Marco, and now apparently, post-career. The void left by those absences was so large I couldn't see what was beyond it.

I was surprised I wasn't terrified of that. Instead, I felt calm, ready for the unknown, even a little optimistic. I climbed into the car and put on the Verdi again. The music now felt wrong, an imposition. I turned it off and drove home in a meditative silence.

Chapter Thirty-Four

On the way home from Topanga Canyon, a cloud of peaceful acceptance enveloped me. It wrapped me in its comfort all night long and greeted me in the morning.

I was still in its glow as I went through the photos I'd taken. It took me a couple of hours to select half a dozen of what I thought were the best ones and send them to Laurie with a description of what I'd done. Then I selected a couple of those to be made into prints for framing, telling her I'd be happy to send some to her if she was interested.

As good as that felt, I wasn't finished. If Juergen was right, someone at Staviscor was having a business-as-usual morning, unthreatened and guilty of Stef's murder. Chisholm was fucking some eager intern or making a speech, pretending he'd never met Stef.

Maybe I didn't know what justice would look like, but I knew I'd recognize it when it presented itself. In the meantime, life went on.

I got up from my desk and stretched. Now would be a good time to go to the gym.

My phone rang; the screen showed it was a private number.

"You bastard," a woman's shrill voice began. It was Arianna, Marco's red-clawed sister, probably out for my blood just as she'd promised. It certainly sounded like she was.

"Hello, Arianna. How are you?"

"You should be asking how my brother is, you arrogant pig."

Arrogant pig? So many jokes could be made out of that, but I wasn't in the mood. "Just say what you have to say so we can get on with our lives."

"I told you what I'd do to you if you hurt Marco, and that's exactly what you deserve."

"Wait a minute. Marco walked out on me...." And then it hit me. Marco would never have given her this number. At least, I didn't think he would. "How did you get my number?"

"The Internet's a powerful thing, jerk. But that's not the point."

I'd never used this number on the Internet. For online accounts, I had a dummy landline that forwarded voice messages to a server, with notifications sent to an e-mail address. "But it *is* the point right now. This number isn't available on the Internet. How did you get it?"

"Shepherd thinks he lives in a rich man's bubble," she sneered. "Don't think you can hide from me, you son of a bitch."

A phone number. I had Chisholm's phone number. "I'm truly sorry your brother is unhappy we split up, Arianna, even though part of me is glad I'm not the only one who's hurting. I'm unhappy too. Very. Please don't call me again, or I'll take legal action. That's a promise. Good-bye."

"Don't you dare hang up! I'm not done with you yet!"

"Actually, yes, you are. I'd be surprised if we talk again. Thanks for your call, though. I really mean that. You've given me an idea I've been reaching for, and I'm grateful." I ended the call and put her number on silent ring tone.

What was I thinking? Was I really so ready to die? A wild happiness took me; it made me shiver and laugh out loud. It was the same euphoria that swept through me in the botanical garden, and again watching Stef's ashes blow up into the tree.

That old voice had always whispered that love could get you killed, and now I saw it was quite true—and a perfectly acceptable risk. Sometimes, that's just the way it was. Death didn't count. Love did. Love mattered.

I WATCHED the screen on my phone go dark. The flow of life that I belonged to would continue, eternal. What mattered was how I played my little Shepherd part in that eternal flow. I'd made so few real promises—promises that counted—in my life. The insight startled me. They hadn't seemed necessary. But I'd made a promise to Stef, and now I knew how to keep it. I was astonished I hadn't seen it before now.

Whether I lived or died keeping it didn't make much difference. In fact, it made no real difference at all. The vast river of life flowed around and through me and would continue, with or without my current self. Keeping my promise made a difference.

Slow down, a voice inside my head called out. *Maybe there's a better way than getting yourself killed.*

I went into the bathroom and splashed cold water on my face. I drew a glass of water and drank it slowly. I slowed down my breathing, waited for my pulse to follow suit. I stared out the living room window, my gaze returning to the patch of botanic garden as if magnetized by its gentle greenness.

By the time I'd calmed down, I knew there wasn't a better way and, what's more, I didn't need one. I'd found a way that could work, and I was grateful beyond words that I had.

I dug out Chisholm's phone number from Stef's records, and sent a text, attaching a selfie close-up of my mouth, tongue extended. *Hey. Stef told me how hot u were, left me ur #. Want 2 get 2gether? Im as much fun as him, dig older guyz big time. Only 175. Lets do it.*

I expected to wait a while for the answer, but I had plenty of work to do in the meantime to square matters away before anything serious occurred.

Chapter Thirty-Five

My old preoccupation with the fear of death seemed laughable now. The little voices that urged me toward personal survival rang selfish and petty when they spoke up. I'd always assumed some kind of contract with life, a set of guarantees, and now I knew there'd never been anything of the kind. It wasn't possible. For anyone. That was just an illusion I'd held, my personal selfishness. False entitlement.

I sent off some instructions to the Trust, along with summaries and passwords to my online accounts, and made out a final check to Camilla. I put all my sensitive data about Stef's murder in an envelope and had it couriered to Marco's home, signature required. That way if I didn't make it back, there'd be nothing left in my apartment to raise questions about his professional conduct.

I made an espresso, pulling the aroma into my nostrils as if I could empty the cup just by inhaling, savoring the flavors with slow appreciation that approached reverence. I made another. I wrote an e-mail to Peter, thanking him for our friendship. It sounded classically suicidal, so I scheduled its delivery for later in the day so he wouldn't raise a premature alarm.

My phone clinked, announcing a new message. Before I looked, my adrenals knew it was the one I'd been waiting for. My heart began to hammer. Sure enough, it was from Chisholm's number. The killer had taken my bait. *Good! Will be at Century Tradewinds LAX, W Cent Blvd betwn mtgs 4:00 today. Call Robert Pierce from house phone in lobby by 3:45.*

So that was that. All set. I could simply not show up if I changed my mind, but I knew that wouldn't happen.

I sent Marco a text: *Appt today w Stef's killers Century Tradewinds LAX, Cent Blvd 4:00 today, name Robert Pierce. Could use help. Call me.*

Would he read the message? If he did, he'd try to stop me before I got there. Maybe he'd ignore this message like all the others. I had no way of knowing if he'd even read them, although I knew he'd act if he read this one.

I forwarded the text exchange between Chisholm's number and mine to Marco's e-mail. I could wait for his reply for another hour before I had to head out, and he'd have another half hour to organize while I drove to the hotel. But I had no control over whether he would. And oddly, it didn't feel that important.

I showered, rubbed some sandalwood oil on my chakras, and folded myself onto my meditation mat. Within a few breaths, the serene flow of universal life enveloped me, lifted me, received my tears of gratitude for all I'd experienced. It filled me with a clarity and calm that I would carry for the rest of my Shepherd life, however long that might be.

When I was done, I checked my messages. Nothing from Marco. He hadn't read my text, I could feel it. I was a little sad about that, not because I was about to die to expose Stef's killer, but because I couldn't share this triumphant moment with him.

I knew that was selfish of me and that he still loved me. That knowledge had to be enough. I wasn't doing this for points with him anyway. I wasn't even doing this for Stef anymore. I was doing it simply because I had to. It was my promise, and I would keep it.

I got dressed in old jeans and a compression muscle shirt that didn't quite meet the jeans. It had a high crew neck, the kind I'd worn to hide my birthmarks at the gym. I checked the look. In the gym, nobody would raise an eyebrow. On the street, it would make me look suitably cheap.

I drank a glass of water. I wondered if I'd be taped to a chair long enough to make me pee on the carpet like Stef had. I doubted it. Chisholm wouldn't even be there, was my guess. So no need to wait for him to make a getaway.

I checked messages once more, car keys in hand. Nothing. I sat and sent off a quick e-mail to Juergen, letting him know what I was doing. Maybe he'd call Marco, who would read something from him if not from me. No guarantees, none requested. I turned off the computer, put my phone on silent, but left my locator on, just in case.

By the time I was in the car, I was whistling "Va, pensiero" again, content and free. I'd never felt so good about keeping a promise. It felt like going home to a big family dinner, even more wonderful than Marco's.

IT WAS 3:42 when I put the house phone back on its hook. Room 538. I texted the room number to Marco and Juergen, and then erased all the messages in case the killer looked at my phone. The self-preservation voices in my head took another turn, appealing to the part of me that wanted to stay in the life that I'd only recently come to appreciate. While they didn't lack conviction, they lacked strength, as if they were talking from somewhere far away, somewhere irrelevant. Life would go on. I would go on in some other form.

I followed a cluster of people into the elevator, making way for their bright shopping bags and carry-on luggage with American eagles on the tags. I smiled at their soft Southern accents as they discussed tomorrow's trip to Disneyland. They got off on four, and I rode the last few seconds alone. The quiet was welcome.

I knocked on the door. A forty-ish man who wasn't Chisholm opened it immediately and motioned me inside. I looked around. Everything looked perfectly normal. I smiled to myself, wondering what I'd imagined I'd see. Maybe a chair and a roll of duct tape? Who knows.

The man pointed to a chair at the desk. I sat.

"So, Shep. Are you a cop?" he asked.

I licked my lips and grinned. "Shucks, no. I'm not a cop."

"Are you working for the police?"

I laughed, shook my head no. "I'm what you call an entrepreneur."

He nodded. "So nobody knows you're here?"

"You and me. Here all on my own."

"Then in that case, you can take off your clothes."

I made a worried face. "But you're not Mr. Chisholm."

"No, I'm not. He couldn't make it today. I'm taking his place."

"He's cool with this? I don't want any trouble."

"I promise you," he said calmly, "I'll make sure there's no trouble."

A pang of pity passed through me. He was so sure. "Same price, though," I said.

"Oh, yes. Exactly the same price."

"Should I call you Robert, or Mr. Pierce?"

"Call me Pierce."

I stood. Pierce sat on the end of the bed, just a few feet away. I tugged my tee up a bit and grinned at him. "You want a little show, Pierce?"

"Sure. Knock yourself out."

I started a little striptease, beginning with my shirt. He was probably waiting to make sure I wasn't wearing a wire, and I realized I wanted to take some time—not because I was hoping to be saved, but because I wanted this chance to say good-bye to my body. I wanted to thank it for all the wonderful gifts it had given me.

My shirt was tight enough to make it really slow to take off. When finally I pulled it over my head, I saw Pierce's eyes go hard.

"Stop," he ordered. "Put your hands down."

I did. He came up to me and ran his thumb over the raised red spots at the base of my neck, not gently, pressing each of them. Maybe he thought they might disguise a transmitter.

"Birthmarks," I said, smiling as if I was embarrassed by them.

Pierce sat back down and made a little circular motion with his right index finger. "Keep going."

I ran my hands up and down my torso and across my nipples—standard stripper moves—but my hands tingled with the love and gratitude I poured into my flesh.

"Time for the pants, Shep."

I kicked off my shoes and opened my fly, thumbed down my jeans. My whole body burned, celebrating life, life eternal. When I'd pulled off my pants, Pierce had his gun trained on me. I'd never seen him move at all, but there was the gun. With a silencer. It was dense and dark. I was surprised it didn't seem ugly. It was perfect for its purpose, a thing of beauty in its own way.

I tossed my jeans aside, holding eye contact. "What's that for?"

"Put your hands on your head, Shep. Right now." I did as I was told.

He turned me toward the chair I'd first sat in. "Bend over. One more place to look for a wire."

I heard the snap of a latex glove. His finger shoved in, no lube, and was joined by another. Clinical twist and probe. "Sit in the chair. Make this easy on yourself. It'll be over soon."

I stared at him. "You killed Stef."

His answer was a thin smile. "Good-bye, Shep. You should never have called that number."

I twisted to one side a little, just as the gun made a sneeze. I felt the bullet hit me below the left shoulder. My chest burned, convulsed. I could hear myself scream. My pulse pounded. No, something else was pounding, I couldn't think what. Then another thud in my body. The pain blossomed, unbearable. I closed my eyes and drifted away.

CHAPTER THIRTY-SIX

THE PAIN melted away quickly. I was surprised at that. I found myself floating, bobbing against the ceiling looking down. I was fascinated—there was my body lying on the floor next to the chair, alien in the otherwise perfectly predictable hotel room. There was a lot of blood. I felt kind of sad, seeing my blood.

The door shattered open; police swarmed in. Marco in the middle of everything. Pierce shooting, then shot. Medics crouching over my body. So much crazy activity, all with the sound turned off.

I reached down and touched Marco's shoulder as he leaned over the medic talking into the radio. I wanted to thank him for coming, to tell him it felt really good to have kept my promise to Stef, that everything was okay. To tell him I loved him. But he was focused on them setting up an IV. I couldn't get his attention, no matter how I tried.

Intrigued, I watched as they strapped me onto a gurney and wheeled me down the hall toward the elevators. Marco took off alongside the gurney, but I didn't really feel like going with them. I was content to stay where I was and watch the police bustling around the room.

In a while I got restless, or maybe just bored, as if I itched somewhere I couldn't reach. Then the hotel just dissolved, and I wasn't there anymore. A path appeared under my feet, and I knew I would follow it, find out where it led, even though I wasn't in a hurry. As I ambled along, it widened, curving through a dense stand of conifers—spruce, cedar, and fir. Their pungent, healing scent settled on me like a soft cloak. Beyond the trees, I came to a fast-flowing stream pouring around smooth boulders.

On the near bank, a slender black-haired youth sat against a rock, busy with a picnic spread all around him—red and white cloth, silver and crystal, the works. He seemed oddly familiar, but I didn't recognize him until I got closer.

He pushed his long hair back behind an ear and flashed a smile, one I remembered well. "Hi, Shepherd—long time no see."

"Danny!" He still looked like he was seventeen, but there was none of the old torment in his face. He seemed genuinely happy, and I couldn't help but smile back. "Are you still dead?"

He patted the grass next to him. "Yeah, I am. Come sit for a little while. Like old times." He laughed happily. "No, better than old times. Much better."

"Am I dead too?"

"Not yet. Maybe soon. Want something to eat?" he asked, offering me a baguette and a slice of paté. "It's really good."

"Hmm." I didn't know how, but I could tell he was asking me to make a choice. "Is this like in the old fairy tales we used to read? If I eat something, I have to stay?"

"Pretty much. It's not a bad deal, though. Hungry?"

"Not really. I hope you're not insulted."

"Nah. Probably means you can go back if you want. It'll hurt, though. Bad. I wouldn't recommend it."

"How do I decide?"

"You'll get called. They'll help." He took my hand and leaned back against the rock, closing his eyes to the bright sunlight. "Just sit with me for a little while, okay? Please?"

"Sure." I relaxed against the rock and listened to the river. I wasn't in a hurry to go anywhere. "I'm really glad to see you again."

He pulled my hand into his lap and smiled into the sun's warmth, his eyes still closed. "I haven't missed anybody from the old time except you."

My throat began to ache. A tear tickled my cheek as it wandered toward my chin. Another followed it. "I really loved you, you know."

Danny turned and kissed me hard, then settled his head on my shoulder with a sigh. "I know—more than I loved you. I'm sorry for that. You deserved better, but I couldn't help myself," he said, his voice soft with regret. He burrowed against my neck. "I still don't understand, but I really am sorry."

I put an arm around him to pull him closer. "Nothing to be sorry about, nothing to forgive. I was just glad to be with you. Glad to be with you now, too. Very."

We sat nestled together for a little while, bathed in the sun, silent. Then Danny pulled away and smiled at me, his face shining. "Thank you," he whispered, his lips inches from mine. "Hearing you say that really helps."

I was going to ask what he meant, but a pulse rang through my body, rolling like a chord of music, overtaking thought. Instead, I just said, "Oh. I have to go somewhere, but I don't—"

Danny nodded and drew away. "That's your call. Don't worry, it'll lead you." He stroked my damp cheek. "I've been so afraid you were mad at me. I'm glad you're not. Maybe we'll see each other again sometime."

He kissed me and faded—along with everything else. I was standing on nothing, in nothing. But the nothing was warm and held me in impossibly vast tenderness.

A QUESTION shimmered, soundless light. *Welcome. Do you choose to stay?*

I knew whatever my answer, it would be honored. Before I could form words to ask if I'd suffered brain damage, my answer formed in the same language. *I'm not done yet. Too much unfinished work. Relationship. And I want a chance to grow old. It seems so long since I have. There's more beauty for me to explore there, growing old. I'd like to experience that. Maybe even with someone else.*

Something like music lifted me, carrying me I didn't know where.

Chapter Thirty-Seven

There was something stuck in my throat. And it wouldn't move. And it hurt. Not just my throat. Everything. So heavy.

I forced my eyes open. A hospital room. Marco slumped in a chair, sleeping.

I tried to say hello to him, but all that came out was a croaking sound. He must've been only drowsing because my noise woke him up immediately.

He jumped up and stood beside the bed, bloodshot eyes wide, lips parted as if he couldn't decide what to say.

"You look terrible," I said. And he did, except he looked beautiful too.

He laughed quietly and stroked my fingers, avoiding the tubes taped to the back of my hand. "You don't look so great yourself, to be perfectly honest."

I wanted to laugh, but it took more effort than I could manage. "What happened?"

"You nearly didn't make it. That was a very, very stupid thing to do, you know."

I tried to shake my head no, but it hurt too much. "Actually," I whispered, trying to smile, "it was the only thing to do."

He caressed my arm. "It'll take a while, but it looks like you'll be okay. You lost a section of lung, and they're going to finish rebuilding your shoulder when you're stronger. Titanium joint. Apart from that, you're still in one piece."

"Glad. The bad guys?" I was so tired I could barely form the words.

"The shooter's in custody, we've got the Staviscor guys." Marco sat gingerly on the edge the bed and leaned forward to kiss my forehead. "Chisholm's withdrawn from the race. Don't worry about them right now, babe. We're taking care of it."

"Babe?"

"Oh, yeah. It's babe." His eyes glowed as he sandwiched my hand with both of his. "You probably have no idea how happy I am that you're back."

"Had to come back," I mumbled, trying to stay focused on his face. "You haven't sung for me yet." I gave up trying and sank.

WHEN I broke surface again, I was in a fog of good drugs, deeply content. Harp music drifted around me, lilting and sweet. Not harp. Marco sat beside the bed, one foot on the rail, playing his guitar. So good. He'd changed clothes and shaved. Maybe not in that order, but he'd done it. And brought his guitar.

I waited until I thought he'd finished. "That's really nice," I said, wishing I could put together the words for a more adult response. "Beautiful."

He looked up and grinned. "Your resident minstrel, reporting for duty," he said. "At least for the next little while."

He sat up straighter. "I was once asked if I could sing this song. So by way of proof...." He began an intro of rolling arpeggios, and sang Happy Birthday, wrapping me in a honeyed baritone that warmed me, made me forget where I was. I was in tears by the time he was done. So was he.

"Beats the hell out of Hvorostovsky, I promise you," I said, feeling leakage trickle into one ear. "Thank you."

He bent over and kissed me—chapped lips, tube-breath, and all. Now that's love. I hoped the grin I felt inside had made it to the parts of my face that could move.

Someone rapped on the open door, and Marco sat back in the chair again as a man with skin dark as espresso roast introduced himself as Dr. Wilson, strode to the bed, and pulled out his tablet. He scrolled through a couple of pages and asked how I was feeling, pain on a scale of one to ten. I told him as long as he let Marco keep kissing me, my endorphins would take care of most of it.

He laughed. "Not sure I can put that on your treatment plan, but I'm not going stop him." His voice dropped to a conspiratorial whisper. "As soon as you got out of surgery, I realized that trying to stop the good detective from doing anything he was set on doing would probably be a serious mistake."

I tried laughing again, but the tube still wouldn't let me do more than cough. "I understand exactly what you mean, doctor."

Dr. Wilson rattled through the nature of my injuries and what they'd done to repair me. More surgery ahead, when I was stronger. He approved of my progress. On his way to the door, he stopped and turned.

"Oh," he said. "When we were closing you up, I excised those birthmarks from your neck. You really should've had them removed years ago, just to be safe. Anyway, the biopsies came back negative. You're all set."

"That's good," I said. "Thanks."

Dr. Wilson lifted his tablet in salute and disappeared.

Marco sat on the edge of the bed again. I could tell he wanted to say something but was holding back.

"What?" I asked, reaching for his hand with my free one.

He took a while longer, but I didn't mind. I wasn't going anywhere at the moment. "Sitting here the last two nights gave me time to think. Mostly about how I walked away and almost lost you." His mouth twisted. He cleared his throat. "I let down someone I loved. My greatest fear. And shame. I abandoned you, and I'll regret that for the rest of my life. If you'll have me, I want to pick up exploring with you again," he said, his voice thick with emotion. "More than ever."

Looking boyishly fragile, hopeful, he shrugged. "We know there'll be issues. Do you think we could?"

I filled with possibility, some kind of happiness new to me, and I knew it wasn't just the drugs. "You're a big part of why I came back. Babe." I added the last as a kind of joke, but when it came out as a rasping whisper semi-cough, it wasn't a joke at all.

I squeezed his hand as hard as I could. "I'd really like to try."

LLOYD A. MEEKER can't help what he writes—stories arising from the between places, the mystical overlapping between the worlds of matter and spirit, and the eldritch beauty that dwells there. It's his natural habitat.

He's in love with the adventure and magic of living there, loves plunging into stories full of both, and wants to take you along. Mostly he's in love with love and believes deeply in the power of love to overcome any challenge. He's known it in his own life and seen it in the lives of others.

In addition to his written work, which includes novels, essays, poetry and short stories, he has served since 2008 as a judge in the Queer Foundation's annual National High School Seniors Essay Contest, promoting effective writing by, about, and/or for queer youth, and awarding scholarships to the winners. Finalists are selected from schools across the United States by members of the National Council of Teachers of English.

Happily ensorcelled by music, subtle energy healing, and the wonders of nature, Meeker lives with his very understanding husband in southern Florida, among friends and family, orchids, and giant hibiscus that take his breath away every morning.

The Companion is his fourth novel. You can e-mail him at lam@lloydmeeker.com, follow him on Twitter at LloydAMeeker, or visit his website at www.lloydmeeker.com.

Also from DREAMSPINNER PRESS

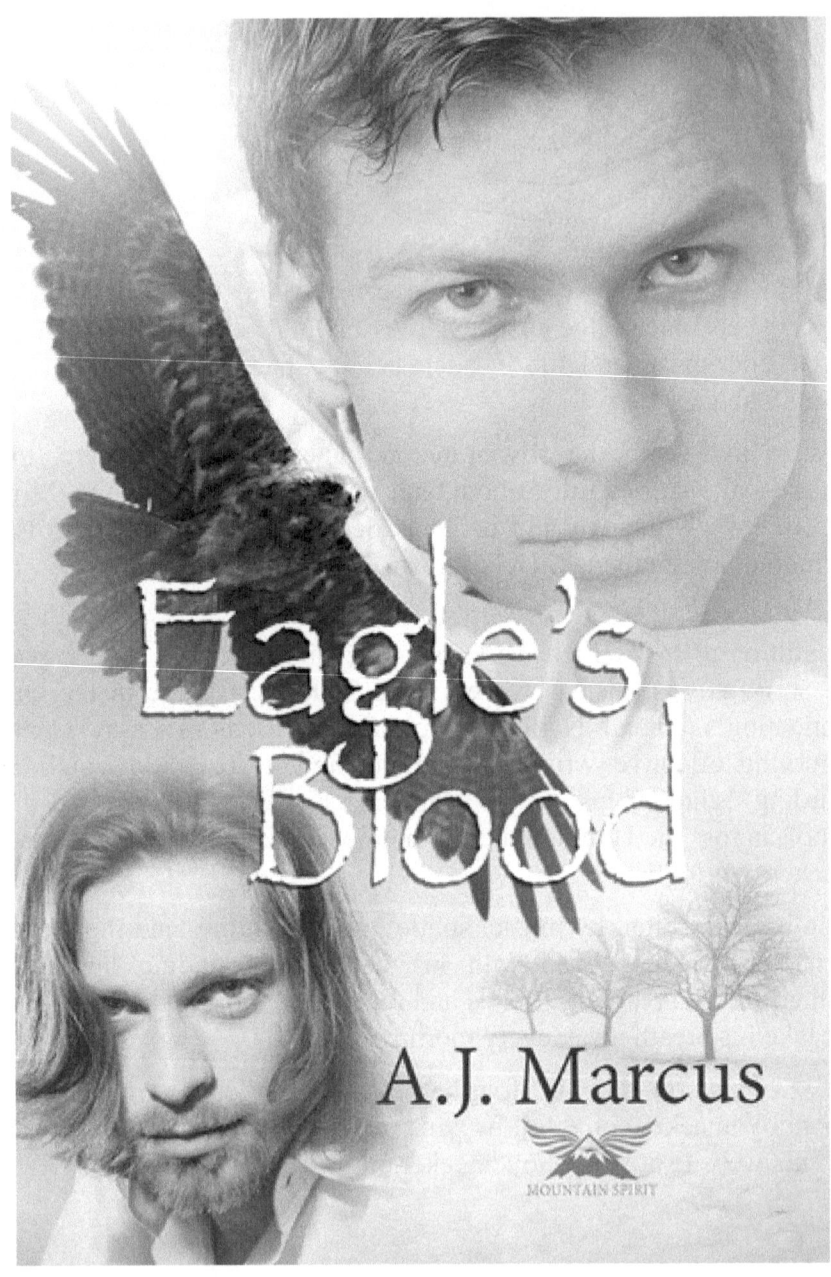

http://www.dreamspinnerpress.com

Also from DREAMSPINNER PRESS

http://www.dreamspinnerpress.com

CPSIA information can be obtained at www.ICGtesting.com
Printed in the USA
LVOW01s2341200315

431365LV00012B/103/P